HOW
YOU
GROW
WINGS

HOW YOU GROW WINGS

Rimma Onoseta

Algonquin 2022

Published by
Algonquin Young Readers
an imprint of Algonquin Books of Chapel Hill
Post Office Box 2225
Chapel Hill, North Carolina 27515-2225

a division of
Workman Publishing
225 Varick Street
New York, New York 10014

LIBRARY OF CONGRESS CATALOGING-IN-PUBLICATION DATA
Names: Onoseta, Rimma, author.
Title: How you grow wings / Rimma Onoseta.
Description: Chapel Hill, North Carolina : Algonquin Young Readers, 2022. |
Audience: Ages 14 and up. | Audience: Grades 10–12. | Summary: Sisters
Cheta and Zam's paths to break free of their oppressive home diverge
wildly—one moves into an aunt's luxurious home and the other struggles to
survive on her wits alone—and when they finally reunite, Zam realizes how
far Cheta has fallen, leaving Cheta's fate in Zam's hands.
Identifiers: LCCN 2022004612 | ISBN 9781643751917 (hardcover) |
ISBN 9781643752891 (ebook)
Subjects: CYAC: Sisters—Fiction. | Wealth—Fiction. | Kidnapping—Fiction. |
Family life—Nigeria—Fiction. | Nigeria—Fiction. | LCGFT: Novels.
Classification: LCC PZ7.1.O658 Ho 2022 | DDC [Fic]—dc23
LC record available at https://lccn.loc.gov/2022004612

10 9 8 7 6 5 4 3 2 1
First Edition

For me

ONE

Zam

I WATCHED REVEREND Sister Benedicta's mouth and tried very hard to concentrate on what she was saying. She had thin lips that pulled back when she spoke to reveal bright pink gums and a chipped tooth. It was hard to understand her because she spoke as if she had ogbono soup stuck in her throat. Cheta said she sounded like that because her tongue was too big for her mouth. I didn't know if Cheta was telling the truth; I was never really sure about anything Cheta said.

Sister Benedicta folded the piece of paper before putting it in a white envelope and licking the flap. I stared at her tongue, trying to gauge if it was bigger than normal but I couldn't tell.

"Zam, put this in your bag," she said, handing me the envelope.

I unzipped my bag slowly; it had to be done just right or the teeth wouldn't close. "Give it to your parents," she instructed. I nodded but what I really wanted to do was tell her that there was a mistake. I wasn't the person they wanted, there had to be some sort of misunderstanding, but I kept my mouth closed.

It was a Friday and it was also the last day of school. Exams ended the day before, so the only thing in my schoolbag was a pen and a notebook—just in case—but when I slipped the straps on my shoulders, I felt like I would topple over.

The first thing I noticed when I stepped out of the office was how still everything was. I had been in Sister Benedicta's office for less than ten minutes and in that time everyone had cleared out, eager to begin the school break. A heavy silence blanketed the compound. The steady hum that usually thrummed through the walls, floated along the hallways, and threaded through the concrete floors was gone. I hurried towards the open gates, where Baba, the gateman, was sitting at his usual post.

Baba had been doing this job long before I had been born. His tenure started over four decades ago when a wealthy benefactor had bought a generator for the school. Baba was hired to protect the generator from thieves who tried to sneak into the school after dark to steal parts to sell. The generator stopped working almost a decade ago. I wondered if they had let him keep his job because everyone was so used to seeing his smiling face or if they had simply forgotten there was nothing worth stealing in the school.

"Ma a ba," I greeted.

Baba waved at me. "Ndo ó nwam. Greet your parents for me," he said with an uneven smile. His weathered skin was soft and saggy and even though I had never touched it, I knew his face would be as soft and stretchy as my grandmother's had been.

As I walked home, I stared at my feet navigating the bumpy road. The road had been tarred just three years ago by a politician who wanted our votes. The crew paving the road had stopped working the day after he won the election, leaving half unfinished. A few months later, potholes started appearing on the tarred half. I wondered if the rest of the road would finally be completed when election campaigning began next year.

I walked the route from school to the house so often, I didn't have to look up to see where I was going. My feet automatically traced the familiar steps, giving my brain the chance to think of other things, like what I was going to do about the letter Sister Benedicta had given me.

As I got closer to the house, I heard the sound of a generator running. The noise pulled me out of my thoughts and snapped my head up. We had the biggest generator on the street and it was also the loudest—the sound was distinct. And if the sun had not set and the generator was on, that meant we had special visitors. Petrol was expensive and it had become even more expensive since the government removed the subsidy. Last week, Papa had spent seven hours at the petrol station queuing for petrol for the car and diesel for the generator. There was only one person important enough for Mama to consider putting on the generator before the sky darkened: Uncle Emeke.

Uncle Emeke usually travelled with at least three cars, all black, expensive, and bulletproof, but when I turned into the compound, I did not see any car that looked like it could belong to him. Parked in our compound was a baby blue Toyota and a grey Volvo that had seen better days. The Toyota belonged to Father Charles, the Catholic priest at St. Cecilia's church. The grey Volvo was coated in layers of dust, as though it had not been used in months. Underneath the dust and grime, I recognized Uncle Festus's car. A black okada was leaning against the wall and that meant Brother Chudi, my older cousin, was also here.

I could hear raised voices drifting from the open window in the living room. Aunty Ngozi's voice was the most noticeable. Aunty Ngozi, my father's half sister, was the most soft-spoken of all my relatives. Whatever was going on in the house had to be big for her voice to get that loud.

I knew better than to enter the house through the front door with all the visitors present; Mama would be angry if I greeted them and I didn't look presentable. My sandals were caked with red mud that had also splattered on my white socks. I wondered how I had stared at my feet all the way home but somehow failed to notice I hadn't taken off my socks. The Reverend sisters that ran the school insisted we wear clean white socks and clean white shirts, because white signified purity. The cleaner we were, on the inside and the outside, the closer to God we will feel, they said.

4

The red sand was unforgiving and it was impossible to walk to school without getting my socks dirty. This was the first time in years I had ever forgotten to take them off. I would have to soak my socks in bleach overnight to get the stains out.

Behind the house was an ukonu made of laterite with corrugated-metal roofing sheets. This was where the actual cooking happened. The kitchen in the house held a fridge, a deep freezer, and a storage room and was no use for anything else. The cloying scent of fried fish wafted through the air as I got closer. I walked into the ukonu and saw my older sister, Cheta, bent over a pot. Inside the pot was hot yam. She scooped the yam into the mortar and grabbed the big pestle that was almost as tall as her.

"Madam, you're back," she said in that sarcastic way of hers, without turning around. "Of course she came back after I've done all the work," Cheta muttered to herself, but she made sure it was loud enough that I heard.

"I'll go and change out of my uniform and come and help you," I said.

She huffed and began to pound the hot yam. "Take the chin chin to the living room," she commanded. Cheta never simply spoke, her voice always rang with authority. Papa used to say she must have been a military general in her past life.

I was the one who served guests because Mama did not like Cheta spending too much time with visitors. Cheta had the most expressive face I had ever seen. Every emotion, every thought, was reflected in her gaze, in the set of her lips, and in

5

the lines on her forehead—and the most prominent emotion she expressed was disapproval. It oozed off of her in waves. Her presence was so intense, being around her was oppressive.

I tiptoed into the living room, making sure to keep my head out of sight. Scanning the room, I counted seven bodies: Mama and Papa, Aunty Ngozi and Uncle Festus, Brother Chudi and his new wife Sister Blessing, and Father Charles. Everyone but Uncle Festus was seated around the center table. Uncle Festus was standing at the side of the room, gesticulating wildly with his arms. With the exception of Papa, they were all talking at once, a chaotic mix of pidgin and Ika. I couldn't make out what they were saying but I could hear a distinctive and steady thwacking noise.

I carefully poured the chin chin into seven bowls and placed the bowls on the silver tray we used just for visitors. Conversation stopped when I walked into the room. I felt all eyes on me, but I kept my eyes on the tray. As I placed the tray on the table, movement from the corner of the room caught my eye. Ezinne, my older cousin, lay on the floor. Uncle Festus stood over her, his worn-out leather belt in his hand. Her clothes were torn and one eye was swollen shut. My heart beat faster when I realized that the thwacking noise I had heard was the belt hitting her flesh. I quickly looked away, pretending not to see her.

I turned to Father Charles. "Good afternoon, Father," I said. He smiled at me, examining me in a way that made me uncomfortable, like he was remembering the night Mama had summoned him. The night he had spent sprinkling holy water on my head and screaming words of prayer at the ceiling as I trembled in the corner. Maybe that night had been the most eventful night of his priestly career and he wanted a repeat.

I turned to the side to greet Mama and Papa. Papa acknowledged me with a quick nod I would have missed if I blinked. Mama's sharp eyes drifted down to my stained socks and muddy sandals. She said nothing but I knew she would give me an earful once all the visitors left. She might even pull my ears, but she would never do anything that would leave a scar on my body, though sometimes I wished she would. Maybe then Cheta wouldn't hate me so much.

I heeded Mama's silent warning and quickly served the chin chin before escaping upstairs to my room to change out of my school uniform. Walking into my room was like entering into forbidden land. Cheta and I had shared the room our whole lives, but somehow I was still an unwelcome visitor. Even though the room was divided in half by an invisible line, Cheta's personality had somehow managed to leak into all four corners. Her twin bed was at the far right corner by the only window. There were printed-out pictures of her favorite celebrities tacked to the wall and the bright orange curtain she had sewn in clothing and textile class hung over the window. My corner had only my bed and dresser. I had never felt the need to decorate because all my life, I felt as though I was just passing through. I didn't really belong here.

The room smelled like Cheta's body spray. The new one she had bought from Nne Adanna's market stall. The label said

Passion Fruit and Vanilla Blend, but it smelled more like wilted flowers dipped in antiseptic. Not that I would ever voice that thought to Cheta. The expensive perfume Aunty Sophie had given her two years ago at Christmas was reserved for special occasions. The bottle wasn't on the rickety bedside table by the head of her bed, where she kept all her creams and cosmetics. It was in a locked suitcase under her bed.

I changed quickly, knowing that every second I wasn't in the kitchen helping Cheta was another second her anger grew.

* * *

When I walked downstairs, Uncle Festus was still towering over Ezinne. Her head was downcast and she made whimpering noises that resembled the cries of an injured puppy. Everyone was so focused on the display, they didn't notice me standing in the corner. Uncle Festus's brown belt had spots darkened with blood. He stood over Ezinne, calling her ugly names that no daughter should ever hear from her father's mouth. Just like she had taken the beating, Ezinne took the insults in silence and that only seemed to make Uncle angrier. I looked around the room, wondering if anyone would intervene. I couldn't imagine what Ezinne must have done to deserve this. But no one did anything; they just watched. Tears streamed down Aunty Ngozi's face as she watched her husband berate their daughter.

Brother Chudi wore a pained expression, but his eyes were resolutely fixed on the floor. Sister Blessing sat next to him on the couch, her fingers wrapped around his upper arm tightly. Her nails were long and fake and I imagined that her grip had to sting, but he did not pull away. She had a triumphant smile on her face, the look of someone who had won a race. Father Charles said nothing. He stared at Ezinne with that familiar serene expression he wore during Mass. Mama watched the scene with disgust. Her nose wrinkled as if she was smelling something bad. Her hand twitched and knowing Mama she probably wanted to grab the belt from Uncle Festus and beat Ezinne herself. Papa wasn't watching. He was staring out the window, his expression blank as he absent-mindedly chewed kola nut. He didn't seem to notice the scene happening right in front of him, or maybe he didn't care. Uncle Festus cracked the belt in the air so close to Ezinne's face she flinched. "I will beat the fear of God into you today," he said. "So that from now on you will remember that I did not raise an igbaraja." *Whore.*

Spare the rod and spoil the child. That was what Mama said when she broke a cane on Cheta's back. *Spare the rod and spoil the child.* That was what Mama said after she slapped Cheta so hard, her ring sliced Cheta's face. *Spare the rod and spoil the child.* That was what Mama said when she flung a frying pan at Cheta's head and Cheta missed school because she had to get stitches at the hospital. *Spare the rod and spoil the child.* It was for our own good. That's what they told us. But this . . . this was different. It wasn't discipline, it was assault. Uncle Festus literally wanted to beat the sin out of her.

Uncle Festus raised his hand to strike and I quickly turned around knowing that if I continued to watch, I would vomit on the floor. "Uncle Festus is beating Ezinne," I said quietly when I walked into the outside kitchen.

Cheta said nothing, continuing to pound the yam as though she had not heard me speak. She gestured at the bowl on the floor in the corner of the room. "Fry the puff-puff," she instructed.

After washing my hands, I grabbed a stool and sat by the large pot of oil. I scooped the puff-puff dough with my hands and dropped half a handful into the pot. The dough sank in the oil and then almost immediately bounced back up. The scent of puff-puff warred with the smell of the fried fish that still hung in the air.

"They caught Brother Chudi cheating on his new wife with Ezinne," Cheta said dryly after a few minutes of silence passed. "Can you imagine? Useless man. They hadn't even been married three months and he's already sleeping with another woman. *Tufiakwa!*" God forbid.

The thought of our cousins, Chudi and Ezinne, rolling around on a bed with his penis inside her body made me nauseous. "They're related by marriage not by blood," I said, trying to rationalize it, trying to make it seem less disgusting.

"They grew up together so it's basically incest as far as I'm concerned." Cheta circled her hand around her head, then snapped her fingers at the floor in the way people did when they rebuked something. I had asked Mama once why people did that. She said that it was a way to cast curses back to the devil.

"If he cheated why aren't they beating him up too?" It didn't seem fair that they had both sinned but she was the one being punished.

Cheta snorted in that unladylike way of hers Mama hated. "Zam, don't be naïve. He's a man. Of course nothing will happen to him." Her tone was condescending. The voice a frustrated teacher used on a thick student. I opened my mouth to respond but thought better of it. Nothing good ever came from arguing with her.

A sudden loud car horn pierced through the air. It was the sound of a car that was well serviced—a car in its prime. It was not the kind of sound we were used to hearing. Most of the cars in the village were second hand; rusting metals and broken mirrors, barely held together with tape. Father Charles's faded Toyota was the nicest car in the village and it was at least ten years old and the horn sounded like a deflating balloon. There was only one person with a car that could make such a hearty noise.

Cheta groaned. "We are going to have to kill the big chicken for Uncle Emeke, even though he won't stay long enough to eat it."

Uncle Emeke, my father's older brother, was the richest man in the village. He had a house down the road from ours, with a living room bigger than the entire ground floor of our home. It seemed unreasonable to have a house that big when he only came to visit a few times a year. Even though he sometimes came with his wife and children, four people didn't need that much space.

"Go and get the drinks, you know how Mama gets when we don't serve Uncle on time," Cheta snapped at me.

I quickly wiped my hands on a rag and went into the in-house kitchen. I grabbed the drinks from the back of the fridge where they were kept specifically for Uncle Emeke. He usually showed up without warning and so Mama always wanted to be prepared. The drinks weren't cold because the generator was not powerful enough to run both the air conditioners and the freezer. I searched through the kitchen cabinets for our nice tray and glasses, which we only ever used for Uncle Emeke and his wife. They were in the top shelf of the cabinets covered in a layer of dust. I washed them in the sink, making sure to handle them with care.

But it wasn't Uncle Emeke who came out of the car, it was his half-caste wife. Aunty Sophie was the most beautiful woman I had ever seen. She had magic eyes that were sometimes brown, sometimes green, sometimes both, and skin that reminded me of the champagne we kept exclusively for her and Uncle Emeke. I had tried the champagne once. Uncle Emeke had taken only a sip before leaving. Instead of pouring the liquid back into the bottle like Mama asked, I had gulped down the golden liquid. It was somehow sweet and bitter at the same time, and it made my chest feel warm. The way the champagne made me feel was the same way Aunty Sophie made me feel when she smiled at me.

My favorite thing about Aunty Sophie wasn't her beauty or her generosity. It was her voice. It was so melodic, so unlike anything I had ever heard. I once read a book about beautiful creatures who sat on cliffs and lured men to their deaths with their voices. I wouldn't be surprised if those creatures looked and sounded like her. Sometimes, when I was home alone, I would sneak into Mama and Papa's room, where the only full-length mirror was, and stand in front it, mimicking the way she moved her hands, the way she tilted her head when she smiled, the way her lips curved when she spoke.

"Our wife. Welcome," Papa said. His voice sounded scratchy, probably because of underuse. It was the first time I had heard Papa speak in three days. I kept a tally. The longest silent streak was eight days.

"Sophie! We were not expecting you! Welcome!" Mama said in a tone that implied that Aunty Sophie was not at all welcome.

"I wasn't planning on coming, but I was in Benin visiting my family and I decided to stop by," Aunty Sophie said with a genuine smile. I never could tell if Aunty Sophie knew Mama didn't like her, or if she just chose to ignore it.

Cheta said Mama disliked Aunty Sophie because Mama was jealous that Aunty Sophie married the rich brother. I often wondered how Papa felt, knowing his wife would have preferred to be married to his older brother.

13

"Our wife! It is good to see you again. It has been too long," Uncle Festus said with a huge smile on his face, all thoughts of his wayward daughter forgotten. Aunt Ngozi had already wiped her tears, and somehow the redness in her eyes had disappeared.

Everyone in the room had diverted their eyes from Ezinne to Aunty Sophie. Their attention was unwavering, expressions expectant and eyes slightly dazed, probably already making plans for the money. It was common knowledge that people often left Aunty Sophie and Uncle Emeke's presence with their wallets thousands of naira heavier.

Aunty smiled at Father Charles. "Father! You're here! That's very convenient. I was planning on stopping by the church after." She gestured towards Boniface, the unsmiling man that followed her everywhere. A long strap was slung casually across his body and attached to it was a rifle. Boniface stepped forward, the gun slapping against his thigh as he moved. I wondered if it was really loaded. It made no sense for anyone to hold an object that could kill a person so carelessly. He unzipped the black duffle bag he was holding in one hand and I saw that it was full of crisp naira notes.

"I heard that the church needed to be repainted. I just wanted to make a small contribution," Aunty Sophie said as Boniface pulled out a stack of bills, firmly tied with a yellow rubber band and handed it to her.

"Our daughter! God will continue to bless you and your husband," Father Charles said, stepping forward, wrinkly hands stretched. But he never touched the money, because Ezinne's whimper caught Aunty Sophie's attention.

Aunty's head turned to the corner and she inhaled sharply when she saw Ezinne beaten and bloody on the floor. "What is going on here?" she asked, her voice a whisper.

"It's nothing for you to worry about. She has been dealt with." Uncle Festus waved his hand dismissively at his daughter, eyes fixed on the stack of bills in Aunty Sophie's hand.

"What did she do? What could she have done to deserve this?" Aunty Sophie's soft voice was sharper, her oyinbo accent more pronounced.

"I said she has been dealt with. Please, don't worry about the stupid child." Uncle Festus's voice was less flippant. Although his focus was still on the money in Aunty Sophie's hand and his own hand twitched as though he was barely containing himself from reaching out and grabbing it, he was not a stupid man; he could tell Sophie was not happy with what she saw.

"Father, you condone this? You sat here and watched this?" There was no mistaking the disgust in her voice.

Father Charles opened his mouth and then closed it. Obviously struggling for the right words to say. I could almost hear the wheels turning in his head as he searched for an answer that would appease her. From the way Aunty Sophie narrowed her eyes at him, I knew she could hear it too.

"Some children learn things the difficult way," Father Charles finally said. But he spoke the words like a question, silently imploring Aunty Sophie to understand the situation and be okay with it. Uncle Emeke was St. Cecelia's biggest benefactor.

Aunty Sophie stared at him for a second before turning back to Ezinne. "Carry the child and put her in the car. I will take her to the hospital." No one moved.

"Now!" She shouted with such force, it stunned everyone into motion. Her father reached her first and grabbed Ezinne's arm, pulling her off the floor with a hard yank. It was a wonder her arm was still attached to its socket.

"Don't manhandle the child like that! What is wrong with you?" Aunty Sophie snapped at him. "Boniface! Carry this girl into the car."

Uncle Festus opened his mouth, shock etched on his face. "Look, this woman, this is not even your business." He was not a man used to taking orders from women. It seemed like he was forgetting who exactly he was talking to. Aunty Sophie was not just any woman.

His wife on the other hand had not forgotten. Aunty Ngozi stepped forward and put a hand on her husband's arm, "My husband. It's okay," she said to Uncle Festus, but her eyes were trained on Aunty Sophie, specifically, Aunty Sophie's hand, the one that still held the stack of crisp naira notes.

Uncle Festus stepped aside as Boniface picked up Ezinne and carried her to the car. We all followed them outside and watched as he laid her in the backseat. I wondered if I should point out that Ezinne's blood would stain the seats. Aunty Sophie got in after Ezinne, the stack of bills tucked firmly under her arm. She didn't seem to notice the thick red fluid seeping into the cream leather seats and slowly making its way towards her light green dress. Or maybe she noticed and didn't care. She could always replace the dress and the car.

Uncle Festus stepped forward. "This is not necessary. You know how children can be. The girl needed to be disciplined." Aunty Sophie responded by shutting the door in his face. The convoy sped out of the compound, leaving a cloud of red dust in its wake.

"No respect. She thinks because her husband has money she can act anyhow," Uncle Festus said. His hand went into his pocket and dug out his key. "I hope she knows she's paying for the hospital bill and petrol. That hospital is far." His face was twisted into a scowl and he spat on the ground before shouting at his wife. "Enter the car, let's be going."

"I dare him to say that to her face. Coward," Cheta whispered beside me as we watched him and his wife get into their dust-covered Volvo and reverse out of the compound.

"At least now we don't have to kill the chicken," Cheta said before heading back inside.

TWO

Cheta—
then

I WAS TEN years old the first time my mother hurt me so badly, I had to spend a week in the hospital. I sat at Aunty Nneka's dining table, my hands braiding my Barbie's blond hair, listening to Mama and her sisters, Aunty Nneka and Aunty Chidera, talk in the living room. I wasn't supposed to be listening but I had already finished my homework and their voices were loud, so it wasn't really my fault. They always had the best gist. I liked knowing what other children at school didn't know.

"Blackie, you know Ebele just bought a store in town. I hear she's going to start selling snacks and soft drinks," Aunty Chidera said. Mama hated it when her younger sister called her Blackie. Mama was the darkest in her family, and sometimes her sisters joked and said she must have been adopted.

Whenever they did, Mama always tried to smile and act like it didn't hurt her, but I knew it did. I could see it in the way her face pinched like she was smelling rotten eggs.

"She's going to be out of business soon. Nobody wants to eat dry meat pie," Mama said with a forced laugh.

I frowned. I liked Aunty Ebele. She was a nice woman. She brought lollipops, hot buns, and ice cream when she came to visit. And when she asked me how I was, she actually listened when I told her about my day, and after she would smile at me and tell me I was the smartest ten-year-old she knew.

"Her meat pies are not dry," I heard my voice say. I knew I wasn't supposed to speak but I wanted to defend Aunty Ebele. Besides, our social studies teacher said smart people always stood for what they believed in and I believed that her hot buns were the best. Even better than Mama's, but I was smart so I knew better than to say the last part out loud.

Mama's eyes cut to me and I knew she was telling me to shut up. She had that look in her eye; the one that appeared when she was waiting for you to misbehave so she had a reason to get her cane. I pressed my lips together and bowed my head.

"When have you tasted her buns?" Aunty Nneka said. I looked up to see her narrowed eyes on me.

I widened my eyes and said nothing. Nobody was supposed to know that Aunty Ebele came to our house every Tuesday and Thursday, while Mama was in her shop and Zam was at maths lesson. Papa and Aunty Ebele were working on a secret project they didn't want anyone to know about, not until it was

19

ready. I promised them I wouldn't say anything. I liked that they trusted me to keep their secret. It made me feel important and grown up.

"Eh. Answer your aunty. How do you know what her meat pies taste like?" Mama said.

"She brings it for me?" I said, but it came out as a question.

"When?" Aunty Chidera asked.

"On Tuesday and Thursday. When she and Papa work on their secret project." I felt bad for telling them Aunty Ebele's secret, but next time I saw her, I would just tell her it was an accident. She had met Mama so she would understand; everyone knew how scary Mama was. I hoped she would still give me sweets.

No one said anything. Aunty Nneka and Aunty Chidera looked at each other and then looked at Mama. Mama was frozen. Her eyes were stuck somewhere above my head. I turned around trying to look for what she was staring at, but there was nothing there.

"Where do they work on this secret project?" Aunty Nneka asked. Her voice was soft.

My eyes went to hers but then snapped right back to Mama. Why was she so still?

"In Papa and Mama's room," I answered.

They all inhaled, sucking the air from the room.

Mama defrosted. She unfolded herself from the couch so quickly, the bottle of malt she held spilled on her hand and dripped onto her dress. "Cheta, get up. We're going home."

I must not have gotten up quick enough because she grabbed my arm, yanked me off the chair, and dragged me to the car.

Mama's anger was physical. It was in her and around her; it took up all the space in the car. I wondered if her head would burst open like the cartoons on TV. I squirmed in my seat, clenching and unclenching my buttocks, preparing them for a beating. Mama had that look that she wore in public, the one that told you once we passed the threshold and were in the privacy of our home, holy hell would be unleashed.

"Go to your room," Mama said when we got inside the house.

"Mama?" Why was she this angry? It wasn't the first time I had spoken when I was not supposed to. Usually I got an ear pull or a light slap. When she was really angry, she would tell Zam to fetch the cane she kept under her bed. She liked to cane the palm of our hands or our buttocks. Never less than ten but never more than twenty. I always counted.

This wasn't the kind of anger I was used to, this was a quiet rage that made the air around her vibrate. She said nothing. My heart hopped in my chest when I remembered I had seen Mama like this once before. We had come home early from church one Sunday morning and saw the house girl wearing Mama's clothes and jewelry, admiring herself in the mirror. That night, while we lay in bed, we had listened to her screams. The next morning her things were gone. Mama never hired another maid. She said Zam and I were old enough to do the housework.

I scrambled up the stairs and went to my room to wait. Mama came in twenty minutes later holding a travelling mug.

"Take off your clothes."

My heart jumped to my throat. My hands shook as I slowly undressed. I shivered when I was completely naked.

"When adults are speaking, you do not add your mouth."

"Yes, Mama."

"When I tell you to shut up and sit down, you shut up and sit down."

"Yes, Mama."

She opened the lid of the mug and before I could blink she tossed its contents on my naked body.

It took a second for the pain to register and when it did, it started in my belly. It was white hot and exquisite. Unlike anything I had ever felt before. It travelled up my spine and from there spread to the rest of my body. I screamed. The sound unfurled from somewhere deep within me. I didn't realize I was capable of making that kind of sound. In the back of my mind, amidst all the pain, I thought to myself, *This is what that housemaid sounded like.* Somewhere far away I heard Zam crying and Papa asking if she was trying to kill me. I wanted to reach out to them, touch them and maybe give them some of this pain because it was too much, but I couldn't because the pain swallowed me whole.

When I woke up, even though it was dark and I couldn't see a thing, I knew immediately that I wasn't at home. My body was wrapped in white gauze and the smell of iodine and TCP irritated my nose. Zam's warm body was pressed to my side.

Light came in through the slightly opened door. Voices floated through the crack. I heard Mama tell someone how her daughter was careless, how she would have to keep a closer eye on me when I was in the kitchen, how I was lucky there wasn't that much oil in the frying pan I had accidentally knocked off the stove.

Zam shifted and her body curled into mine, her warm breath tickling my cheek. I focused on the feel and smell of her and not on the pain throbbing through my body. I closed my eyes and let the tears fall silently so I wouldn't wake Zam.

Mama had never done anything like this before. Never hurt me so badly I wished I could crawl out of my skin and leave the pain behind. It wasn't until many years later that I realized it wasn't Papa's infidelity that broke Mama, it was the embarrassment.

THREE

Zam

WE SAT AT the wobbly dinner table—another hand-me-down from Uncle Emeke. The sun had set and the visitors had left but the house still pulsed with the drama from earlier.

I didn't like dinnertime. It was the one meal we shared as a family and it was usually the only time we were all in the same room and although some dinners were better than others, they all felt like punishment. Almost as if it was my penance for whatever sin I had committed during the day.

Cheta was shoveling her food into her mouth so fast, I wondered how she didn't choke. She always ate like that at home, and I knew she did it because she wanted to finish her food quickly and get away from us all. Sometimes, I would watch her in school during lunchtime as she talked and laughed with her friends. There, she ate at a much slower pace, taking her time to chew.

"She brought rice but common sense did not tell her to bring petrol. She no know petrol price don go up? Does her husband not own petrol stations across the country? Ordinary petrol, she cannot give," Mama complained. One of the cars in Aunty Sophie's convoy had returned a few hours earlier. The driver offloaded a bag of rice and some other food items. He also handed Papa a thick envelope that we all knew was filled with money. Mama snatched the envelope from Papa as soon the car left.

As Mama spoke a piece of food fell from her mouth into her lap. I wanted to tell her to eat with her mouth closed. Like every dinner, we ate together and like most nights, Mama was the only one talking. As expected, her topic of choice was Aunty Sophie. As annoying as Mama could be, there was also something slightly comforting in knowing what to expect.

"But Mama, I saw the stack of money her driver brought. Can't you use some of that money to buy petrol?" Cheta asked. She sounded genuinely curious but a glance at her face showed me that she was deliberately baiting Mama.

Why did she have to do that? Why annoy Mama and make dinner more unpleasant than it had to be.

"Shut up! Do you know how expensive things are in the market? You that you like to eat all the food in the house, that money will be gone in a week," Mama said before turning to me to ask, "Zam, didn't your report come out today?" It was an obvious attempt to change the subject. She never liked being questioned, especially by Cheta.

"Yes, Mama," I answered in a low voice.

"Go and bring it. Let me see."

I had been hoping that with all the excitement from earlier, Mama would have forgotten about the report. "It's upstairs Mama. I'll go and get it after dinner." When Cheta wasn't there, I didn't add.

"It will only take a minute to get it. Go, let's see how you did," Cheta said, excitement in her voice. This was her moment to shine. She had always been the smarter one. I continued eating, pretending like I didn't hear her, when a foot kicked me under the table.

"Are you deaf? Go and bring your result, let's see," Cheta said sharply. I reluctantly pushed away from the table and headed upstairs to get the report from my schoolbag.

My hands shook as I unzipped it. I ignored the envelope that Sister Benedicta had given me and instead picked out the envelope that had my results. I opened it hoping that my results had changed but it was still the same. Father Charles always spoke about miracles and how God was able to do the impossible. If God could do that, why hadn't he changed my results? It had been almost five hours from the time my results were handed to me, wasn't that enough time to perform a miracle? My mind went back to the oily puff-puff I had stuffed in my mouth when Cheta wasn't looking. Maybe I should have fasted to show my devotion to God. Or maybe, he had not helped because during school assembly, I had imagined what Mr. Oyeyemi's thick lips would feel like pressed against mine. How could I expect God to perform a miracle for me when my mind was impure? I walked downstairs slowly, delaying the inevitable by a few seconds.

When Mama opened the envelope, her eyes immediately went to the top right where the overall position was written.

"*Eziokwu*? Is this true?" Mama asked me, surprise in her voice. "My daughter came first overall! Praise God!" Mama said, raising her hands in the air and swaying them as though she were waving to God. "Nedi Cheta, see your daughter's result." She thrust the paper towards Papa. He hadn't been paying attention and it almost landed in his soup.

"Let me see," Cheta said. She leaned over and snatched the paper from Papa before he had a chance to even glance at it. Papa didn't seem to mind; he continued eating his food.

"You came first," Cheta said slowly.

I didn't look at her because I didn't want to see the anger in her eyes. On a good day, Cheta's mood was like water simmering on low heat. On a bad day, it was like hot stew bubbling over, ready to blow off its lid, eager to burn everyone and everything in the room. My skin crawled and I sat on my hands so I could resist the urge to crack my knuckles. I kept my eyes firmly on Mama, whose eyes and hands were still cast to the ceiling as she praised God.

Cheta had come second overall when she was in my year. I wanted to tell Cheta that I wasn't trying to come first. I didn't want to take her position as the smart one in the family. I knew how much it meant to her. But I wasn't sure if it would make things better or worse. Would she hate me more if she knew I had bested her without even trying?

It took some time to gather the courage to look at Cheta but when I opened my mouth and turned to her to say something to make her understand, she wasn't looking at me. Her gaze was firmly fixed on her plate.

This was all Mr. Oyeyemi's fault. He was the new maths teacher who had been posted to our school for his NYSC service. When he spoke, everything made sense. During the exam I had thought of his plump lips that reminded me of a ripe udara. I thought of the shapes his mouth made when he explained the functions and expressions and vectors and theories. The numbers and letters I never understood suddenly seemed so easy and I felt foolish for never understanding maths before. I craved Mr. Oyeyemi's approval, so I studied harder and listened better and somehow managed to crawl my way from my usual position, which hovered around sixth overall, to first, the position that had always eluded Cheta. She had always come second behind Ndidi, the smartest girl in her year.

Cheta didn't say anything else until she finished her food. "Thank you, Mama, thank you, Papa," she said quietly as she carried her plate to the kitchen.

I waited for Mama and Papa to finish eating their food. When they were done I carried their plates outside to where

Cheta was sitting on a little stool by the tap. Her forehead was resting on her knees. Water was trickling from the tap onto her toes.

"Do you want any help?" I asked Cheta as I placed the plates on the ground beside the wash basin. The plate Cheta used was already washed and in the drying rack.

I held my breath as I waited for a response. She usually answered one of two ways, and it was never with a simple yes or no. Nothing was ever simple with her. She would either command me to do something and walk away without thanking me or she would ignore me entirely. It bothered me that she hated me. It was not my fault Mama was the way she was.

"Go away," Cheta said softly.

With everything that had happened today it should not have surprised me when she went off script. Cheta had the confidence of a conqueror who had won many wars. Her shoulders were always straight, her head always high, she never stuttered, never broke eye contact. When she spoke, her words were like a gust of wind that swayed you no matter how firmly you dug your heels into the ground. So when she spoke the words, so gently, I complied without hesitation because I was not interested in finding out if a soft-spoken Cheta was as dangerous as a loud Cheta. Tonight was not the night to wander into unknown territory. I was too tired.

I walked into the living room and saw Papa was sitting in his armchair, reading the newspaper. He looked up when he heard me come in. Our eyes locked. I opened my mouth even though I had nothing to say, but before I could find words his eyes were back on the newspaper.

I wanted to shake him. I wanted to scream until my throat was sore, but I didn't, because that was not the way good children behaved. A familiar feeling of helplessness washed through me. I knew what was coming next but it didn't make it any easier. It felt like there were hundreds of fire ants crawling on my legs and biting me. I stumbled up the stairs to my room, I would have run but my vision was spotty and I knew if I fell I wouldn't be able to get up.

I flung myself on my bed and dug my hand in my pillow-case until I found the rosary I kept in there. I rolled the tiny beads between my fingers, the smoothness helping me to focus as I recited the first Our Father in my head. By the end of first mystery, it no longer felt like ants were crawling over my body. I could feel my legs by the end of the third mystery and by the fifth, the pressure on my chest was gone and I could see properly again.

I started over because my heart was still beating faster than it should. I was halfway through the fourth mystery when I heard Mama calling my name. I quickly stuffed the rosary back into my pillowcase before standing up. My legs were shaky and I had to concentrate on putting one foot in front of the other.

"Come and help me open this new bottle," Mama said when she saw me standing at the door.

I collected it from her and tried to twist it open. It didn't work. I covered the cap with the end of my shirt and tried again until I heard a click. I handed the opened bottle to Mama and watched as she poured it into a measuring cup before pouring it into a bowl. She did the same thing with the bottle of hair developer, carefully measuring it out and pouring it into the same bowl. I watched her mix the creams together with a spoon.

Mama used to use just bleaching cream but a few months ago, she met a woman at the salon who told her hair developer helped the bleaching cream work faster. Mama was always looking for a product that could make her skin lighter faster and she wasted no time going to the market. She had used the mixture that night and every night since.

Cheta and I used to take turns rubbing the cream on her back, but Mama stopped asking Cheta to help the evening Cheta came into the room and started reading a newspaper article about the harmful effects of bleaching. Cheta's disapproving frown was too much for Mama to handle.

Mama untied the wrapper that she had knotted over her breasts, stood naked in front of the mirror, and watched herself. She started from her hands, worked her way up to her shoulders, then worked down her body. Her heavy breasts lined with stretch marks swayed like the pendulums in physics class as she bent over to rub the concoction on her legs.

As always her movements were slow and methodical. She took her time to rub the mixture into every angle and under every flap, paying special attention to her knuckles, elbows, and knees. When she was done she turned around and handed me the bowl and I dutifully started rubbing it on her back. My touch was slow and firm, the way she liked it. The concoction was warm to the touch and I always felt the residual heat on my palms, no matter how many times I washed my hands, for hours afterward.

"Mama, what is going to happen to Ezinne?" I couldn't help but ask. Aunty Sophie had only delayed the inevitable. Ezinne would eventually be discharged from the hospital and Uncle Festus would be right there with a belt in his hand waiting to finish what he started.

Mama hissed, "Please, I don't want to talk about that stupid girl. You know this is Festus's fault. He was too gentle with the girl. Some children need heavy hands. Children like your sister. If you don't discipline strongheaded children, they think that can do whatever they want. If not for me, Cheta would probably be an igbaraja like her stupid cousin."

I said nothing as I rubbed the cream into her skin and silently said a prayer for Ezinne.

"This developer is working, *eh*?" Mama asked after I was done. Her eyes were on her reflection as she twisted and turned, trying to get a good look from every angle.

"Yes Mama. It's working." I told her what she wanted to hear. It would have made her angry if I had told her that the bleach didn't make her look light-skinned, it just made her look like an overripe banana. Her skin was a motley shade of yellow with patches of brown on the body parts the cream couldn't penetrate.

She turned to me and wrapped her hand around my wrist, lining up her forearm against mine, as she compared our skin tones. "Yes. Yes. It's working. Very soon I'll be a yellow paw-paw like you," she said with a satisfied smile on her face, as she used her hip to nudge me. I knew Mama liked me more than Cheta, but I sometimes was not sure if it was because I was the child who never talked back or if it was because I was light-skinned.

Papa came into the room just as I had finished rubbing the concoction on Mama's back. The white singlet he wore was stretched out tightly over his big belly that seemed to get bigger everyday. He said nothing to us as he unrolled the straw mat on the floor. I once made the mistake of asking Mama why Papa slept on the floor when the bed was big enough for four people. She pinched my lips closed with her fingers and told me to not ask about things that did not concern me.

"Goodnight Papa," I said. Did he notice that my legs had almost given out in the living room? Had he noticed that I had stumbled up the stairs with my hand clutching my chest like a drunkard having a heart attack? I waited a few seconds for him to respond but all I got was a low grunt.

FOUR

Zam

A SHARP STING on my arm woke me up. I opened my eyes to see Mama's discolored face staring down at me.

"Mama, it's Saturday," I said, rubbing my arm. It was the only day I got to wake up after the sun had risen.

"Is that how to greet your mother? You want to start behaving like this your wayward sister?" She glanced at Cheta's bed.

"Sorry, Mama. Good morning, Mama," I said quickly. It was too early to listen to her rant about Cheta's rudeness. It was her favorite topic and if allowed, she could go on for a while. Mama was very good at keeping track of Cheta's transgressions.

"Get up and start sweeping the sitting room. Your Aunty

Sophie called this morning. She is coming to visit before she heads back to Abuja."

"But she came here yesterday, what is she coming to do again?"

"Dodo, stop asking me questions and start sweeping the floor."

"I did it yesterday. It's Cheta's turn to sweep the compound."

"Then wake her up and tell her to sweep," Mama said, walking out the door.

Sometimes, I wondered if Mama was more terrified of Cheta than I was.

I stared at Cheta's sleeping form, silently debating whether or not to wake her up. After last night, I was not sure what kind of mood she would be in this morning. An angry Cheta I could handle, a sad Cheta, I could not. I changed out of my nightgown and into an old T-shirt, with holes in the neck, and tied a wrapper around my waist. By the time I finished sweeping the compound and the first floor, the sun had come out and sweat dripped down my back.

I walked up the stairs slowly, my back aching from being bent over for so long. When I entered the room, Cheta was still on her bed but I knew she was awake from the unnatural way she was positioned; flat on her back, her legs pressed firmly closed, arms at her sides in tight fists. As quietly as I could, I stripped out of my clothes and wrapped my fraying towel around me.

* * *

Aunty arrived around 1 p.m. There was no mistaking the sirens of her convoy.

"Why does she have to use the sirens? She wants to wake up the entire street?" Mama asked. I didn't mention that it was midday and everyone in the village was already awake.

From the window I watched as Mr. Boniface stepped out of the car first and opened the door for Aunty, his gun swaying as he walked. Aunty Sophie's hair was down today, the loose waves framing her face.

"Our wife! Welcome," Mama said with a fake smile. "Please sit down. What would you like to drink? Zam, bring the champagne," Mama called out to me without waiting for Aunty Sophie to actually tell her what she wanted. I didn't understand why Mama bothered to offer. Aunty Sophie never drank or ate anything and afterwards Mama would complain that she just wasted the champagne. "It's because her husband has money, that's why she thinks it's okay to come to somebody's house and waste their food. Or does she think she's too good to drink in our house?"

I didn't know if Mama forgot that it was Aunty Sophie that gave us the money we used to buy food, or if she chose to ignore that fact. If I were Aunty Sophie, I wouldn't want to drink in our house, either, because it was not hard to imagine Mama poisoning her.

I wiped my hands on my dress after I set the tray on the side table beside the sofa. "Good morning, Aunty," I said.

"Zam. How is school? I didn't get to talk to you yesterday."

"F-fine, ma," I stammered. I wanted to ask her what happened with Ezinne but my tongue couldn't form the words.

"She came first in the entire school. Zam, go and bring your result," Mama said proudly. Mama grabbed any opportunity to boast, which always made me feel uncomfortable. But this time when I walked up the stairs to grab my result booklet, I didn't feel the dread that wrapped around me the night before. I wanted Aunty Sophie to be proud of me.

I thrust my result into Aunty Sophie's hands. I wanted to feel that lightness in my chest when she tilted her head and smiled at me. I watched her scan my results, my heart beating hard from the anticipation.

"You're a very smart girl," Aunty Sophie said. When she looked up at me and smiled the pressure in my chest loosened. Her teeth were perfect; white and even.

"Thank you."

"What do you want to be when you grow up?" she asked me.

"I don't know yet." I didn't tell her the reason I didn't know was because I wanted to do whatever she did, though I wasn't exactly sure what that was.

I didn't have to turn around to know that Mama was frowning at me because I had given the wrong answer. Mama wanted Cheta and I to work in the oil and gas industry like Uncle Emeke, because apparently that was where the money was.

"Well, whatever you choose, I'm sure you'll be great at it," she said. I didn't think my smile could get any wider, but it did, and it felt like my face would crack.

Cheta came home a few minutes later, a bucket of water on her head. The water had stopped pumping upstairs by the time Cheta woke up, so she had to fetch some from the neighborhood well down the road.

"Cheta! Congratulations! I heard you got into University of Nsukka and UNIBEN," Aunty Sophie said when she noticed Cheta standing by the door. She patted the space next to her. "Smart girl! Come and talk to me."

Cheta cautiously placed the bucket of water on the floor before walking over to Aunty. Her movements were rigid and unnatural. Aunty asked Cheta about school and choir and I watched as the tension slowly eased out of Cheta. I wondered how Aunty Sophie did it; how she made people feel so at ease. Was she just born that way or could it be learned? Mama was the only person I knew who didn't like Aunty Sophie but Mama was like utazi, no matter how you cooked it, it would always be bitter.

After a few minutes of talking to Cheta, Aunty Sophie reached into her bag and brought out two envelopes and handed one to each of us. "Here, go and buy biscuit, while I talk to your parents."

"Thank you Aunty," Cheta and I said in unison.

"Thank God," she replied.

I slowly opened the flap and, without needing to count, I knew that the money she handed to us was enough to buy a hundred biscuits and still have change to buy soft drinks, but

I didn't want to leave. I only got a few minutes with Aunty Sophie every few months.

Her visits were very quick and she had never wanted to talk to my parents alone before. She usually handed my parents money, talked to us for a few minutes, and then got back into her car and left. I didn't blame her. If I didn't live here I would want to leave as quickly as possible too. There was something draining about the house. Sometimes it seemed the walls had absorbed all the negativity and would cave in on us.

Cheta and I stood up to leave. From the look on her face I knew she was thinking the same thing. What didn't Aunty Sophie want us to hear?

Cheta walked fast and I knew it was because she didn't want me following her. I watched until the harmattan haze swallowed her. Then I turned and walked in the opposite direction to Munachi's house.

Munachi was sitting on a low stool on her veranda bouncing one of her six sisters on her lap. Her mother, Nne Munachi, was pregnant again and I really hoped for everyone's sake it was a boy. Nne Munachi always looked angry when I saw her in church kneeling before the altar and praying furiously for the son her husband, Nedi Munachi, wanted so badly and Munachi was tired of being a second mother to her siblings.

"Nani," I greeted her.

"Nhu nma. Zam, you always come at the perfect time." Munachi said with a smile, lifting the baby's hand and using it to wave at me. The baby reached out for me and I picked her up.

"Thank you," Munachi said gratefully. "Abeg, can you help me watch her, she's been crying and I need to sweep the house before Mama comes home with the other ones."

She didn't wait for a response before running inside. Munachi was one of the few friends I had and sometimes I wondered if it was because I helped her with her siblings or if she genuinely enjoyed my company. I would never actually ask her though. I wasn't sure I wanted to know the truth.

I sat on the verandah and enjoyed the breeze and the baby's babble and imagined how I would tell Mama I forgot the letter Sister Benedicta had given to me yesterday. Mama would read it and she wouldn't be able to resist telling Aunty Sophie that her daughter had been chosen to be the next Deputy Head Girl of St. Margaret's Secondary School, and then Aunty Sophie would smile her beautiful smile at me.

I hoped Cheta wasn't there. There was a prefect hierarchy at school. The Head Boy and his deputy and the Head Girl and her deputy were at the top. Then the hostel, the social, and the sports prefects. The food, the library, and the assembly prefects were at the bottom. Cheta had been chosen as assembly prefect. We were all so sure the Reverend Sisters were going to appoint Cheta as the Head Girl, so when they didn't it was the only thing the entire study body talked about for weeks.

Of course, Cheta never played by anyone's rules and although her position was one that shouldn't come with any real power, Cheta ran our school. Teachers listened to her, students listened to her, even the Reverend Sisters listened to her.

When the Head Girl gave orders students did as they were told but when Cheta gave orders people stumbled over themselves in their haste to do her bidding. But it didn't matter to Cheta that she practically ruled the school, all that mattered was she didn't have the title. She wouldn't care that she had already graduated and was heading off to University in a few months, all that would matter to her was the fact that I got something she wanted. I was still convinced the Reverend Sisters had made some sort of mistake. I was not Deputy Head Girl material. I didn't have an authoritative presence. I could imagine giving junior students orders and having them ignore me or—worse—laugh.

But Aunty Sophie was gone by the time I got back home, the tire tracks on the sand the only sign she was ever here, so there was no need to show Mama the envelope in my bag. Papa was sitting on a chair on the veranda, his head against the wall, his eyes closed. I wasn't sure if he was awake but I still greeted him when I passed by.

I found Mama in her room, sitting on the edge of her bed and counting money.

"Mama what did Aunty want?" I asked.

"She wanted to see if you could live with her and Emeke in Abuja," Mama said without looking up from the bundles of naira in her hand.

It took a few moments to make sense of her words. I was sure I must have misheard her. How could she speak such life-changing words so casually?

"Ke iku?" I asked softly. *What did you say?*

"I said yes."

She misinterpreted my question. I was asking her to repeat her sentence because I was sure I heard wrong, but those three words, *I said yes,* meant I hadn't heard wrong.

"She wants me to live with them in Abuja?"

"Yes," Mama said.

I wanted to ask why but I bit my tongue before the word spilled out. I didn't want to know why. I didn't need to know why.

"When?" I asked instead.

"She's coming to pick you up next Saturday."

* * *

Cheta's bitter laugh made me stiffen. Nothing good ever came after a laugh like that. We were at the dinner table and Mama had just told her I was moving to Abuja. Another day, another confrontation between Mama and Cheta. But this time, I didn't feel the familiar sensation of helplessness crawling up my spine because I knew I wouldn't have to deal with either of them for much longer. It was just a matter of days.

"Why her? Why does she get to go to Abuja and live in a mansion and go to a fancy school? Why does Aunty Sophie want her? Why didn't she ask me?" The words poured out of Cheta's mouth, a torrent of rapid Ika and English, as though her brain couldn't decide what language to speak. Cheta's words always tumbled out of her mouth in a rush to shut someone up or prove someone wrong. But there was a different type of edge in her voice. It was the same way Nne Dorcas had sounded when she found out her daughter had been arrested in Italy for prostitution.

"Why would she want you when she can see all the grey hair you have given me with your wahala? You're a stubborn child, everyone can see that. I would not even have agreed if she wanted you, too. A child like you needs a heavy hand. Do you think I would just give Sophie my child to spoil? Why can't you just be happy for your sister?"

"Because she always gets everything and it's not fair," Cheta said in an unusually solemn voice.

"Eh? So na jealousy dey worry you?" Mama asked, her sentence punctuated with a mocking laugh.

It was like this almost every day. But the argument was different tonight, because for the first time I saw tears fill Cheta's eyes.

No one spoke for a few minutes. Forks scraping against plates and the songs of crickets coming through the open window were the only sounds in the room. So when Cheta started to laugh slowly, an odd-looking smile stretching her face, everyone froze, even Papa who never paid attention to anything, paused and looked at her.

"This child. I'm tired of your nonsense. Finish your food and shut up. Your sister is going to Abuja. End of story."

"Mama—" Cheta didn't get to finish her sentence because Mama picked up the fork by her plate and threw it at her head.

Cheta was quick; she ducked before the fork hit her. She had plenty of practice dodging the objects Mama threw at her.

Cheta rose up slowly, her breathing quick and shallow, her eyes watchful. When she was sure Mama was done throwing things, she straightened to her full height, laughing as she did. I looked at her fingers gripping the edge of the table. I held my breath. Was today the day Cheta would throw something back?

"Kiror?" Mama asked. "Why are you laughing like a devil?"

"You. Mama. You. You are funny." Cheta shook her head and laughed into her food. "It's funny how much you hate Aunty Sophie but you try so hard to be like her. You hate her and yet you're sending your precious daughter to live with her."

"My God. Cheta, so you have the boldness to open your mouth and speak to me like that? Nedi Cheta did you hear what your daughter said to me?"

Papa grunted, his eyes trained on the plate in front of him. He carved a ball of eba, rolled it in his hand, and dipped it in his soup before putting it in his mouth.

"Eh? Zam haven't I tried? Haven't I?" She looked at me, expecting a response.

I didn't have to turn around to know that Cheta was staring at me, waiting for me to say something wrong. I said nothing because as scary as Mama was, Cheta was scarier.

Cheta was a carbon copy of Mama. They had the same big brown eyes and long lashes, thick lower lips and high cheekbones. They not only looked alike, they acted alike too. Their immediate reaction to anything and everything was argue first, reason later. I suppose that was why they never got along—they were too similar.

I had once witnessed a chicken fight in the market. I did not understand the appeal, but one day in the market I came across a group of men and some women standing in a circle screaming, yelling, and laughing. Through a gap in the sea of bodies, I saw two chickens battling it out. The fight was vicious. Claws and beaks, scratching and pecking, wings flapping as they jumped as high as they could. In the midst of the chaos, feathers floated in the air, landing softly around the birds. The fight ended when one chicken pecked the other's eye out. But the victor had a broken wing that trailed limply at its side, so I'm not sure there was really any winner. Cheta and Mama reminded me of that fight. They just kept pecking at each other relentlessly, viciously.

Cheta slowly pushed away from the table and walked upstairs.

"Where do you think you are going to? Come back here!" Mama shouted.

Cheta kept walking.

Mama sat back down and turned to me, "Can you see your sister? She wants to use stress to kill me." She picked up the chicken on her plate and started eating it angrily.

I glanced at Papa, silently willing him to say something, but he quietly ate his food. Could he not feel the tension floating around the dining table? Did it not wrap around his neck and threaten to choke him the way it did me? I wanted to reach across the table, pry his mouth open with my fingers, reach down his throat, and pull words out.

I picked up my fork and continued eating. The food tasted odd. It had been Cheta's turn to cook and, not for the first time, I wondered if she was slowly poisoning us all.

When I got back to the room, Cheta was lying on her bed curled into herself. She made no sound but I knew she was crying from the way her shoulders shook. Sometimes I wished we were like normal sisters. If we actually got along, I would go over to her, wrap my arms around her, tell her that everything would be fine, maybe laugh about Mama's madness. But we weren't close and Cheta would probably slap me for touching her. I sat at the edge of my bed and watched her. I wondered if Mama had finally broken her.

As quietly as I could, I changed into my nightgown and got ready for bed, the lightness that had filled me when Mama told me Aunty Sophie's plan had condensed into a tight rock at the bottom of my stomach.

"Papa never says anything," I said quietly as I lay down on my bed. I knew better than to expect a response, but just before I drifted to sleep, Cheta said softly, "That's because Papa is a shell. Mama has already sucked his soul out of him."

I slipped a hand under my pillow and rolled a rosary bead in my fingers. I decided that tonight, I would be sad for Cheta, but tomorrow I would be happy for myself because I was escaping this house and its sad walls.

That night I dreamt Mama gouged Papa's left eyeball out of its socket, put a straw through the hole, and drank his blood.

FIVE

Cheta—
then

WHEN I THINK of all the adults in my life, I'm filled with deep disappointment. Especially the ones I expected more from. Like Sister Benedicta. I used to think she was one of the better ones but I knew she was just like everyone else. Especially after that scene with the music teacher, the week before prefects were announced.

I was on my way home when a juvie I recognized as one of Zam's classmates told me Zam was in the music room with Mr. Henry. Everyone knew what that meant. I hesitated. I should just let her be, let her learn things the hard way—the way I did. Zam needed to stand up for herself. But I found my feet walking towards the door. Sometimes I didn't know if she was purposefully naïve or if she was just an idiot. Everyone in school knew you weren't supposed to be alone with Mr. Henry. I peered through the window. I could see the tops of their heads but the piano blocked their bodies.

I tried the doorknob, and found it locked. I pounded on the door loudly and obnoxiously, the way landlords did when their tenants owed them rent. "Zam, come out. Let's go home," I shouted. Their heads snapped up at the noise.

Mr. Henry stood and opened the door, his hand resting against the door frame, blocking my entry. "Don't you know how to knock properly? Is that how you knock on doors in your father's house?"

I ignored him and ducked under his arm. "Zam, pack your things, let's go."

"Can't you see that we're having a lesson?" Mr. Henry said testily.

"Our mother is waiting for us and it's just music lesson. It's not as if it's important. If you want to teach her, you can teach her when other students are around."

I grabbed Zam's arm and tried to brush past him but he used his body to block our exit. Mr. Henry wasn't a big man. He was tall and slender and his oversized shirts made him look even skinnier than he was, but I knew he was still stronger than I was. He grabbed Zam's other arm and tried to drag her to his side.

"Stop touching her!" I shrieked. Everyone knew the kind of man he was. I tried to tug Zam away from him.

"Who do you think you're talking to like that?"

"Mr. Henry leave her alone, o!" I knew men like him. Men who had been given leeway to do whatever they wanted by other men in power and by women who chose to look the other way. Men like Mr. Henry were used to getting what they wanted and when they didn't, they usually reacted in one of two ways: they slunk away unused to being confronted or they exploded, their egos unable to handle the indignity of being confronted. Mr. Henry was the latter.

He grabbed my arm and locked the three of us in an awkward circle.

"What sort of nonsense is this, Cheta? What kind of disrespect? How can you march into my office and act like this?" His nostrils flared as he shook us.

"You think we don't know who you are? What you did to Mary? I'm not leaving you alone with my sister," I yelled at him. I released Zam's arm and tried to pry his fingers off mine.

He let go of Zam and dragged me out of the music room and into the corridor.

"Rapist. You no dey shame? You no see woman your age? Agbaya, as big as you are, you're chasing *small small* girls. No woman your age wants you, so you follow fifteen-year-old girls." I taunted him as he dragged me in the direction of the administrative office. Probably to report me to Sister Benedicta.

"Shame. Shame. Shame," I chanted loudly.

The school was mostly empty but a few stragglers stepped into the corridor or stuck their head out of their class windows to see what the commotion was about.

He abruptly stopped, making me slam into him. He smelled musty, like palm wine and ofe oha. I pushed off him just in time to see the hand that wasn't latched to my arm fly at my face. My head spun from the force of the slap. It took a few seconds for me to get my bearings and when I did the anger in me exploded in the most vicious way.

I kicked and punched, all the while screaming "rapist" at the top of my lungs.

"What is going on here? Cheta, stop it. Stop this nonsense at once!" Sister Benedicta's thick words penetrated the fog of rage in my head.

"This rapist hit me." I panted as I spoke. I felt like I did after I ran the 400-meter race during inter-house sports.

"Sister. This child came into my music room and started accusing me of nonsense. What kind of rubbish is this? In my entire life, I have never been disrespected like this. Never. Am I her age mate? How can she open her dirty mouth and speak to me like this?"

Father Charles was right behind Sister Benedicta. "*Eziokwu?* Cheta, is this true?"

"Why wouldn't I insult him? We all know what he did to Mary. If I left them in the music room, only God knows what he would have done to my sister. Why have you not fired him? Why is he still here?"

"We looked into the accusations. Mary confessed that she lied."

"Because you people pressured her!" I screamed. "Because the school's reputation is more important than doing what is right! What kind of Man of God are you?" I pointed a finger in his face and then turned that finger to Sister Benedicta. "You too. After all the prayer, has God not granted you the ability to know right from wrong?"

Sister Benedicta made a choking sound.

Father Charles frowned. "Cheta, watch how you talk to us."

I was sick of this. They were all the same. Just like Papa. Spineless. Never doing anything that needed to be done.

"How is that important? Why are you more bothered about how I'm talking instead of how your music teacher is touching small girls?"

"Cheta. What kind of behavior is this? I expected better from you. As the next Head Girl, you need to learn how to be diplomatic. You need to know when to listen and when to talk," Sister Benedicta said. The way she looked at me when she said "Head Girl," the way her eyes narrowed, I knew there was a threat in there somewhere but I didn't care. They could keep their stupid prefect badge.

I took a deep breath, trying to calm the fury that pounded in my chest. "If I come to school tomorrow and this man is still here, I'll call Aunty Sophie and tell her everything. I'll tell her how you willingly employed a pedophile who likes to touch little girls. I'll tell her. And you know Uncle Emeke would do anything for his wife. You know that there will be repercussions."

I turned to the skinny man at my side, who looked like he wanted to slap me again. "And you. I dare you to try any nonsense with any other girl in this school. I will finish you in this town. Do you hear me? I will make sure my uncle puts you in jail. Just try it again. I dare you."

The crowd around us had grown. Wide eyes and open mouths surrounded me. I searched through the crowd and found Zam cowering in the corner, trying to go unnoticed by making herself smaller. It's a strange thing, hating someone and wanting to protect them at the same time. "Zam, bia, let's be going." I pushed my way through the crowd, ignoring everyone looking at me. I didn't look back to see if Zam was following me, I knew she would.

The walk home went by too quickly. Mama was standing still at the front door, her eyes trained on us. Sister Benedicta had probably already called her and told her what I had done. Even from a distance I could see the air vibrating around her. This was the kind of anger I was weary of. It was the kind that left scars that were too deep. Quiet rage usually meant she was getting creative.

Mama hated me. I figured out a long time ago it was because she couldn't beat me into submission. I refused to give her that satisfaction. I would rebel till the day I died. God forbid her turning me into a zombie like Papa or an nzuzu like Zam.

I couldn't deal with Mama right then. I had used too much of the rage that constantly simmered in my blood. All I had left was a bone-deep weariness. I turned to Zam, who was trailing behind me. Tears were streaming down her face. She had not spoken a word since I saw her in Mr. Henry's office. I hated her meekness. I hated that she never, not once in her life, ever tried to speak up for herself or for me. She just stood there and let things happen, trying to blend into the shadows and ignoring everything happening around her.

"Jesus Christ. Why are you crying?"

She shook her head, her chest heaving as she tried to contain her sobs.

"Look, Zam, God gave you a mouth. Next time when someone is doing something you don't like, use that mouth. When I graduate next year what would you do? You need to learn to save yourself. People aren't always going to be there to save you."

She nodded.

"Go home. I have something I need to do." I knew I would have to face Mama at some point, but that could wait.

I walked down the street to Uncle Emeke's house. Years ago, I had stolen the key Papa kept in his bedside table and made a copy. I made sure no one was paying attention to me before I rounded the house and scaled the wall that surrounded the compound. Through trial and error, I had learned the best place to climb to avoid the barbed wire that lined the top of the wall. The empty house was the place I went to when life got to be too much and I started to wonder what was the point of it all.

I lay on the bed and I finally let the tears leak from my eyes. I cried until it felt like my body would wither away from dehydration. I screamed until my throat hurt too much to make another sound. I broke down in all the ways a person could and when I had nothing left in me, I went home to the punishment that awaited me.

SIX

Zam

I WOKE UP before the sun rose because my body wouldn't stop shaking. I couldn't pinpoint the exact emotion. I was happy, scared, and relieved at the same time. It had become almost unbearable to breathe in the house. Some days I woke up gasping for air because I dreamt I was suffocating. I wasn't sure if leaving meant the dreams would stop, but at least it wouldn't make it worse.

I made sure to make as little noise as possible as I got ready; I didn't need a confrontation with Cheta the day I left. My suitcase had been packed for days, my outfit set aside and ironed the night before. I even used the lip gloss I had bought years ago but never touched. It was sticky and tasted artificial but it made me feel like a woman. I wore my newest sandals, the white and gold ones I had begged Mama to buy because they reminded me of some I had seen Aunty Sophie wear—not that I told Mama that was the reason I wanted them.

I carefully combed my hair. Mama had relaxed the thick undergrowth into submission the night before and my scalp still burned from the chemicals. I tried not to cry as I sat on the floor between Mama's thighs. It was hard not to squirm while she roughly combed the relaxer through. I had to press my hands against my bladder because the pain made me want to pee. Mama had been relaxing my hair for as long as I could remember, and I had learned not to bother begging her to wash it out even when my scalp felt like it was on fire. "That's how you know it's working," she would say. My scalp always tingled for days after.

After combing my hair, I carefully applied Vaseline to the chemical burns around my nape and edges, before joining Papa on the veranda. Papa spent most mornings on the veranda, chewing kola nut and humming.

"Good morning, Papa."

He made a sound with his nose in response. I had not heard him speak since Aunty Sophie's visit over a week ago. I dragged a chair from the dining table and set it beside him. I could feel him watching me, but I didn't turn to look at him.

Papa's silence didn't happen overnight. It was a gradual process and I didn't notice until it was too late. I wasn't sure Mama noticed. She spoke enough for both of them. I often heard her carrying on conversations with him as if they weren't one-sided.

I think it was Grandma's death that broke Papa. Grandma was the smallest woman I had ever seen. I could see over her head by the time I was twelve. Even though she only passed away two years ago, sometimes my brain can't put her individual features together to create her whole face and I have to look through our photo albums to remember what she looks like. I do distinctly remember her ears. They were different shapes: the right one looked like a normal ear but the left was pointed at the top like the elf in a Christmas movie I once watched. She said it was a gift from God so she could hear when he spoke to her.

Her eyes were brown with a thin blue ring around the outer edges. You had to be standing really close and looking right into her eyes to notice the blue. Aunty Ngozi said it wasn't always like that. The blue ring had appeared as she got older. Her nose was small and pointy and there was a bump on her right nostril. I had her nose but without the bump. And she always smelt like talcum powder and the flowery perfume that Uncle Emeke bought for her whenever he visited.

Grandma was everyone's favorite person; she was kind, she remembered everything you ever told her, and best of all, she had given birth to Uncle Emeke, the richest, most generous man in the village. The man every mother hoped their son grew up to be.

She died on a Saturday. I remember because there was no school or church that day. I was sweeping the compound early in the morning when I heard screams. I looked up to see her houseboy running. Chuks was only a grade below me in school but he was tall for his age with a face that had matured before his peers. But right then as I watched him run towards me with panic twisting his features and tears streaming down his face he looked like a child.

"Mama don die! Mama don die!" he cried out. He lived with Grandma in her compound, helping her to do housework and run errands. Grandma used to live with us, but her arthritis had gotten worse and she could no longer climb the stairs to her bedroom. Uncle Emeke and Papa didn't like the idea of her living alone, and she refused to move to Abuja to live with Uncle because Alihame was her home, so Uncle Emeke built the bungalow opposite our house. She was close enough that we could check in on her every day.

Chuks's screams had Mama and Papa running out of the house.

"What is happening?" Papa asked, his chewing stick hanging loosely from his mouth.

"Grandma is dead," Chuks said, the words coming out in between hiccups. It was clearly the first dead body he had ever seen.

Mama slapped him hard across the face. "Gbankiti! Don't you know not to say such things. Stupid boy."

Papa was already running towards Grandma's house. I wondered if he realized he was only wearing one slipper. Mama followed, her bonnet still on her head, wrapper flapping behind her.

I stood there not knowing what to do, the broom still in my hand. A part of me wanted to follow them and see for myself if Chuks was right, but another part of me was terrified he was. We sat underneath the mango tree and watched Grandma's house. Cheta joined us a few minutes later. "Kiror? I heard shouting while I was bathing."

"There's something wrong with Grandma," I said. I didn't want to use the words *death* and *Grandma* in the same sentence. I didn't want it to be true. I didn't say anything else; Cheta could figure out from the way Chuks was crying and the crowd of elders that had begun to form outside Grandma's house that whatever was happening was serious.

She sat with us under the tree and we watched the crowd grow bigger. It wasn't long before we heard women's screams drift through the air. Mama's wail was the loudest—the most distinctive. I would recognize that sound anywhere. A mortician's car pulled up.

Papa came out of the house soon after the black car of death left.

"Papa what happened?" Cheta asked even though we already knew the answer.

"My mother is dead." His words were low and somber and had a finality that shook me. For some reason, Papa's soft words made it all real in a way that the houseboy's hysterical screams, the mortician loading the body into the car, and Mama's distinctive wails hadn't. It was like I had been watching people act a scene from a play. Death wasn't something I ever associated with my grandma, it wasn't something I thought would ever happen to her.

Papa changed that day. The Papa that came out of Grandma's house was different from the Papa that went in. This Papa looked deflated, like he had lost several kilos in the span of a few hours.

"When last did you hear Papa speak?" Cheta whispered to me about a month after Grandma's burial. We had just come back from school. Papa was sitting on the bench on the veranda. When we greeted him he hadn't even acknowledged us.

I opened my mouth to say it was yesterday when he asked me to bring his dinner early, but I realized I was wrong. He hadn't actually told me to bring dinner, he made a gesture with his hand in the direction of the kitchen and I somehow knew what he was talking about. "I can't remember," I answered.

We stood there and watched Papa eat his kola nut. We didn't say it out loud but deep down I knew we were wishing for the same thing: for Papa to call us over and ask us what we learned in school, the way he did before Grandma died. It was as if Papa's words had been buried with Grandma's body. We didn't move until Mama came back home from her shop and told us to go inside to start preparing dinner. That was when I started counting how many days went by without Papa speaking.

As the sky lightened that morning while I waited for Aunty Sophie to take me to Abuja, Papa and I sat in silence, listening to the next-door neighbor's child cry and the chickens in our backyard cluck. For days I had planned what I was going to say to Papa. I wanted him to know how angry I was that he stopped speaking. He wasn't the only one who lost Grandma. I missed the Papa that used to tell us stories about his childhood and make faces at us behind Mama's back when she was on one of her endless rants. I wanted to tell him I was happy that I was leaving because living under the same roof as Mama and Cheta made my chest hurt. I wanted to tell him I was sorry for whatever was causing him pain.

But I didn't say any of those things. A part of me hoped he would speak first. A part of me wanted him to tell me not to leave because it would mean he would be stuck here with Mama and Cheta. I wanted him to tell me he was sorry for not speaking. I wanted him to tell me he would try his best to be more like the Papa I used to know. But he said nothing, so I said nothing, and together we sat in silence, watching the sun rise.

"Zam, come and rub my back," Mama shouted. Her loud voice carried clearly from upstairs, interrupting our silence.

I left Papa on the veranda, dragged the chair back inside and put it in its proper place before heading upstairs. Mama was standing in front of the mirror turning round and round, examining her body from different angles like she always did.

"My Zam, who is going to help me now that you're going?" Mama asked while I rubbed the cream on her back.

"Cheta can help," I said.

Cheta chose that moment to step into Mama's room, a broom in her hand. It was her turn to sweep the house. She greeted Mama without looking at her. I had no doubt she was counting down the days until she left for university just like I had been counting down the days leading up to today.

After rubbing Mama's back, I left her and Cheta in the room together, silently praying today was not the day one of them killed the other. I didn't want anything to interfere with me leaving.

I went back to my room and lay on my bed, running my fingers over the rosary around my neck. I didn't get up until I heard the loud car horns—the unmistakable sounds of Aunty's convoy.

When I walked downstairs, Aunty Sophie was standing in the middle of the living room talking to Mama.

"Zam. Are you ready?" she asked with a smile when she saw me.

"Yes, ma. Good morning, ma," I said. I couldn't help the wide smile that spread across my face. This was really happening.

"Where's your luggage?"

"That is it, ma," I said, gesturing to the old, peeling suitcase in the corner, with a missing wheel. It was the only suitcase we had.

"That?" she asked, eyeing the suitcase.

She said it in such a way, that I was not sure what it meant. Had I packed too much or too little? Before I could reply Cheta said, "Good morning, ma."

She came down the stairs, still in her nightgown, a broom in her hand. I wondered what would happen now that I was leaving. The housework had always been divided equally between us. Cheta still had four months before she left for university. What would happen when she left? I had never seen Papa touch a broom or a mop and Mama hadn't done any housework since

Cheta and I were old enough to help. Sometimes when we cooked she came into the kitchen to supervise, even though her supervision wasn't necessary.

"Ah! Cheta. There you are. I have something for you." Aunty reached into her big bag and brought out a phone box. It was the latest iPhone.

"Thank you, ma. Thank you so much, ma," Cheta said, sounding stunned.

"Thank God," Aunty Sophie said before turning to Boniface and asking him to put my suitcase in one of the cars. "Zam, take one more look around and make sure you didn't forget to pack anything important."

I nodded and went back upstairs even though I had already triple-checked that I had everything I needed. When I was done, Papa was standing in the middle of the living room with Mama, watching me as I walked down the stairs.

Papa bent his knees so he was at my eye level. He grabbed my shoulders and pulled me close to him, his nails digging into my flesh. When he spoke his kola nut breath fanned my face. "My daughter. Don't ever go somewhere that if anything happens the first thing people will ask is, 'What were you doing there?' Do you understand me?" he said softly. His voice was hoarse from underuse.

"Yes, Papa," I replied. It was the most Papa had said to me in a long time and I was too shocked to tell him I did not understand what he meant.

Papa's eyes searched mine as if he was looking for

something. He must have found it because he gave me a small smile and nodded before heading upstairs.

Mama drew me into her. We rarely hugged and I didn't expect to find comfort in her hold, made even more strange by the unique chemical odor that oozed from her, but I did. "My pikin is going to chop life in Abuja," she whispered before heading outside to talk to Aunty Sophie.

It was only Cheta and me left in the living room. The space suddenly felt smaller. For the first time in our lives Cheta and I were going to be apart. How do you say goodbye to someone you had lived with your entire life but didn't know and didn't like? We stood there, neither of us knowing what to say.

Cheta spoke first. "Zam, be very careful in Abuja. Rich people are not like us. They have different rules." She moved forward and for a second it looked like she was going to hug me but then she abruptly took a step back and turned away. I watched her disappear up the stairs. Her words had sounded like a warning. Why were they doing this to me? Why would Papa and Cheta leave me with words that made my already tingling scalp tingle a bit more? If Papa had said nothing and if Cheta had walked away without looking back, I would have left Alihame feeling calm because I would have known things were the way they had always been. I didn't want to go to the car anymore. I wanted to stay and shake Papa and Cheta and make them explain.

SEVEN

Zam

"YOU'RE VERY QUIET. You don't talk much," I heard Aunty Sophie say beside me. We were in her car and my house had long since disappeared in the horizon.

I didn't know how to tell her I didn't like talking for the sake of talking. Maybe it was because I was always around Mama, who never stopped talking, so I appreciated quiet when I had it. Maybe it was because whenever I spoke, Cheta found a way to make me feel foolish. Or maybe it was because sometimes when I opened my mouth to speak to people I was unfamiliar with, my tongue stuck to the roof of my mouth and I had a hard time getting the words out.

I cleared my throat and said, "I don't know what to say." My voice came out feeble sounding and I hated it. Why didn't I have

Cheta's confidence? My mouth felt dry and I knew it was because Auntie's mami wata eyes were focused on me. It was as though her undivided attention was making my salivary glands malfunction.

"It's okay to be shy."

"Yes, ma."

She smiled at my robotic answer. Leaning closer she said, "I know what it feels like to move to a new place. I went to boarding school when I was a teenager. Moving from Benin to England was such a culture shock. I really wanted to make friends so I told people about the wild monkeys that roamed my neighborhood hoping they would think I was cool."

"Did they?"

Aunty laughed. "No. They called me monkey girl and made monkey noises when I walked by. It was very racist."

I thought this was supposed to be an uplifting story. "Did you make friends at the end?"

Aunty laughed again. "God no. I hated that place. I called my mum crying every day until she got tired of it and moved me to a different school."

I blinked and waited for the moral lesson, not sure what it was supposed to be.

"Looking back, yes I was teased, but I probably could have gotten through it if I had a friend to turn to. You and Kaira will both be in the same year. So, you'll have a friend in class. You'll have the whole summer to get to know each other very well before school starts."

I smiled. I liked the thought of having a best friend when I started a new school. "What about Akubundu?" I asked.

"Aku just graduated. He got accepted into MIT. He will be travelling around Europe this summer before he heads off to school." She smiled when she mentioned MIT. There was no mistaking the pride in her voice.

"That's good," I said, though I wasn't sure what MIT was.

"Yes. Very good. We are proud of him. He's very disciplined. But Kaira has not been as focused. You're doing well in school so you'll be a really good influence."

I nodded, excited at the thought. Kaira and I could do homework together, talk about boys, do each other's hair. We could have the kind of relationship Cheta and I never had.

I rubbed my arms against the seats that no longer had any trace of Ezinne's blood. The leather was firm and supple at the same time, nothing like the worn-out seats in Papa's car, with yellow foam peeking through the cracked leather.

"Are you cold?" Aunty Sophie asked when she saw me shiver. She didn't wait for me to respond before reaching over to the air vent. She pressed a button and I watched as the numbers on the screen went up. It was strange riding in a car with air conditioning. I wasn't sure if the air conditioner in Papa's car had ever worked. We always rode with the windows down. I was used to tilting my body towards the window so I could feel the breeze on my face.

* * *

After the plane leveled and the weight in my belly eased, I spent most of the flight with my face pressed against the window. The clouds were so close, so white and fluffy and so unbelievably beautiful, I forgot about my fear. But it came rushing back when the plane began to descend. My ears popped and my belly felt like it was being stretched. I closed my eyes, grabbed the armrests, and said a quick prayer. I didn't open my eyes until I felt the plane come to a stop. And when I stepped off the plane with shaky legs, my body humming with leftover worry, it didn't stop the smile that stretched my lips and made my cheeks hurt. I was in Abuja.

The air was dryer and lighter. It smelt different too. I inhaled a lungful before stepping into the car. The ride was smoother than I was used to.

"There are no potholes," I whispered. I rested my forehead on the tinted windows as I watched the road.

"Honestly, I'm not sure if that's a good thing. Abuja drivers are crazy. The roads are good so people speed anyhow. On top of that a lot of the streetlights don't work so driving in Abuja at night is basically a death trap," Aunty said with a laugh.

I knew exactly when we reached Uncle's neighborhood. It was when the houses turned into mansions. Mansions protected by gates that looked like they were reinforced with some sort of specialized metal only rich people could afford. One house had two statues of angels on either side of the gate. Each house was so different and so beautiful. I thought back to our village, to the rows of brown gateless bungalows all built the same way and all crumbling the same way.

The car came to a stop in front of a black and gold gate that protected a three-story house. We drove into the compound and the first thing I noticed was a water fountain made of white marble. In the middle, a cherub sitting on a pillar held a pot. Water poured from the pot into the fountain.

The front door opened to a beautiful room that belonged in a magazine. Everything looked new and untouched, like the pieces had just arrived from a showroom. There was a small side table in the corner that had a white phone on it. Aunty picked it up and dialed a number. "Come downstairs and bring your sister with you," she said.

"We have a phone in every room in the house. It's easier than shouting," she explained when she saw me looking at her.

Kaira was the first to appear. This was not the Kaira I remembered. We were the same age but somehow she looked older than me, more put together, like the rich women on the cover of the glossy magazines Mama refused to buy. Her lips were painted red and her brown eyes were framed with lashes so long they had to be fake. Her hair was shiny and long and fell in cascading waves. I knew her hair was probably a wig or a weave—I wasn't sure which. Whichever one it was it had to be very expensive. Mama had let Cheta get a weave for her secondary school graduation and the nest of synthetic hair that was sewn onto Cheta's head was nothing like what graced Kaira's head. Cheta's extensions had been an unnatural shade of black, the strands stiff and unyielding; nothing like the softness that framed Kaira's face. I wanted to reach out and run my hands through it.

Her eyes scanned me from head to toe and from the way her lips twisted, I could tell she didn't like whatever she saw.

Akubundu walked in behind her. "Hey," he said, smiling with only one side of his mouth.

If they hadn't been my cousins, I wouldn't have known they were related. Aku had the same fair skin, curly hair, and changing eyes as his mother, and Kaira looked nothing like them. She had dark brown skin and a slight dimple in her chin. Underneath her expensive wig or weave, I knew her kinky coils were chemically relaxed like mine.

"Give Zam a tour of the house," Aunty said to Kaira distractedly, her eyes on her phone. Aku had somehow managed to slip out of the room without anyone noticing.

"Mum, I'm heading to Sola's place now and you know I'm going to that concert later."

"Why don't you take your cousin with you?"

"She doesn't know my friends and tickets are sold out," Kaira said, sounding impatient.

"She can use Aku's ticket." Aunty Sophie turned to me and explained, "We bought the concert tickets before we booked his flight. Aku can't go because he's leaving early tomorrow morning and you know how these concerts can be."

I nodded, though I didn't know how concerts could be.

Aunty's explanation seemed to make Kaira angry. Aunty, whose eyes were on her phone and not on Kaira, didn't notice.

"Zam is tired," Kaira announced like a decree.

"Oh. Of course, Zam. I didn't think of that. You must be tired after all that travelling," Aunty Sophie said, frowning as she typed something.

From behind her mother, Kaira stared at me, arms crossed and eyes narrowed, daring me to contradict her. It was then I realized that living with Kaira could be just as bad as, if not worse than, living with Cheta.

"Yes. I'm tired," I said. With Cheta, I knew when to approach and when to avoid her. I knew how to interpret her laughs, her sighs, the way she pursed her lips. It took years to figure out, years of missteps and misjudgements. I wasn't looking forward to navigating Kaira's landmines, too.

* * *

The first floor had four living rooms and two dining rooms. Each apparently had a different purpose and was decorated in unique styles. The music room had a grand piano and a glass-encased saxophone in one corner. The dark walls and velvet seats gave it a moody feel. The reading room was white and beige and very sparse, as if they had forgotten to decorate it. The game room was a riot of colors and shapes. And the

TV room had large overstuffed couches, dark wood, and the biggest TV I had ever seen.

Between the music room and reading room, a spiral staircase led to the second floor. There were two doors at the landing.

"We call this one the east wing," Aunty said pointing at one door, then she pointed at the other, "This is the west wing. The west wing is your Uncle and I's private quarters."

The door of the east wing opened to a living room decorated in shades of orange. Three couches arranged in a U formation faced the TV. A large wood coffee table in the center was shaped like a cloud and had carvings etched on it.

"There are six bedrooms in this wing. Those are Kaira, Aku, and Annabeth's," Aunty said, pointing at different doors. "That one will be yours." I didn't know who Annabeth was and I didn't ask.

I opened the door to the room that was mine. The walls were cream. There was wallpaper on one wall that had patterns of gold and beige. My suitcase was already by the foot of the bed. Someone must have put it there while we were touring other parts of the house.

"I'll leave you to get settled. If you need anything call me on the intercom. I'm going to be in the west wing. There's a paper on the side table with the list of all the numbers for each room," Aunty said before leaving me alone. Kaira had disappeared early on in the tour.

I took my time to look around the room. There was a walk-in closet that was bigger than my room in Alihame. The bed was twice the size of Mama and Papa's and the bathroom was unlike anything that I had ever seen. There was a complicated-looking bathtub that had a headrest and so many nozzles and nodes I couldn't think what they might be for.

Everything was so expensive and new, so unlike anything I was accustomed to. I wanted to call Aunty back and tell her that I did not know what to do with so much space.

I sat on the bed and bounced a few times, testing it. It was perfect. The mattress at home was so thin, I could feel the iron frame underneath. I lay in the middle of the bed, legs apart, arms wide out, stretching my limbs as far as I could and yet my fingers and toes didn't find the edges.

As I lay on the bed, words that I had heard Father Charles say several times in the past came to me, *Never put a question mark where God has put a full stop.* So, I decided to enjoy the good fortune that had been dropped on my lap. No one, not even Kaira and her obvious hostility, was going to ruin this for me.

EIGHT

Cheta

8:22 P.M.

Twenty-two minutes. That's how long I had been seated at the table—alone. "Eight more minutes," I whispered to myself. Eight more minutes and I was going to start eating. *Do not cry, do not cry*, I chanted in my head as I watched the seconds tick by on the clock. For as long as I could remember dinner was always at 8 p.m., give or take a few minutes. When I was twelve and had malaria, Mama forced a tablet of chloroquine down my throat and dragged me to the dining table. My body was weakened by fever, I could barely keep my eyes open, and I had no appetite. Still, Mama made sure everything on my plate went down my throat. It all came back up an hour later. When I was fifteen, Mama pushed me and I ended up with a sprained wrist when I landed awkwardly on the floor. I couldn't lift a fork with my right hand so Mama insisted I eat with my left. All I wanted to do was swallow a tablet of Panadol and sleep off the pain but, of course, Mama did not allow that.

I hated the dining table. Sometimes I imagined taking an axe to it and chopping it to little pieces. Other times, I dreamt of setting it on fire and watching it burn to a pile of ash. Yet every night, I had to sit at the table with Mama, Papa, and Zam and pretend I wasn't dying inside. Until tonight.

Zam had not been gone up to a day and already things had changed. Mama had never been late to dinner. It was her favorite time of the day. The time where she could gather her family in one place and make all our lives miserable. She never missed it.

8:24 P.M.

The door opened and Papa walked in. He nodded at me before shuffling to his place at the head of the table. Instead of taking a seat, he grabbed his plate and walked back outside.

Don't cry, don't cry, don't cry, I continued chanting. My breath hitched in my chest. I hated that I was upset. I hated that I had thought myself immune to Mama and Papa's actions and they had somehow found a way to hurt me. Again.

Dinner time is family time, Mama always said. Now Zam was gone and she was nowhere to be found.

8:27 P.M.

Papa walked back in, grabbed his glass of water, and walked back out.

8:30 P.M.

I picked up my fork and started eating. I took my time as I ate, chewing slowly and thoroughly and hating myself as I did so, because I was giving Mama time to walk through the front door.

9:12 P.M.

I finished eating, washed my plate, and went to bed. Mama did not show up.

NINE

Zam

I WOKE UP and saw the sunlight streaming in through the windows. I jerked out of bed so fast, my head spun. I didn't know what time I was supposed to wake up. I didn't know if I had chores to do. I showered and got dressed as quickly as I could, before stepping out of the room in search of someone who could tell me what to do.

The living room on the second floor was empty. The tour of the house hadn't included the west wing and I wasn't sure if I was allowed in there. I headed downstairs to check the numerous sitting rooms and dining rooms. They were all empty. As I turned to head back upstairs, I heard sounds coming from the kitchen. I opened the door and saw a man standing at the counter, humming softly.

"Good morning," I said. My voice came out as a whisper.

The man turned around and I saw he was young—just a few years older than me. I stared at his jaw. It was the squarest one I had ever seen.

"Good morning, Madam," he said.

It was strange to be referred to as madam by someone who was obviously older than me. I wanted to tell him he didn't have to say that but I couldn't find the words. We stared at each other. I knew he was waiting for me to speak, waiting for me to let him know what I wanted, but my voice refused to work.

"Breakfast will be ready soon ma."

"D-Do you need help with anything?" I managed to say.

"No, ma." He turned back to the counter and continued chopping the onions.

I stood by the door, my hands twitching by my side. He was dismissing me.

"*Biko*. Please. I need something to do." Something in my tone made him turn around and look at me differently. I needed to prove to be useful. After spending a night on a bed that I could roll around in without fear of landing on the floor, I knew I wasn't ready to go back to Alihame. It didn't matter that Kaira obviously didn't like me. The house was big enough to avoid her.

"You can . . . help me peel the carrots," he said. I didn't miss the hesitation in his voice. He didn't want my help but he didn't know how to tell me no either.

"I'm Ebuka," he said as he handed me a knife.

"Zam."

We worked side by side, peeling carrots. I was peeling faster than he was, mostly so he could see how useful I could be.

The phone by the door rang and Ebuka quickly wiped his hands and answered it. "Morning, *sah*, yes, *sah* . . . no, *sah* . . . okay, *sah*."

After hanging up, Ebuka said, "Aunty, Oga say make you go upstairs. To his floor." His voice trembled as he spoke. How had Uncle known I was here? Had he called every room in the house until he found me?

"*Abeg*, tell Oga say no be me force you do work." There was a mixture of fear and anger in his tone.

"S-sorry," I said without looking him in his eyes. I walked up the stairs slowly, thinking of what I had done wrong and how to explain myself. I hesitated and took a deep breath before I knocked on the west wing door.

"Come in," Uncle's voice said.

I slowly turned the knob and pushed the door open. It took more effort than I was used to. The doors in the house were so thick, nothing like the flimsy doors in our houses, all of them cracked and splintered.

Aunty Sophie and Kaira were seated on opposite ends of a large sofa. Aunty had a large mug in her hands and Kaira was on her phone. Uncle Emeke was standing in the middle of the room, his eyes on the large TV. On the screen was a picture of the living room on the second floor, then it changed to a picture of the entrance of the house, then it changed again to a picture of the kitchen. When I saw Ebuka walking about in the kitchen, I realized I was actually watching security camera videos.

"Good morning," I said, and all their heads turned to look at me.

Kaira rolled her eyes and refocused on her phone. Aunty Sophie and Uncle Emeke smiled at me. It seemed impossible that this man and my father were full-blooded brothers. They were so different, even in the way they carried themselves. Papa's walk was slow—not old-man slow—careful slow. As if he had to think about every step before he took it. Uncle Emeke's walk was bold. He moved with intention and with the assurance that the world would part for him.

Uncle was wearing a T-shirt and jeans. I had never seen my father in jeans. Papa typically wore one of his many once-white-but-no-longer-white singlets with yellow armpit stains that never came out no matter how long I soaked it in bleach. He also tied his wrapper around his waist before pulling the edges up and knotting it round his neck.

Uncle Emeke was four years older than Papa but he looked at least ten years younger. He was lean and he didn't carry the bulk of his weight in his belly like most fathers I knew.

"Zamzam. How are you?" Uncle Emeke said.

The nickname made my heart lurch because it was the name Papa used to call me when I was little. Back then, Papa would put me on his shoulders and carry me around the house. Sometimes when the season was right and the fruit was ripe,

Papa would carry me to the mango tree outside so I could stretch my little hands out and pluck them.

"I'm fine Uncle," I said.

"Good. Good. Very good." He smiled at me again, his teeth the same unnatural shade of white as Aunty Sophie's. I knew no matter how hard I brushed my teeth it could never get that white and I wondered what kind of toothpaste they used.

Uncle patted me on the back, his arm wrapping around my shoulder. "What were you doing in the kitchen?"

"I was helping Ebuka with breakfast."

"Why did he tell you to help him? Don't we pay that boy enough?" Something dark crossed Uncle's face and it reminded me of the day I made a comment about how nice Uncle was. It was after a visit when he had given Mama and Papa two cows, a dozen chickens, and several hampers stocked to the brim with expensive provisions. Cheta and I were standing outside watching his convoy drive away and in typical Cheta fashion she snorted at me and said, "Nice men don't succeed in this country," before walking away.

"No, no," I said quickly. "I was the one that wanted to help. Cheta and I always do housework in the morning. I'm used to having something to do." I didn't tell him I wanted to be useful so they wouldn't send me back home.

Uncle smiled at me. I wondered if the toothpaste I found in my bathroom was the same one he used. "Sophie, I told you we spoil these children. See their cousin, waking up early to work in the kitchen."

Aunty Sophie didn't react to Uncle's comment. She was looking out the window, not paying attention to the conversation.

He turned away from his wife and faced his daughter. His long finger pointed at Kaira. "You, do you even know how to boil egg?"

"Yes, Dad," Kaira replied, her eyes on me. It was the same look Cheta gave me anytime Mama compared her to me. I wanted to reach up and slap my hand against Uncle's mouth. Did he not know that he was only making things worse for me?

"How was your concert?" I asked Kaira.

"It was fine." Her tone was reluctant; I could tell the only reason she answered me was because her parents were there. I couldn't think of anything to say after that so I was happy when Aunty started talking about something she read in the news.

I headed back to the kitchen, but Ebuka was no longer there. Instead there was a man wearing a white cook uniform and hat and a red apron, standing in front of a stove, stirring something in a pot.

"Good morning sir," I said.

The man turned around at the sound of my voice. "Ah. You must be our new little madam. Come and taste this." His apron had *Chef Gideon* written in cursive script on the left breast.

I walked closer and watched as he sprinkled spices into the pot and stirred. He was a short, plump man with skin so dark and a head so bald and shiny, it reminded me of a freshly licked icheku seed.

"Do you like tikka masala?" he asked.

"I don't know."

"It's Indian food, but I put my own special twist in it."

Another man came in through the door that led outside.

"Have you met Romieto? Romieto, come and meet the new little madam." Chef Gideon said to the man in a voice that was too loud to use when speaking to someone that close.

"This is Romieto, the house steward. He's my Oga. *Eh no be so*? He runs the house." Chef Gideon put an arm around the man's shoulders as he spoke. Mr. Romieto was just as fat and just as short as Chef Gideon, but not as bald and not as dark. He had the biggest eyes and the pointiest ears I had ever seen on a human head.

"Good morning, sir," I said to him.

He laughed a deep laugh and his pointy ears moved up and down as his face did. It was hard to stop staring at it. I had never seen ears move like that. "I like this one already. See how polite she is, not like the other one," he said to Chef Gideon, but his eyes were on me. I had a feeling Kaira was the other one he was referring to.

Mr. Romieto went over to a drawer and pulled out a notepad and a pen. "So little madam, what do you like to eat?" he asked.

I hadn't been expecting that question. I wasn't sure I had ever been asked what I like to eat, at home Mama decided what we cooked and at school we ate whatever the Sisters prepared.

"I like everything," I said because my mind had gone blank. I couldn't remember my favorite foods.

For some reason that made Chef Gideon laugh. "You can't like everything because you haven't tasted my food yet." He got a small bowl from one of the cupboards.

Aunty Sophie was having some important guests over and Chef Gideon was preparing little appetizers and pastries for them. I spent the next few hours in the kitchen, tasting whatever he put in front of me. I smiled and ate and told Chef Gideon how great everything tasted and in return he smiled so hard his chubby cheeks wobbled.

* * *

"Is that what you're wearing?" Kaira asked, standing by my open door.

I looked down at my outfit. It was the same one I wore when I arrived in Abuja, three days before. I knew Kaira didn't like it but it was the best I had and I wanted to impress Kaira's friends.

"I have some clothes you can borrow," she said. Her voice had the same authority Cheta's had. I sat on the edge of my bed and waited for her return.

She came into my room about fifteen minutes later, rolling a suitcase behind her. "These are some of my old clothes. You can have all of them. We should be the same size." I watched as she rifled through the suitcase before picking out dark blue jeans and a black peplum shirt. She handed it to me and I headed to the bathroom to change.

I returned slowly, bracing for the criticism heading my way, but surprisingly she gave me a nod of approval then said, "Come and sit down. I'll do your makeup for you."

I obediently sat down.

"My foundation is too dark for you. I'm going to mix my mum's foundation with my own, hopefully it'll be close to your color," she said. She left the room and came back a few minutes later with a lighter foundation.

"You have very good skin," she said softly as she rubbed something silky into my face.

I wasn't sure if it was a compliment or an observation, so I didn't say thank you. It was strange to be this close to her. I could smell her perfume, it was sharp and flowery and hung around her like an invisible cloud. She was so close I could feel her breath on my face. It was the first time she had ever touched me.

"Do you want me to bake to your face?"

"Um . . . you can do whatever you think is best," I said because I didn't know what baking my face meant.

"Do you have to talk like that?" she asked me as she went through her makeup bag.

"Talk like what?"

"With that thick Igbo accent?"

I didn't know what to say. This was the way I had always spoken. Everyone around me spoke like me. This was the first time I was surrounded by people who sounded different.

Neither of us said another word as she finished my makeup. When she was done I went into the bathroom and watched my lips in the mirror as I practiced talking like her.

Kaira's friends were just like her. Their faces were flawlessly made up, eyebrows perfectly arched, cheeks precisely contoured. Like Kaira, they both looked so much older than sixteen. One had medium-sized braids piled on the top of her head and twisted to create a donut and on one side of her nose was a small diamond stud. The other girl was very short and had a long weave that reached down to her tailbone. The weave was just as soft and healthy looking as Kaira's. Despite their obvious differences, Kaira and her friends seemed to look the same. I think it was the thick eyebrows they had drawn on.

"This is my cousin, Zam," Kaira said.

"Zam. That's a really cool name. What does it mean?" the one with long hair asked.

"My full name is Chukwuzamekpere. It means, 'God has heard me,'" I said, elongating my vowels and numbing the consonants, the way Kaira did. The way these girls did too. I saw the girl with the braids' eyes widen and dart to look at her friend before looking back at me and saying, "Sorry, what did you say?"

I repeated myself, my words slower, less sure because I could see the amusement in their eyes, the mocking. The girl turned back to her friend—who was trying and failing to hold back laughter—with a wide smile on her face. My heart started to pound because I knew they were mocking me and I didn't understand why.

"She sounds like all those Nollywood actresses trying to do phonetics," Long Hair said to Nose Ring.

"Zam come here, I want to ask you something," Kaira said. She didn't wait for me to react before grabbing my arm and pulling me out of the room and towards the stairwell.

"Why are you talking like that?" she whispered.

"Like what?" I thought I had been doing what she wanted.

"With that nasty voice. Is that your idea of an American accent? Stop. Just stop," she said before releasing my arm. My heart stuttered at the fierceness in her voice. I stood in the stairway trying not to cry.

"I don't know why she doesn't like me." I did not realize I had spoken the words aloud until I heard a voice behind me say, "It's because you're finer than her."

My head snapped up and I whirled around to see a tall girl with thick glasses and the biggest afro I had ever seen. It was the kind of Afro that people sported back in the day, when my parents were young.

"She's insecure. You are beautiful and she is not. It's that simple," the strange girl said as she walked up the stairs towards me.

Her accent was odd. So similar to Aunty Sophie's—she also had a lilt—but it was a different kind. Not quite Nigerian, not quite foreign, a little bit of both. The strange mixture of accents all rich people seemed to have.

"You have an accent." It was the only thing I could think to say.

An eyebrow rose above the frame of their glasses. "So do you."

I wanted to shake my head and disagree with her, but instead I asked, "Who are you?"

"I am Ginika." She announced her name in a way that made me feel like I had done something wrong by not knowing who she was. "And I'm guessing you're the village cousin Kaira doesn't like."

Village cousin. Was that how Kaira was referring to me? Had she texted all her friends to warn them that she had a village cousin she didn't like living with her?

She stepped closer to me and I instinctively stepped back. She took another step towards me.

"You look like Aunty Sophie." It was a statement, not a question, and I was not sure if she wanted a response.

"But you are related to Aunty only by marriage." Another statement.

"If I saw you, Aunty Sophie, and Kaira together. I would assume that you were Aunty's daughter not Kaira. You have Auntie's fair skin and delicate nose."

My hand reflexively came up to touch my nose. I had never thought of my nose as delicate.

Ginika used a finger to push her glasses back up her face. She looked like what I imagined university professors looked like. "Kaira looks nothing like her mother and her bulbous nose is too big for her face. But she's attractive enough."

She stopped talking and tilted her head as if in deep thought.

"Until she opens her mouth," Ginika said.

"What?"

Ginika sighed impatiently and I felt like a student who had been caught sleeping in class. "Kaira is a reasonably attractive girl, until she opens her mouth. Sometimes I want to poke out her eye with my pen."

My eyes drifted to her huge afro and to the pen almost completely buried in it. Did she have more pens in there?

"Are you friends?" I asked. What was this girl who clearly did not like Kaira doing here?

"I have no friends," she said simply.

I did not find that surprising. I had only been in her presence for a few minutes and I already knew that she was too honest, too forthright. The kind of friend that will tell you things you did not want to hear. The kind of friend everyone said they needed but no one truly wanted.

"Why are you here then?"

"Aunty Sophie and my mother are friends," she said before walking into the living room.

I followed her. Kaira and her friends were sitting on one couch. None of them acknowledged Ginika and she didn't seem to mind. She walked up to Kaira and took the remote that was beside her before moving to the other side of the room to sit on another couch. I wondered how she could be so comfortable in someone else's house.

"What are you doing? We were watching that," Kaira said, but she didn't seem very upset.

"You weren't watching, you were gossiping. If you want it, come and take it from me," Ginika said. But it didn't sound like a challenge, it just sounded like she was too lazy to walk back to hand it to Kaira. Kaira hissed and turned back to her friends.

While Kaira and her friends talked about people I didn't know and places I'd never heard of, Ginika watched something about sea lions and I just sat there, unsure of what to do with myself. My eyes were on the sea lions documentary but my ears were on Kaira's conversation.

When the phone rang, I rushed up to go get it because at least it gave me something to do, if only for a few seconds.

"Hello?"

"Mrs. Ibe is looking for Annabeth," Mr. Romieto said. It was the same name Aunty had mentioned when she was giving me a tour. Annabeth was the person who stayed in the room opposite mine.

I wasn't sure which one of Kaira's friends was Annabeth so I called out, "Mrs. Ibe is looking for Annabeth." None of the girls answered, no one even looked at me.

"Did you say Annabeth?" I asked Mr. Romieto. Maybe I had heard the name wrong.

"Yes."

"They're looking for Annabeth," I said a little louder. Again no one even acknowledged that I was speaking.

"There's no Annabeth here," I said into the phone, ignoring the heat snaking up my neck.

A few minutes later I heard the distinctive sound of high heels on marble. The door opened and an average-height woman wearing a blue dress walked in.

"Annabeth, didn't they tell you I was calling you?" the woman said as she strode into the sitting room, her eyes locked on Ginika.

"Mum. I've told you that my name is Ginika," Ginika said without looking away from the television. Her tone was flippant, as if she was talking to a classmate and not her mother.

"Annabeth, don't start this again."

"Ginika," Ginika said firmly.

"Fine—Ginika. Are you okay with spending the next few weeks here? I have a last-minute deal I need to oversee in Lagos, it may take a while."

Ginika gave her mum a thumbs-up with one hand. That seemed to be a good enough answer for the woman, who turned around and left. Her high heels announced her exit, the same way they had announced her arrival.

When the sound faded, Kaira turned to Ginika and asked, "Why don't you want to be called Annabeth?"

"Because Ginika is my name."

"It's your middle name," Kaira said.

"First name, middle name, whatever position it is. I answer only to Ginika now," she said in a firm voice that sounded like a warning. If she had been talking to me I would have dropped it. But Kaira and her friends weren't like me.

"Why? What's wrong with Annabeth?" Nose Ring asked.

"Nothing. It's a perfectly good name. But I am a Nigerian, why should I bear a white name. I personally think it's a cop-out. It's sycophantic. There are millions of beautiful Nigerian names."

Kaira rolled her eyes.

"I have a white name," Long Hair pointed out.

"Congratulations," Ginika said without looking away from the TV screen.

"Why do you suddenly care about your name being Nigerian? You've answered to Annabeth for years," Kaira asked.

"They've taken so much from us, our history, our art, our religion, our language. Why should I willingly hand over my identity too? Call me Ginika or don't call me at all," Ginika said.

Her agitation hung in the air awkwardly and it was obvious that no one knew what to do with it.

Kaira broke the silence with a broken laugh. "Ginika, it's really not that deep."

"It really is."

"What really happened? Let me guess, you watched a slave movie and got all in your feelings?"

Ginika sat up straighter. She looked like someone gearing up for a fight.

Kaira must have noticed it too because she quickly said, "I'm really not in the mood to argue with you." She rolled her eyes and turned back to her friends. "Let's go to my room."

Ginika didn't seem to mind. She settled into the couch and continued flipping through channels. I wasn't sure what to do with myself. A part of me wanted to knock on Kaira's door and another part of me wanted to stay here and talk to this strange girl who clearly didn't care what anyone thought of her and walked into someone else's home like she owned the place. In the end I headed to my room.

TEN

Cheta

I WOKE UP with a headache the morning after Zam left and punished myself by not taking any Panadol to ease the beating in my skull. Why couldn't I learn that Mama did not deserve my tears?

"Mama, dinner was at eight p.m., you were not here," I said when I saw her seated at the dining table, drinking her morning cup of Bournvita.

"Ehen? And?" she said, not bothering to look at me.

I said nothing. If this was how she wanted to act, then I could show her that I was better at this game. I wore my shoes and got ready to leave.

"Where do you think you're going to?"

"Out."

"Better cook breakfast before you go anywhere."

"I cooked dinner last night. It's Zam's turn to cook breakfast."

"Are you stupid? Can you not see that your sister is not here?"

"That is not my problem," I said, before walking out the door.

I heard Mama scream behind me. I knew she wouldn't follow me out of the house. She had learned I was unwilling to tolerate her nonsense two years ago. It had been early in the morning. She had taken off her slipper and threatened to beat me with it because I had not ironed her clothes to her satisfaction. I just couldn't handle it. I couldn't take one more hit and for the first time in my life I defended myself by grabbing her wrist instead of curling into a ball and letting her do as she pleased.

"*Heewwooo!*" Mama had screamed. "You have the guts to grab me like that? Nedi Cheta have you seen what your daughter has done?"

I released Mama's wrist and she instantly brought it up to her chest, cradling it with her other hand as if she was in pain.

"This child is trying to kill me o! Cheta, I did not kill my mother, so I will not let you kill me! Did you hear me?! I will not allow it!" Mama shouted.

She stopped hitting me that day and started throwing objects, usually the closest thing to her, like textbooks, knives, shoes, remotes, and even a half-eaten chicken wing. She had good aim but I had quicker reflexes; it was a skill I had to hone fast.

She kept her evil concealed behind closed doors, lying to people about how I got my scars. Acting like the other mothers—strict but dutiful. The kind of mother that hated to discipline her children but had to because it was the godly thing to do. Everyone probably assumed she was heavy-handed with me because it was what was best for me, not because she was a sadistic witch.

I walked the distance to Ms. Okoye's house. Ms. Okoye was my Primary 3 teacher who got married, changed her name to Mrs. Ochuba, and moved with her husband to Anambra. She came back to Alihame three years ago, husbandless and with burns covering the left side of her face, insisting everyone refer to her by her maiden name. No one knew what happened to her. At first the rumor was she had been in a car accident that killed her husband, but as rumors go that wasn't juicy enough. When Ms. Okoye refused to confirm or deny anything, new rumors began to spread. Some said that she had been caught with another man and her husband, in a fit of rage, poured boiling water on her. Others said the wife of the man she was sleeping with burnt her face with an iron. There were many rumors, each much worse than the last.

I learned not to ask Ms. Okoye questions. The first and only time I did, she shook so hard, her teeth chattered. I had tried to let her know that I knew what pain felt like. Tried to show her that I understood what it felt like to live with scars. I raised my shirt to show her mine and she immediately withdrew from the land of the living. She wrapped her hands around herself and started swaying from side to side, a loud keening noise coming from her closed mouth. It took me a moment to realize she was crying without tears. I learned to keep my thoughts to myself after that. She was half of the reason I wanted to study psychology; Mama was the other half.

I used my key to enter the house. She had given me the key a year ago when I started cleaning for her. On the kitchen table, I found a list of items she wanted me to buy and a stack of notes on top of it. How did she make money when she never left her room?

"Ms. Okoye," I called out, knocking on her door. "It's Cheta. I'm going to the market."

There was no verbal response but I heard the thump of her knuckles hitting the bedside table. We had come to an agreement. If she didn't want me to burst into her bedroom to make sure she was alive, she had to respond in some way when I spoke to her.

The first time I shopped for Ms. Okoye was the day I had found her unresponsive on the market road, mud seeping into her clothes as she rocked and muttered nonsensical words. There was a crowd gathered around her, watching and shouting for someone to help her, yet no one did. They probably thought whatever she was going through was contagious.

I elbowed my way through the crowd to get to her. She didn't seem to know who I was but she followed me as I guided her home. I forced her to drink a bottle of water, unsure if it would help but sure it wouldn't hurt. She came back to herself after she lay on her couch for a few minutes. I offered to return to the market and finish her shopping because I had noticed how empty her fridge was when I fetched the water, and she was in no shape to go back there. She offered me a job when I returned.

I loved going to the market. The air was thicker, it smelled like spice and sweat and dirt. Voices mingled and clashed in the air as vendors called out to customers, each one trying to outshout the other. I liked the controlled disorder of the market. There was so much happening, so many scents, so many voices, it overwhelmed me in a good way because it matched how I felt inside.

As I walked through the market, hands reached out of market stalls, trying to grab me. Voices called to me, telling me they knew what I wanted, they had the lowest price, their product was the best. I ignored them all, expertly navigating the stalls.

"How much is your tomatoes?" I asked.

When the woman told her me her price, I laughed. "Are you here to sell your market or are you here to play? Dodo, be serious."

"Sister, times are hard, o. Price don go up," the woman said, the edge of her lips pointed downwards in an exaggerated frown that made her face look like it was melting.

"Hmm," I said, my tone conveying I didn't believe her.

"*Ehen!* Make I even show you this shoe I dey sell." She bent down to riffle through the Ghana Must Go bag by her feet and brought out a brown leather shoe with a ridiculously high heel.

"Look at this shoe. Fresh from Italy. Very good quality. Will last you ten years." She hit the shoe on the ground twice before lifting it and knocking on the sole twice with her knuckles.

"See. Strong material," she said, and thrust the shoe at me. "Which size you be?"

This was one of my favorite things about coming to the market. The hustle. Everyone was working hard, doing what needed to be done to make money to eat and keep a roof over their heads. "Wetin concern me, concern Italy shoe? Is that what I told you I wanted to buy?"

The girl put the shoe back in the bag, muttering under her breath about how I would regret not buying the shoe when I see all my friends wearing it.

"The heat is too much for this nonsense. How much for tomato?" I asked, impatience making my words come out in huffs.

I was a good negotiator. I got good deals and always convinced them to add a little jara. It was why I didn't feel guilty when I pocketed a quarter of Ms. Okoye's change. I earned it.

I liked Ms. Okoye but the money she paid me wasn't enough for the plans I had, and as a rule, I generally don't regret actions that are for my benefit even if it puts someone else at a disadvantage, because no one put me first. I had to put myself first. Every moment of the day something in this bloody country tried to kill my spirit and I was too stubborn to allow it. I refused to leave this earth before I got a chance enjoy my life. If I had to cheat Ms. Okoye in the process, so be it.

* * *

Mama was in the living room waiting for me. She sat on the couch, her legs crossed and her foot shaking with anger.

"If you want to live in this house, you will do housework."

"Okay, Mama."

I watched her eyes widen in surprise before narrowing. Then I smiled and continued, "But only on the schedule that we've been using for the past six years."

"So who is supposed to do the work on Zam's days?"

I knew she was daring me to point at her and say she should do it but that was a fight for another day. Instead I shrugged and said, "Hire a house girl."

"What will people say? I have a daughter and I'm hiring a house girl? How do I explain that?"

"Daughter, not indentured servant, Mama," I said.

ELEVEN

Zam

"CAN YOU HEAR me?" Mama shouted.

I held the phone away from my ear and inhaled. "Yes, Mama, I can hear you," I said, bringing the phone back to my ear. I was standing on the balcony because it had the best mobile reception. The connection in some areas of the house was spotty. Mr. Romieto said it was because of the tall hills that surrounded the estate.

"Didn't I tell you not to use that broom? Go and get the other one," Mama said.

It took a moment to realize she wasn't talking to me. Mama was very good at carrying on several conversations at the same time.

"Somto, not that one the other one. Hello, hello. Zam, can you hear me?"

I closed my eyes and released a slow sigh, "Yes, Mama. I can hear you. Who is Somto?"

"The new house girl. I need someone to take care of the house now that you're not here."

I was confused. "I thought the house girl's name was Ada?" When I spoke to Mama two days ago, in between telling me how someone had the audacity to challenge her position as the head of the church council, she had yelled at Ada to wash the bathtub.

"I sent that stupid girl away. She was worse than your sister. I'll tell her to sweep and she'll be frowning her foolish face. What is it with you children of nowadays? No respect. Anyway, I hired this new girl yesterday. Nne Eze recommended her," Mama said.

"What do you think you're doing?" Mama yelled. "If you break my vase, the money will come out of your salary."

This girl was definitely not going to last long.

"*Ehen*, Zam, what was I saying? Mm . . . Oh yes, your sister! Do you know that I have not seen that girl since yesterday? She thinks because she has finished secondary school she can do whatever she wants."

"Sorry." I apologized on Cheta's behalf because that was what I had always done. I hadn't spoken to Cheta since I left. She hadn't called me and I hadn't called her. I wondered if she missed me. I definitely didn't miss her and I wasn't sure if I should feel guilty about that.

"Is Papa there?" I asked. I hadn't spoken to Papa either.

"No. He's sitting on the veranda." I knew Mama was in the living room because she just told Somto not to break her vase. It was the blue figurine that sat on the middle of the center table. If Papa was on the veranda, then he was just about ten steps away. Mama could have called to him and asked him to come get the phone or she could have stood up and walked the ten steps, but she didn't offer and I didn't ask.

When the phone call ended and I turned around, I saw Ginika standing behind me, licking a lollipop and looking at me with a thoughtful expression. I hadn't heard the sliding doors open, so I didn't know how long she had been behind me.

"Your Igbo sounds different," she said.

"I wasn't speaking Igbo. That was Ika."

"It kind of sounded like Igbo."

"It's similar, but it's not the same."

"Will you teach me?" she asked, bringing the lollipop out of her mouth with a pop.

"Teach you Ika?"

"No, Igbo."

"Why?"

"Do you want to live in a world where most people speak the white man's language? How boring," she said, her nose wrinkling.

"My Igbo is just okay. Maybe Ebuka can help you," I said.

She did that eyebrow thing where one went up. "Who?"

"The boy that helps Mr. Romieto." I wasn't exactly sure what his title was.

She tilted her head, as if thinking about it, and then shook it. "You can teach me. I'm sure your Igbo is more than adequate."

She turned around and headed back inside and I followed her. On the dining table were several notebooks, pens, a laptop, and an iPad. The black leather notebook she always had with her was open to a blank page. I wanted to ask her what she was always writing in it but another question that had been bothering me came out instead.

"Why do you hate white people?" I asked abruptly, the question that had been on the tip of my tongue bubbling out of my mouth fast before I lost the nerve to ask.

She looked up from her notes in surprise, taking a moment to answer. "Because I read."

I wasn't sure what she meant by that.

She sighed. "I'm joking. I don't hate white people. I just want to learn how to love my people, but a lot of our culture and history has been eroded. The harder it is to learn about our past, the angrier it makes me. But I don't hate white people."

I nodded even though I didn't really believe her. Instead I said, "Will you teach me how to talk like you?"

"Talk like me?"

"Kaira said my voice is too Igbo. Teach me how to pronounce words the right way."

"You can't talk like me. I grew up in Germany, and pronouncing words the Nigerian way isn't wrong." She sat on the chair, opened her laptop, and began to type. I watched, fascinated, as her hands flew over the keyboard using all of her fingers. She didn't even need to look at the letters. There were only two computers in our school, and I had only ever typed on them a few times, carefully picking out the letters with just three fingers.

"You really shouldn't listen to Kaira, she's very pretentious," Ginika said. She tilted her head up to look at me, her fingers still flying across the keyboard. I wondered if she could actually type without looking at the keys or if she was just typing nonsense.

"I have this app on my phone and laptop that teaches languages. Obviously, Igbo isn't one of them, or I wouldn't need you. We can use the format the app uses."

It was obvious she had already planned this out, and I didn't know if it meant I was predictable or she was so confident she would always get her way.

"Let's start from here," she said, turning the laptop towards me and pointing at her screen.

I hesitated for a moment, not liking the way she expected me to do what she wanted. But I had nothing better to do and it was nice to be needed for something, so I pulled out a chair and sat down.

* * *

I entered the kitchen and saw Ebuka rifling through the pantry, a notebook in his hand. Every few minutes he paused to write something down.

"What are you doing?" I asked.

"I'm seeing if there's anything I need to add to the list of things to buy in the market tomorrow," he answered without turning around, like he knew I had been standing there watching him.

"Can I come with you?"

"I'm not sure—"

I cut him off before he could finish his sentence. "I'm coming with you. I like going to the market," I said in a firm tone. I needed to be more like the people around me. Ginika wouldn't ask. She never asked, she just took. Besides it wasn't his permission I needed.

He turned around and finally looked at me. "Okay," he said, his lips twisted in amusement. I spent most of my time in the kitchen because that was where I felt most comfortable. It was hard to feel anything other than comfortable in Chef Gideon's presence. Ebuka didn't talk as much but he had warmed up to me. Sometimes I found him smiling at me, his deep dimples on full display.

The next morning, I was up early, eager to be out of the house and heading somewhere other than church. "Madam said to give you in case you see anything you want to buy in the market," Mr. Romieto said, as he handed me a stack of bills bound together with a yellow rubber band. It was so strange how easily money was given out in this house. I tucked it into my blue purse that was slung across my body.

Mr. Romieto and I walked outside, where the black Range

Rover and the white Hilux truck were. Ebuka was in the Hilux with a driver whose name I didn't know.

"Festus will be with you in the black Range Rover," Mr. Romieto said.

"Why can't Ebuka ride in the car with me?"

"You're the new little madam. Madams don't ride with staff," Mr. Romieto said with a laugh.

The Hilux was the only vehicle in the compound that wasn't tinted. I could see Ebuka talking with the driver and laughing. I wanted to put my finger in his dimple.

"Zam, he's the staff. You are Oga's niece. Do not forget that," Mr. Romieto said in a serious voice. I turned around in surprise. He had never said my name before, it was always little madam. He wasn't looking at me; he was staring at Ebuka with a frown.

"Don't get that boy in trouble," he said before turning around and heading back into the house.

* * *

The first thing I noticed when we got to the market was the smell. The scents in the air were familiar: fresh fruit, sweaty bodies, rotting fruit, fried foods, cheap perfume. But it was also different—spicier, less earthy than the market in Alihame. Loud conversations floated past me, but the rhythm was different and it took me a moment to realize it was because there were more languages being spoken. I heard snippets of Hausa, pidgin, Igbo, Idoma, Esan, and even French.

"Where are we going to first?" I asked Ebuka.

"To buy tomatoes." He paused before adding, "I buy it from my mother."

Ebuka's mother was a thick woman with ample folds and wobbly cheeks very much like Chef Gideon's.

"My boy," she said when she spotted Ebuka. She got up from the wooden bench she was sitting on to hug him. Her folds seemed to wrap around him, engulfing him in what I imagined was a very warm, very soft hug.

"Who is this?" she asked when she noticed me standing there, watching them.

"This is Zam. She's Oga's niece."

"Hmm," she said as she stepped in front of Ebuka, almost as if she was protecting him from me.

"Wetin she dey do here?" she asked Ebuka even though her eyes were on me.

Ebuka didn't answer and it took me a few moments to realize he was waiting for me to answer for myself. "I like coming to the market," I said.

"Hm," she said again before turning to Ebuka. "Ebuka, I need you to stay here, I need to go and collect the money Cynthia is owing me. Mama Jonah said she saw Cynthia buying shoes from Mama Kechi. Can you imagine the useless girl? She's buying shoes when she owes me money." She tapped her foot in time with her words.

"Mama. Biko. I don't have time. Oga dey wait me."

"I'll be quick. I just want to ask her how she has money to buy new shoes, but does not have the money to pay me back."

"Mama, you know you sabi gist. By the time you stop to greet everybody in the market one hour will have passed."

"I can help," I said without giving myself time to think about what I was doing.

His mother turned to me and looked me up and down twice before laughing.

"My mama get shop. I've helped her before," I said. I didn't mention that Mama had never actually let me haggle with customers because she didn't think I was tough enough to negotiate. Sometimes after school when it was not my turn to cook dinner I would walk to Mama's shop and do my homework at the back. It was a better option than being home with Cheta and Papa.

Ebuka's mother narrowed her eyes, assessing me. I tried not to fidget under her inspection. A few moments passed and I was fully expecting her to say no when she gave me a sharp nod. There were several baskets of tomatoes on the floor, the table was piled with carrots, cucumbers, oranges, tomatoes, and a variety of other fruits and vegetables. It took a few minutes for her to explain how much everything was. Ebuka silently slipped away while she spoke.

"If the person looks like they have money, tell them it's double the price, let them price it down, but if they look like they don't have, just give them the normal price. But don't sell

it to anybody for less than what I've told you. Understand?"
She brought her hand up to her ear and tugged on it.

"Yes, ma," I said with a wide smile, unable to control my
excitement. I had never been on the other side of the market stall.

"Put any money you make into this bag." She handed me
a red bag filled with crumpled notes. "Call me Mama E," she
said as she looked at me with narrow eyes. I could tell she was
already second-guessing her decision. As she walked away she
kept on glancing over her shoulder at me, a frown on her face.
I watched her until the crowd swallowed her up.

I had three customers in twenty minutes. The first one was
a man who looked like he was in his thirties. He bought one of
the already peeled oranges. I sliced it in half and handed it to
him. I watched him as he walked away and saw when he turned
his head to the side to spit out the seeds. The second one was a
girl that looked just a few years older than me. She didn't even
bother to price it down. She was probably like Ebuka, a house
girl shopping for her madam. It wasn't her money she was
spending, so she wasn't interested in saving it. The third one
was a middle-aged woman that had the same multicoloured
skin as Mama. She simply laughed and walked away after I told
her the price for a basket of oranges.

I was humming to myself and enjoying the weight of the
responsibility when I heard an accented soft voice ask, "How
much be this?"

I looked up quickly at the sound of the stilted pidgin. The
sun was behind the person who spoke and I had to squint to see

her. When my eyes adjusted, I saw it was a white woman. The first one I had ever seen in real life. The missionary that came to visit my school a year ago didn't count because I had not seen her up close. But I could make out this woman's features clearly. Her eyes were bright blue, the same shade as my bag, and her nose was long and pointed. She wore a yellow spaghetti-strap dress that reached her ankles. Her neck and chest were red, I wondered if it was because of the hot sun or if she always looked like that.

I opened my mouth to tell her the price when Mama E somehow appeared. I don't know how she had walked up to us without me noticing—she took up a lot of space, I should have spotted her from afar. Mama E's shoulders gently pushed me out of the way as she came to stand closer to the woman, who was examining a tomato. When Mama E told the woman the price of a basket of tomatoes, the white woman laughed. "No be yesterday I first come. Give me last price."

"Aunty, you never hear of the disease wey dey kill tomatoes. Tomatoes is cost now, o. The economy dey very bad," Mama E said in a solemn voice. The kind of voice that people use when they are talking about a sick relative.

"Wetin be the last price," the white woman said. I tried not to laugh at how funny she sounded speaking pidgin.

When she bent down to inspect the tomatoes, her hair tumbled down her face. I couldn't help myself, I reached out and touched the ends, rubbing it between my fingers. I had always wondered what oyinbo hair felt like. It felt a little like Kaira's weave.

"My tomatoes fresh *well well*. See the body, no bruises. You go cook betta stew for your husband with my tomatoes."

The oyinbo woman gently stroked the tomato as she turned it around in her hand.

"Your price is too high," she said before putting it down and turning to leave.

Mama E reached out and grabbed her arm, "Okay, how much you wan pay?"

It didn't take long for them to settle on a price. The woman smiled as Mama E made a show of grumbling about not making any money off the sale.

The wheelbarrow boy the white woman had hired looked like he was maybe twelve or thirteen years old. The T-shirt he wore was filthy, his feet caked with mud. He rearranged the items in the wheelbarrow, so he could have space for the basket of tomatoes.

We watched them go. The woman had looked so pleased with herself. I wondered how she would feel if she knew she had overpaid by a lot. They were far away when Mama E turned to me and said, "You almost spoilt my market. You have to times the price by ten for oyinbos."

"I know," I lied. I would have given her the rich people price. I wondered what price she charged Ebuka for the tomatoes he bought for the house, rich people price or oyinbo price?

"All these white people they all have money. Their husband all work for oil companies, you know."

I nodded even though I didn't know.

"Do oyinbos usually come here?" I asked. I had expected white people to shop at places like the big supermarkets with air conditioners, where the foods were already chopped and diced. Or to send their house help, the way Aunty Sophie sent Ebuka and Mr. Romieto.

"They have been coming more and more. Dem don sabi our matter. They know that they can get it cheaper here than in those fancy stores. Didn't you hear that woman speak pidgin. See as she priced my tomatoes down," Mama E said. Her voice had an odd tone. It was like she couldn't decide if she found it annoying or amusing that oyinbos now knew how market women operated.

"I don't know what they're looking for here. Na only suffering dey this country. See, before I die, I must see abroad. My leg must touch America or London or Dubai. Just wait and see."

"One of my friends said that abroad is not that great." It was something Ginika had said during one of the dinners with Uncle and Aunty. Ginika wasn't exactly my friend but I didn't know how else to refer to her.

"Is she rich?" Mama E asked.

I nodded. Anybody could tell from the way she spoke and acted that Ginika came from money. Besides, people tended to stick with their own kind. The rich befriended the rich, the poor befriended the poor. If her mother was Aunty's friend, then her mother definitely had money. That was the way it was.

"Eh, of course she'll say that. Rich people don't need America because they are enjoying life here. That's why they'll open their big mouth and say that abroad is not all that. As if it's only them that should enjoy life." She turned around to look at the white lady. She was far away now, but I could make out her yellow dress weaving through the crowd, the wheelbarrow boy right behind her.

"One day when we have saved enough, Ebuka is going to go back to university and graduate and become a big man. He'll take me abroad," she said it with such conviction, I couldn't help but believe it too. So, while Mama E haggled with the next customer, I slipped the money Mr. Romieto handed to me that morning into the red bag.

After the market, the next stop was a small white building. It had a sign with a feather logo over the entrance.

"You didn't have to come down here. It's only going to take a few minutes," Ebuka said when I got out of the car and met him at the door.

"What are we buying?" I asked as we stepped into the building. It was so cold; goose bumps immediately broke out on my skin. It was a small room with freezers lined up against all four walls.

"Chicken. Romieto already called ahead to order it."

A woman wearing a T-shirt with the same feather logo from the sign in front of the building came out of a door marked EMPLOYEES ONLY. "Ebuka, you're back again."

She handed him a receipt. "The boys are already loading the chicken in the truck," she said, writing something into a notebook. I looked out of the only window in the room and saw the driver standing on the truck bed and arranging the plastic bags two young boys were handing to him. I envied her easiness, the way she smiled and put her hand on his arm. So carefree, no second-guessing, just action. My body had never been that free, that loose. Ebuka smiled at her, but it was a small smile. His dimple didn't show and that made me a little happy.

TWELVE

Cheta

"WHERE DO YOU think we'll be in ten years?" Anita asked, her mouth full of Cabin biscuit. She was lying on a bench, her head on Ikenna's thigh. They were back on again.

"Far away from here," Anwulika muttered. She was standing by the window, looking out into the road. We were in an old abandoned building a few plots away from our school. Someone had started building a home and had run out of money halfway through and since graduation a month ago we met up there almost every day to talk about our futures. It was the only thing on our minds. Where would we go? What would we be? Would our dreams come true? Leaving the safety of secondary school and going out into the world was scary and the only way we could cope was talking about it over and over again, letting our imaginations run wild.

"I'm going to be a world-famous afro-beats artist," Ugonna said. He was slouching on a chair, eyes on the ceiling, fingers absently tapping a beat on his knee. Ugonna's answer always changed. Last week he wanted to be a soccer player, the week before that a politician.

"I'll be your manager. We'll tour the world," Ikenna said, running a hand through Anita's weave.

Anita smacked his hand away and leaned up on an elbow to look at Ugonna. "We'll be your backup dancers and go on tour with you. Anwulika can shake her big bumbum."

"Mba. I'm going to be an actress but don't worry I'll come to your world tour," Anwulika said. She had been the most unwavering about her future. She already had a plan to move to Lagos and start working towards her dream of being a big Nollywood star. I was envious of her certainty.

"You can be my plus-one to the Grammys," Ugonna said to Anwulika. "Anita and Cheta will be my backup dancers."

"Ah! You want Anita to get on stage and disgrace her ancestors with her lack of rhythm? She can be your publicist. You know how she likes to talk. I'll be the director of choreography," I said.

Anita threw a piece of her biscuit at me. I laughed and dodged it.

"Don't forget to mention us in your acceptance speech, sha," Ikenna said.

"No shaking. I got you, bros," Ugonna said with a smile. We all knew he was going to end up apprenticing with his uncle in his small shop, but we fed each other's dreams no matter how ridiculous.

"Oya, Ugonna, sing for us, Mr. Pop Star," Anwulika said.

"Ikenna, drop a beat," Ugonna said. Ikenna started pounding on the bench.

Ugonna nodded his head in time to the beat and turned to me. "Cheta, I need a harmony."

I started humming to Ikenna's beat. Ugonna cleared his throat and began singing.

Ohhhh, yeah. Oh, oh, oh, na, na, oooh.
They call me Ugo, I like to play Ludo,
you can catch me in the streets,
making money with my beats,
After the party we head to my crib,
see the pretty girls dancing in my crib,
they call me Mr. Glow,
because I shine everywhere I go,
yeah, yeah, after the party,
there's another party,
because they call me Ugo and anywhere I go,
you go, we go, we all gooo, with Ugo. Na, na, na.

Anita got up and started moving her rhythmless body to Ugonna's yeye song. We burst out laughing. When summer ended and we all headed in different directions to start our lives, this was what I was going to miss the most.

THIRTEEN

Zam

GINIKA WAS AN eager student. Her pronunciation was still horrible and needed a lot of work but she was picking up Igbo faster than I expected. Probably because we spent hours at the dining table doing lessons.

I hardly ever saw Kaira. If she wasn't out at some event, she locked herself in her room. She only came out to eat and occasionally to watch TV.

It was early in the morning and Aunty was in the living room, typing away on her laptop. Ginika and I were at our usual spot working on her pronunciations when Kaira came in, wearing an expression that made it obvious she wanted something.

"Mummy, can I start taking driving lessons?" she asked.

"No," Aunty answered, not even taking a moment to think about it.

"But Aku took lessons when he was my age," Kaira said in a way that was clear she had expected that answer and had prepared her argument.

"Akubundu was more responsible."

Kaira made a strange sound, like she was choking and laughing at the same time. "More responsible? More responsible?" she repeated, her voice going higher with every word.

"Kaira, please, I have a headache," Aunty said, trying to end the conversation.

Kaira wasn't ready to let it go. "How is Aku more responsible? Or did you forget that the reason you even got him driving lessons was because he stole your Mercedes keys and bashed the car into the gate when he was trying to reverse out of the house?"

My mouth dropped. Opposite me, Ginika mouthed, "Yeah, it was bad."

"Kaira, I'm busy. We'll talk about this when I get back." Aunty said, closing her laptop and putting it in its bag.

"But Mummy," Kaira whined.

Aunty was already walking out the door.

For days after that fight Kaira was even more bad-tempered than usual, so I was surprised when, on a Saturday morning, instead of walking past us like we didn't exist, Kaira actually spoke to Ginika and me. "What are you guys doing today?" she asked.

Neither of us answered immediately. Me, because I was shocked, and Ginika, probably because she didn't want to.

Kaira kicked the table, making everything on it rattle. "Are both of you suddenly deaf? What are you doing today?"

"What do you want Kaira?" Ginika asked in a bored voice.

"Let's go to the Ridge today."

"Why?"

"Aren't you tired of sitting in the house doing nothing?"

That seemed like a good enough reason for Ginika, who said yes, and since I didn't want to be the one left at home, I said yes, too.

"Why is she always angry?" I asked Ginika when Kaira headed back into her room to get ready.

"She's just upset that Aku is in England while she's here. She didn't do well in school last semester, so she's not travelling abroad for summer. That's her punishment."

I wondered how living in a mansion with servants and drivers at your disposal and unlimited access to money was punishment.

"So they travel abroad every summer?"

"Yeah, sometimes Easter and Christmas too."

"Are you being punished? Is that why you're here?"

"I'm here because my parents travel a lot. So they dump me here."

It took an hour to get ready because when Kaira saw my outfit and my makeup she announced that I wasn't going anywhere with her looking like that. She rummaged through my closet, where I had hung and folded all the clothes she gave me, until she picked an outfit she liked. Then she wiped off my makeup and reapplied it. She would have done the same thing with Ginika, but Ginika told Kaira that if she came near her with the makeup brush she would break it. As she did my makeup, Kaira explained that the Ridge was a fancy hotel in Maitama where all the expatriates and rich people stayed and we might bump into people she knew so we shouldn't embarrass her.

We piled into the backseat of one of Uncle's Range Rovers. The driver and one mobile police sat in front. The MOPOL held his gun the same careless way Mr. Boniface did. The car ride was quiet. It was the kind of silence that happened when everyone mutually decided to ignore each other and get lost in their own world.

When we got to the Ridge, a doorman wearing a suit opened the car door and greeted Kaira with a smile. "Welcome back, ma'am."

The lobby looked and smelled expensive. The gleaming surfaces reflected the lights of the massive chandeliers that hung from the high ceilings. In one corner, a man on a raised platform played a grand piano. The soft notes filtered through the air, giving a soothing vibe. Kaira led us through the lobby, to the pool area. On one side of the pool was a fancy-looking hut that had a sign that said TIKI BAR hanging from the ceiling. Kaira didn't bother to read the menu, she simply announced, "I'm ordering Chapman and pizza for all of us."

There was something oddly relaxing about the atmosphere, even though we were all ignoring each other. Kaira was on her phone, Ginika was writing in her notebook, and I was watching everyone. There were two young olive-skinned, dark-haired children playing in the pool. Probably Lebanese. I had overheard Aunty talking about how there were so many of them in Nigeria. I wondered if their hair felt the same as the white woman's hair I had touched in the market. My hand itched to investigate.

At the other side of the pool area, there were stairs that led to a basketball court and a tennis court. No one was on the tennis court, but there were two young boys shooting hoops on the basketball court.

We were halfway through the pizza when a shadow fell on us. I looked up to see a man smiling down at us.

"Hello ladies, how are you all doing today." His eyes bounced from Ginika to Kaira before settling on me.

None of us responded. I could tell from the way his smile dimmed a little that it wasn't the reception he was expecting. This was a man who was used to his smile clearing a path.

He cleared his throat, his confidence slipping a little. "So, what are you—"

"No one here is interested," Kaira said, cutting him off.

"Look, I just came here to—"

Again Kaira cut him off, raising her voice as she said, "I really don't care. The police commissioner is my uncle, do you want me to call him and tell him that there is a man here disturbing underage girls, *eh*? *Agbaya*, don't you have shame?"

The man spun on his heels and walked away without saying another word.

"And they say I have a big mouth," Ginika mused when the man was a good distance away. "Kaira, one day that mouth of yours is going to get you in trouble. How do you know that man does not have his own police commissioner on speed dial?"

Kaira snorted, "Please. He was at the bar with an older woman when we first arrived. I saw the way he was eating. He was stuffing his face as if the chicken was going to come back alive and run away. Only poor people eat like that, because they're not sure where their next meal is going to come from. He's probably here to look for a sugar mummy or a rich young girl he can scam. That man does not have money or know anybody important. I can bet anything that he's a yahoo-yahoo boy. Everything about him was fake, the sunglasses, the shoes, the watch."

"He wasn't wearing a watch," I pointed out.

"Well if he was, it would have been a Rolex and it would have been fake," Kaira said, crossing her arms.

We stayed at the tiki bar until it started to get dark. "I want to check out something behind the tennis court before we go," Kaira said when we got up to leave. "Come with me."

I looked at Ginika who shrugged, chugged the rest of her Chapman, and stood up to follow her.

The hotel was built in front of a hill thick with tall and untamed land. The tennis court was next to an iron-link fence that separated the hotel from the wild bushes.

"Do you know where you're going to?" Ginika called out

to Kaira as she led us through a gate with a rusted latch and into the thick vegetation.

"Shut up," Kaira said.

"Don't tell me to shut up. You shut up. Where are you taking us to?"

"Why are you so annoying?"

They continued quarrelling as we trudged along. I walked with my hands out in front of me, parting twigs and leaves, but the bushes still brushed against my arms and legs. The ground was soft and squishy beneath my shoes. I heard the sound of rushing water and saw a little stream ahead of us. Kaira expertly hopped over it, almost like she had done it many times before. Ginika and I traced her steps, stepping where she stepped. We walked for about ten minutes before the bushes began to thin. Ahead, I saw a small clearing. Someone had taken their time to create this little slice of calm in the middle of the lush wild.

Four men were sitting in the middle of the clearing. One was lounged lazily on the ground as if he was in a spa. The others were lying on wooden benches that looked like they had been ravaged by termites. They all had cigarettes in their hands.

As we got closer, the sharp smell of kpoli hit my nose and I realized it wasn't cigarettes they were holding.

"Did you come here to buy weed?" Ginika didn't wait for a response before asking, "Do you think the hotel managers know what is going on here?"

"Ginika, shut up, why are you always so loud?" Kaira hissed as we walked closer to the men.

I could see that all four men had bloodshot eyes. Their smiles were too lopsided, their limbs too loose, as they watched us approach.

"Stay here," Kaira said to us.

Just as she was about to take a step closer to the men, the bushes came alive.

I jumped in shock as figures holding guns ran out of the bushes.

"Don't move. Hol' it! Hol' it!" a voice shouted.

The four men lounging in the clearing scrambled, running in different directions.

Someone grabbed my arm and I looked up to see a police officer. She was standing so close I could see the hairs on her chin. Her other hand held an AK.

"Are you deaf? I said hol' it!" an officer screamed. His voice cracked at the end and I knew he would have a sore throat tomorrow.

An officer with a baton had a hold on Ginika. Kaira was in the middle of the chaos looking incredibly confused and incredibly scared.

"Fine girls like you smoking kpoli like touts? You be ashawo? I thought ashawos do their work at night?" the officer holding me asked, looking from Kaira's tight dress to my tight shirt. The frown on her face deepened when she looked at Ginika. There was no way Ginika could be mistaken for a prostitute with her oversized T-shirt, oversized glasses, afro bigger than her head, and makeup-less face.

"We're not ashawos," Kaira said. Her voice was different, softer. It was a tone I had never heard from her.

"Hmm. You can explain yourselves at the station."

There were three policemen standing around two men sitting on the ground. One was handcuffed while the other's hands were tied behind him with a rope. The other two men had run deeper into the bushes. The police officers made no effort to run after them. I didn't know if it was because they believed the ones they captured would sell their friends out or if their bellies prevented them from running.

"Ma, we were not doing anything," Kaira said in that same childlike tone.

"Move. I said you can explain yourself at the station." The policewoman placed her hand on Kaira's back and pushed her forward. One of the policemen prodded the cuffed men with his baton. We walked through the bush, down the dirt path, past the tennis court, and towards the lobby.

A wheezing noise made the policewoman turn around.

"What is wrong with her?" she asked Kaira but her eyes were on me.

I realized then that the wheezing noise was coming from me. I couldn't breathe and I had to stop walking to lean forward and rest my hands on my knees.

"Na kpoli dey do am like that? How many she smoke?" The male officer poked me in the ribs with the baton.

"Look sir, we are sorry. We didn't know what was happening. We saw people walking there and we just wanted to see what was going on."

"Didn't your parents teach you not to do *follow-follow*? If you see people doing something, must you do it? Eh? You're following us to station, you can write statement and explain what you were doing there."

That was when I remembered what Papa had said the day I left Alihame. *Don't ever go somewhere, that if something happens people will ask what you were doing there.* Christ! What was I going to tell Mama? I reached up to my neck, trying to reach my rosary, but it wasn't there.

"What is wrong with your friend?" one of the male officers asked Kaira.

"Nothing. She's fine," Kaira said. "Zam, tell them that you're fine." Her long, fake fingernails pinched my side.

"She's not fine. There's something really wrong with her," Ginika said. Her hand touched my shoulder lightly.

"Na asthma dey worry am?" someone asked. Their voices seemed to be fading. My vision blurred and the pounding in my ears made me feel like there was an angry drummer in my head but I was alert enough to hear Kaira latch onto the police man's explanation "Yes. I almost forgot! She's asthmatic. She must have forgotten her inhaler at home," Kaira said.

"She's hyperventilating," Ginika said. That was when my eyes and my legs gave out.

* * *

I opened my eyes and saw Ginika standing beside me, holding something cold against my forehead.

"Are you okay?" Ginika asked.

I nodded. She opened the bottle of water she had been resting on my forehead and handed it to me. I gulped half of it and wiped my mouth with the back of my hand.

"You're in the staff lounge, they carried you in here after you fainted. They were going to take you to the hospital but I told them you'll be fine because I think it was just a panic attack. Kaira agreed about not going to the hospital but I think she was just scared that her parents would find out."

There was one window in the office and I could see Kaira, the police officers, and one other man standing in a circle in the lobby.

Ginika saw me looking and said, "Kaira is trying to bribe the officer. The other man is the hotel manager. He's trying to explain that he did not know what was going on behind the hotel."

It took some time for Kaira to bribe the officers. From the way her hands were gesticulating wildly, it didn't seem like the conversation was going in her favor. She plucked her phone out of her pocket and spoke to someone. Minutes later the MOPOL that rode with us to the hotel appeared and joined the small circle. With the MOPOL there, things seemed to move faster. Kaira pulled out a bundle of money from her handbag, money changed hands, and she left the circle.

"You're awake," Kaira said, walking into the office. "I hope you're happy, the officers thought you were on drugs because of your fainting nonsense. I had to double the bribe."

"Kaira, shut up. It's not like she begged to follow you here. You're the one that brought us here and then took us into the bush."

"Whatever. She's paying me back the money."

"She's not paying you back anything. You're the one that got us into this wahala in the first place."

The car ride back home was silent, but it was different from the silence that filled the car on the way to the hotel. This silence was strained. It was the kind that happened when everyone wanted to speak but no one knew what to say.

I was seated by the window this time, and the windows were down because Ginika said the fresh air was better for me. The faint Hausa words from the radio presenter filtered through the car speakers. The drive back home seemed longer even though there was no traffic. When the car finally pulled up to the house, I opened the door and ran inside before the driver had completely stopped the car.

I had only had a few minutes to myself when I heard a knock on my bedroom door. I didn't answer. I tried to remember if I had locked the door; I was not in the mood to deal with anyone. I got my answer a few seconds later when the door creaked open.

"Zam?" Ginika said. Her voice was somewhere in between a whisper and her normal volume. I didn't respond. I heard her footsteps walk into my room. I knew it was only a matter of time before she found me in the walk-in closet. I was sitting on the floor, my forehead resting on my knees that were drawn up to my chest. The footsteps got closer and the closet door slid open. I heard her lower her body and sit beside me. I just wanted her to go away, but I knew Ginika wouldn't leave unless she wanted to.

"I have never seen anyone have a panic attack. It's actually kind of fascinating. You must have really bad anxiety," she said.

"Anxiety?" I said the word out loud, slowly, tasting it on my tongue. I had never thought of putting a name to the body-numbing chaos that churned in me. It came, it passed, and I tried to forget it ever happened. I didn't know if other people experienced it. I never asked because I was scared that if I was the only one it happened to, then it meant there was something seriously wrong with me.

It was cold in the closet. Ginika had very hairy arms, and her hair brushed against me, tickling me, but I didn't move. I found the contact comforting. When my breathing calmed down and I had control of my limbs, I pulled my phone out of my pocket, opened the search engine, and started typing in the word she said. My thumb hovered over the screen, as I thought about how to spell it. I sounded out the word slowly in my head. *An-ZIGH-eh-tee.*

"A-N-X-I-E-T-Y," Ginika spelt out.

I didn't say thank you because it would mean acknowledging that I didn't know how to spell it. The first thing that I saw on the page was the dictionary definition. *Concern, tension, fear, worry.* For some reason reading the definition made the knot in my chest loosen a little. I read article after article. Some of them were scientific, others were personal accounts of people who had had anxiety attacks. The knot in my chest loosened a bit more. I didn't realize I was crying until a teardrop fell on my phone screen.

"I thought it was a spiritual attack," I heard myself say.

"What?!" Ginika asked, surprise in her voice.

"I thought God was punishing me for something," I whispered.

The small space was quiet for a moment. I hadn't turned on the light in the closet, it was dark except for the ray of light coming from the small crack where the door wasn't shut properly. I watched the dust particles dance in the light.

"Why would you think that?" Ginika asked.

"The first time it happened, I couldn't breathe, I thought I was dying. Mama must have thought I was dying too, I remember her shaking me and crying, I can't remember what she said because it felt like I was drowning. It was one of the worst ones. I don't remember what caused it but I remember Papa drove to the church to get the priest, after that I think I fainted. When I woke up the priest was rubbing anointing oil on my head and praying for me. After he did that, he anointed the house too.

"Mama didn't let us sweep or mop the house for a week after that. I think she was afraid we would clean the anointing away before it had time to seep into the foundation of the house."

"They went to the priest and not the hospital?" Ginika asked, not bothering to hide her confusion.

I nodded.

"So anytime you had a panic attack your parents called the priest?"

"No, it was only that time."

"So what did they do the next time it happened?"

"Nothing. They didn't know."

"You hid it."

"Yes," I said, even though she hadn't asked a question. We were silent for a while. I could hear the faint sounds of explosions and guns coming from the television in the living room.

"The priest said we needed to pray more. I thought it was my fault that evil spirits attacked me. That night Mama stayed up all night casting and binding any evil force. But the phone says that it happens to millions of people around the world and there's even medication for it. It can't be a demonic attack if there's medicine for it."

Ginika stared at me for a moment before taking my trembling hand in her cold one. "I'm happy for you," she said quietly.

As I looked at our interlocked hands, the peace in my chest exploded like fireworks and I could feel the happiness spreading to every inch of my body. A part of me had been afraid of what she would say, afraid that she would laugh and tell me I was silly for thinking it was a demonic attack or launch into a lecture about why the white man's religion was a bad thing. I closed my eyes and leaned my head against the drawer, and even though one of the handles dug into my back I couldn't be bothered to move.

Then laughter bubbled up my throat and out of my mouth, as if the happiness was too much for my body, and it had to be let out. Beside me I heard Ginika laugh. It was the first time I had ever heard a real laugh from her—not the sarcastic laughter that was like acidic bubbles of judgement, but real laughter that was woven with joy. We stayed in the dark closet for hours, holding hands, laughing, and talking.

FOURTEEN

Cheta—
then

A MONTH AFTER my sixteenth birthday, I was selected as the head of the youth choir and just six months later, the position was taken from me. I don't think I could ever forgive Zam for that. There were very few places that made me feel safe and happy, and the church before dawn was one of those places. That was why when my alarm went off at 4:30 a.m. every Sunday morning, I didn't feel tempted to hit the snooze button. Sunday Mass was at 7 a.m. but choir members had to be at church an hour and a half early to practice.

The day I lost the position, I got ready quickly but loudly, slamming doors and drawers and stomping around. Zam grumbled, turned around to face the wall, and covered her head with her duvet. I knew it was inconsiderate but she could either speak up or continue to be annoyed in silence.

My church outfit had been ironed and laid out the night before. I had selected one of the five church outfits I had on rotation. They were all fitted but not too tight, with high necklines that were far away from the swell of my breasts and sleeves that covered my upper arms. The hemlines all grazed my ankles. They had all been sewn by Mama's tailor. She had chosen the style but I got to pick out the fabric. I tied my scarf tightly over my head, making sure none of my braids escaped. I made the knot tight enough to make my head throb. The Reverend Sisters were very strict about hair not showing.

Papa was sprawled on the couch in the living room, snoring. Sometimes he slept on the mat on the floor of the bedroom he shared with Mama and sometimes he slept on the couch. Three empty bottles of Gulder were littered on the floor next to him. He didn't stir as I walked by him and left through the front door.

It was a ten-minute walk to church. The sky was still dark and without the morning sun heating the air, there was a slight chill. A few choir members were already there by the time I arrived. The first five pews on the left side were reserved for us. Ikenna was sprawled out, his hymn book open on his belly, eyes on Anwulika's bumbum as she leaned over the choir director's chair flirting with Ugonna, the drummer.

I smacked Ikenna's arm with my hymn book. "Stop looking at nyash in church."

He smiled at me. "I'm just appreciating God's work."

Anita, who was sitting two pews behind him, hissed. The sound of her sucking her teeth carried through the church. I grabbed a stack of hymn books and dumped them on Ikenna's belly.

"Oya, make yourself useful," I said, pointing to the other side of the church. "Distribute them. Three per pew."

He grumbled but did as I instructed. Anita eyed him evilly the whole way. As the assistant to the choir director and president of the youth choir, I was charged with keeping things running smoothly in his absence. Sometimes that meant leading practice and other times it meant keeping bitter exes away from each other. We were all in the same class in school so I had learned how to deal with Ikenna and Anita's on-and-off drama for a few years.

"I don't even know why he's still here," Anita said to me.

I shrugged. Ikenna had a really good voice but it was obvious he didn't care about the choir—not like I did. He spent half of the time trying to annoy Anita and the other half staring at Anwulika's big nyash. Several times, Anita had come up to me and tried to convince me to tell the choir director to kick Ikenna out. Every time I lied and told her I would see what I could do. I had no intention of letting Ikenna leave. The choir needed him. His deep bass voice rounded out our harmonies.

"Just ignore him. Don't give him the satisfaction of knowing that he's annoying you," I said. It was the technique I used with Mama. Anita, like always, did the opposite and turned in Ikenna's direction to glare at him.

I shook my head and continued setting up. The choir members filed in over the next few minutes. Everyone had their duties. We had to sweep the church, light candles, dust the altar, and wipe the windows. There were about forty of us, so it didn't take long.

When it looked like we were done with cleaning and setting up, I said, "Okay. We're all here. Let's start practice."

Everyone shuffled to their assigned seating position. Ugonna counted down on the drums and Anwulika came in with the piano.

"Great is thy faithfulness," I sang and the other voices followed.

My voice wasn't great but it was good enough. And I loved the choir. I loved when it all came together—the voices, the instruments, the clapping. Morning practice was special because as we sang, the sun rose. The sunlight made the stained glass windows sparkle and the colored rays bounced off the floor and walls. There was something magical about watching the church light up as our voices twined together to make beautiful music.

As we rounded up practice, the congregation began to filter in. Even as the church filled up with hundreds of people, something in me knew and stiffened the moment Mama walked in. I was attuned to her presence. But not even Mama could diminish the magic of the choir.

When Mass began, I tuned out Father Charles. I liked the routine of church. Everyone knew when to stand, when to sing, when to kneel, when to listen. It was constant and predictable and I found comfort in that, but I wasn't there for the sermon. I was there for the music and the camaraderie with my friends.

At the end of the service, a lector stood at the podium and announced the names of families who had signed up for the after-Mass thanksgiving. Thanksgiving at the end of Mass was always my favorite part. We saved the best songs for it. Everyone was on their feet clapping and singing along as people danced their way to the altar bearing gifts. I watched as a particularly stubborn goat had to be dragged down the aisle, shitting on the floor in the process. Two boys carrying a sack of rice followed the goat, stepped on the shit, their shoes spreading it along the aisle. We sang at the top of our voices and shook our tambourines as Ugonna banged on the drums. It was loud and frenzied—but more than that, it was fun.

The third Sunday of every month, Mama's church group met for their monthly meeting. The women were all loud and argumentative and could never come to a decision about any-thing, which meant what was supposed to be a forty-minute meeting often took hours. Zam and I had to wait for Mama before we could go home. Why we couldn't just head home by ourselves, I did not know. Mama was unnecessarily difficult like that. Most of my friends had left and only a few people remained, so I found a corner in the shade to sit and wait. I closed my eyes and rested my head on the wall.

I don't know how long I had been dozing when a small com-motion startled me awake. I turned my head and saw Belinda cornering Zam. It wasn't the first time I had seen the girl on Zam's case. She had it out for Zam for some reason. I had never bothered to ask what that reason was. She had Zam's bag in her chubby hands and was rifling through it. Zam grabbed the strap and tried to pry it away. Belinda yanked it back—hard.

Zam said something, but her voice was quiet and I was too far away to hear what she said. Whatever it was seemed to enrage Belinda. She got in Zam's face, her big frame towering over Zam menacingly. Even from the distance I could see Zam shaking. She did that sometimes—shake when she was scared or overwhelmed. It was so irritating.

Zam's mouth moved. Belinda shoved Zam's shoulder. "What did you say?" she demanded.

"Orobo, leave me alone," Zam said, her voice a notch louder, so it carried to me. Her hand reached for the rosary around her neck. I watched in fascination. It was unusual to see Zam standing up for herself.

I hated violence. I couldn't even watch boxing. I wanted to leave it alone, wanted to close my eyes and pretend I didn't notice what was happening, just like everyone else was doing. But I couldn't. As much as I didn't like Zam, I had never raised a hand to her and there was no way I was going to sit by and watch someone else do it. I knew what it felt like when someone committed violence against your body. The shock, the pain, the anger, the helplessness—it all blended into a heated feeling of outrage right below your breastbone.

I sighed and walked towards them. "What is going on?"

Belinda swung her head to look at me, her nose flared. She probably wanted to hit me too for interfering but she knew better. I might have only been a year ahead of her in school but that year difference demanded respect, even if we weren't on school grounds. As her senior, I could punish her or have my classmates punish her. And we could get creative with punishments.

"We were just talking," Belinda grounded out. Her fists clenched. What had Zam done to the girl? Most people liked Zam, to my annoyance.

My presence seemed to ginger Zam. "The orobo was disturbing me," Zam said. Her chest was rising and falling quickly and the words came out weak and squeaky but the insult was there.

Belinda, who was probably sensitive about her weight, lunged at Zam. I stepped between them, but Belinda's momentum was too much to hold back and we fell to the ground. She scrambled to get off me, eyes still on Zam, her intent written all over her face. I locked her legs with mine and tried to hold on to her. She was not having it.

"Leave me alone!" she shouted, furiously trying to arch away from my grasp. I held on tighter.

"What is going on here?" Sister Benedicta's thick words made us freeze for a moment. The shock wore off after a few seconds and our bodies sprung into action. Belinda and I quickly drew apart and got to our feet. I tried to brush off the dried grass and soil that clung to my outfit as I looked around. While I had been trying to contain Belinda a small crowd had gathered.

"You are fighting on holy grounds?"

Belinda and I said nothing. I looked around and Zam was nowhere to be found. She had probably gone to a dark corner to hide.

I opened my mouth to explain but Sister Benedicta wasn't having it. "Chetachi, to my office, now!"

I sighed and complied, while she berated Belinda in front of the crowd.

It wasn't my first time in Sister Benedicta's office. After the incident with the music teacher, I had spent a lot of time there.

"Chetachi, I'm very disappointed in you," Sister Benedicta said when she walked in about fifteen minutes later.

She sat behind her desk and leaned forward to look at me.

"I wasn't fighting. I was separating a fight." I tried to explain but I could tell from the look on her face that she wasn't interested in listening to me.

"Stop arguing. You're just making things worse for yourself. Nobody likes an argumentative woman. You are the head of the youth choir and the assembly prefect at the school. Everyone looks to you for guidance. You are to be like our Mother Mary. Meek and humble. A paragon of virtue and honor. What kind of example are you setting when you're rolling around on the ground like a hooligan?"

I felt tears prick at my eyes but I refused to let them fall. My nails dug into my palm. I hated it when adults did things like this. They never listened, never took the time to get the full story. They just drew conclusions from limited information and refused to budge once they had made up their minds. They acted like admitting being wrong would kill them. If she just gave me time to explain, she would see that I had been doing the right thing.

"Sister Benedicta, what you—"

She cut me off, "For atonement, I want you to go out there and apologize to everyone who saw you. Tell them that you are sorry for setting a bad example and that you will strive to do better in the future."

I had spent a good portion of my life apologizing to Mama for any slight infraction, real or imagined, my fault or not, and every time it left a bitter taste in my mouth. Apologizing for things I hadn't done was something I was used to, but for some reason I couldn't make myself say the words.

"I didn't do anything wrong," I said, hating how whiny I sounded.

Sister Benedicta shook her head and sighed. "Your strong head will be your downfall Cheta," she said.

She sat back and studied me. I felt her eyes scan my face. This went on for a moment before she said, "If this happened in school, I would have you debadged."

I clenched my jaw at her words. I wasn't Head Girl but I was proud to wear the assembly prefect badge.

Sister Benedicta continued, "After the behavior I witnessed today, I think it's best that you step down from your position as head of the youth choir."

"But . . . but . . ." I didn't know what to say. Leading the youth choir made me feel accomplished. I had worked towards it for years. That position belonged to me.

"I want you to go home and think about your behavior and the consequences of your actions."

"Sister—"

"I have said all I have to say."

It took everything in me not to slam her door when I left the office. Zam was standing in the corner at the end of the hallway, clutching her rosary and looking at me with worried eyes. I walked past her and the only thing running through my mind was—I should have let Belinda beat her up.

FIFTEEN

Zam

"WHERE ARE YOU going?" Ginika asked me after I cut an Igbo lesson short one morning.

"To the kitchen. Chef Gideon is trying a new recipe and I'm his official taste tester and helper," I said proudly.

"Can I come with you?" she asked. Her voice was softer than I was used to.

I blinked. Ginika didn't ask for anything. If she wanted to do something, she did it. If she wanted to take something, she took it. Her question was reluctant and hopeful at the same time, almost as if she was afraid I would say no.

"Yes," I said slowly. I tried to keep the smile off my face, acting like it wasn't a big deal.

When we walked into the kitchen, Chef Gideon, Mr. Romieto, and Ebuka were at the corner table playing cards. Chef Gideon noticed me first. "Little madam. You're late o. We should have started five minutes ago." The smile on his face dimmed when he noticed Ginika standing behind me.

The men were hesitant around Ginika for the first few days. Their words were more measured, their laughter not as loud. I couldn't blame them, Ginika had been staying at Uncle's house for years and not once had she ever bothered to talk with any of them. Chef Gideon warmed up to her first. He was a man who liked attention and Ginika gave him just that. Her endless questions about Sudan and food quickly made her one of his favorite people.

It was fascinating watching Ginika navigate the world. She had the kind of confidence that moved everything from her path. It wasn't Cheta's kind of confidence, the kind that made you feel foolish and resentful at the same time. It was a quiet confidence, the kind that gripped you by the throat and demanded you listen. It was a confidence that made you wish you were better, smarter, more like her. I was in awe of the way she spoke, the opinions she had.

I wasn't the only one who felt that way. I could see that Chef Gideon and Mama E were just as fascinated with her. The first time Ginika followed me to the market, Mama E gave her the same dubious look she had given me. When Ginika opened her mouth and spoke with that foreign accent that made her stand out as an ajebutter, Mama E's wobbly face squeezed in an ugly way. But as we sat under the shade of her umbrella and Ginika asked questions about market life, her interest genuine and intense, I saw the watchful look in Mama E's eyes melt and morph into something less suspicious. Mama E, like Chef Gideon, liked talking about herself.

The kitchen and Mama E's market stall quickly became my favorite places in the world. The lightness I felt watching Mama E haggle with customers and laughing at Chef Gideon's stories was a kind of lightness I had never felt before.

But as much as I liked having Ginika with me in the kitchen and in the market, it was nice having something that was just mine. Ebuka's dimple was just for me. My favorite moments were late at night after everyone else had gone to bed and it was just the two of us in the kitchen working side by side.

It was one of those nights, when I was helping him clean up the kitchen, that Kaira found us. Uncle Emeke and Aunty Sophie had travelled somewhere for a conference, so the atmosphere in the kitchen was freer, the way it always was when we knew Aunty and Uncle were not at home, which meant there was no one watching us with the cameras.

We were by the sink washing dishes and splashing each other. We stood there laughing, his soapy hand wrapped around my wrist, trying to stop me from splashing the soapy water at him, when a voice behind us said, "So this is what you're doing?"

Ebuka's touch that had moments ago been the right kind of warmth, was suddenly too hot. I snatched my hand away.

The look on Kaira's face told me that she had seen it all and didn't like what she saw.

"I've been trying to call the kitchen. Why is the phone not working?" She stared at us, her eyes demanding an answer we did not have.

Her eyes went to the phone sitting on its stool in the corner and my eyes followed hers. The phone had not been placed properly in its cradle.

"I want orange juice and plantain," she said. Her nose was scrunched, like she was smelling something bad. "I want the plantain diced not cut in circles and next time make sure the phone is hung up properly. I don't want to have to come down here again," she said before she spun out of the kitchen, slamming the door shut behind her, making the kitchen rattle.

I did not understand why she was so upset. Was it so difficult to climb down one flight of stairs? Ebuka said nothing after she left, his mask was firmly in place. It was the same expression he had anytime Uncle or Aunty were close by. I did not know how to be around him when he was not smiling but I did not want to leave. I sat in the corner and watched him cut and fry the plantain.

I pretended not to notice when Ebuka spat in her orange juice. When he turned to the freezer to get ice, I spat in it too.

* * *

148

I crossed my legs and tried to ignore the sharp pain in my bladder. The familiar pressing need to pee I felt whenever I did my hair, along with the smell of hairspray and fried food mingling in the air of Mama Chisom's shop, was making me very uncomfortable.

Ginika and Mama E were seated on low stools on the other side of the small shop. A small kerosene stove with a frying pan full of oil was between them. Mama E had overripe plantain that would be beyond salvaging in a day, so she had brought it to fry for Mama Chisom's children, who sometimes helped her in her stall. One of Mama Chisom's daughters, Faith, was currently manning Mama E's stall, while Mama E gisted with Mama Chisom and Ginika.

"Do you have a chopping board?" Ginika asked Mama E.

"What do you need chopping board for?"

"To chop the plantain."

"Rich man pikin," Mama E said, laughing. "You don't need chopping board to cut plantain, see I'll show you." She picked up a plantain from the ground and sliced it open with the knife, then started cutting thick oval pieces into the bowl on the floor. Ginika watched closely, her eyes following Mama E's movements, the way she cradled the plantain in one hand and cut it with the other. The way the sharp edge of the knife came close to the palm of the hand holding the plantain, but never close enough to risk injury.

"See, that's how it's done," Mama E said with a flourish.

Ginika picked up another plantain and copied what Mama E did. Her movements were slower, less sure, her eyes fixed on the plantain like it was a puzzle she was determined to solve. Mama E and Mama Chisom laughed at her.

"Finally. We thank God o! We were all about to starve to death," Mama E said, when Ginika finished peeling and chopping all six plantains. Mama E sprinkled salt into the bowl and tossed the plantain.

"I read somewhere that fried food causes cancer," Ginika said, as she watched Mama E.

I wondered why almost everything Ginika read seemed to be so dark. It seemed that anything worth eating ended in death.

"*Abeg!* First it was gala, then indomie, then suya, now it's plantain. Everyday something new is killing us. Look, if something is going to kill me, let it be plantain," Mama E said with a dismissive wave of her hand. Ginika scooted away as the oil began to pop when the plantain came in contact with it, but Mama E didn't even flinch.

Ebuka appeared at the front of the shop. "Mama. I'm going, o."

"Be well, my boy," Mama E said.

Ebuka turned to leave but he paused and said to me, "I like the hair."

I couldn't help the wide smile that spread across my face. "Thank you."

Mama Chisom's hand shook as she braided my hair. Although I couldn't see her, I knew she was laughing silently.

150

"I have to go buy the chicken. I'm leaving with the truck. Raymond will wait for you with the Mercedes."

"Okay."

Immediately after he stepped out of the shop Mama Chisom said in her loud voice, "*Love* and *nwantinti*. So you like him?"

My head felt hot, it was a slow heat that started from the tip of my ears, crawled down my cheeks, and slid down my neck. She was behind me; she hadn't seen my face when I smiled at him. Was it something in my voice that let her know how I felt? And why did she have to be so loud? The people in the next shop probably heard her. Ebuka probably heard her.

Mama E was watching me, a knowing smile on her face. "Yes. You like him. I don't blame you. My boy is a handsome boy. Very good boy."

I said nothing as I silently willed my heart to slow its pounding rhythm.

Mama E tilted her head and tugged her ear, a sign for me to listen closely. "But you have to be careful with boys, o! Face your book, boys will come later."

"But he's your son," Ginika said, as if Mama E needed reminding who she gave birth to.

"Yes. He's my son, but he's still a man."

Ginika opened her mouth, no doubt to ask another question, but a woman came into the small salon. "Do you sell pink oil here?" the woman asked.

Mama Chisom stopped braiding my hair and wiped her greasy hands on the wrapper knotted at her waist. "Yes, o.

Hold on. Ijeoma, go to Blessing's shop. Tell her to give you pink oil." A little girl, about eight years old, popped out from behind a stack of crates on the other side of the shop. I hadn't known she had been here this entire time; her small body had been perfectly hidden. She scrambled to her feet and dashed out. Just like in Alihame, the market people here seemed to have a network. If one didn't have something, they directed the customer to their friend's stall or made a sale on their friend's behalf. They had formed their own little community here, each willing to help the other because they knew the other would do the same for them. Even though I could tell from the way she spoke Igbo that Mama Chisom was originally from Imo while Mama E was from Anambra, they treated each other like kin.

Ijeoma came running back a few minutes later with a bottle of pink oil. Money exchanged hands and Ijeoma was off again, running back to whoever she got the pink oil from to give her the money. Mama Chisom tried to cajole the woman into buying something from her. I had spent many hours in Mama's shop, watching her interact with customers; it was easy to determine which customers could be talked into parting with their money. From the way the woman's feet shuffled, as though she wanted to leave but didn't know how to, I knew Mama Chisom had found a new customer. She talked the woman into buying hair cream after convincing her that it would help her hair grow faster.

As soon as the woman left, Mama E said, "Ehen. What were we talking about?" She rubbed her hands, eager to get back to the conversation.

"Being careful with boys," Ginika said.

"Yes. See the thing is, men are children. That's why you'll see a sixty-year-old man sucking breast. That's all they know how to do. Suck breast and give you headache. Most of them are useless."

"What about your husband?" Ginika asked.

"He was just as useless. They say if you cook for your husband his eyes will not wander. They say if you know what you are doing in the bedroom his eyes will not wander. They say if you submit, his eyes will not wander. I did all that and the man's eyes did not remain in the house. The man's eyes were bigger than his head. Always looking at things he should not look at."

I coughed, choking on my own spit. Mama Chisom thumped my back. The heat returned to my face, I wanted to look at Ginika to see if she was as uncomfortable as I was but I was scared of accidentally looking Mama E in the eye, so I kept my eyes fixed on my toes.

"Did you love him when you married him?" Ginika asked.

"Love. Love? Mama Chisom did you hear this child?" Mama E tilted her head back and laughed louder. A laughter that started from her belly, so deep and hearty, it seemed to shake the entire shop.

"What can love do? Is love going to feed you and your children? Is love going to put money in your bank account? Look at my own husband," Mama Chisom said. "I gave him five children. Three sons. He still wants to marry another wife.

Did I not fulfil my duty? What does he need another wife for? The children he has, we can barely pay school fees and now he wants to bring another woman into our house. I blame this Abuja. Because he sees all these men here with their plenty wives, he thinks he can do whatever he wants." Mama Chisom's hands gripped my hair tightly.

"Can't you divorce him?" Ginika asked.

Mama Chisom snorted. I felt the breath on my neck. "Divorce *ke*? If I divorce him how am I going to feed my children and send them to school. Or do you want me to leave my children with him for another woman to raise? God forbid."

"So you stay, even if you're not happy? Because of your children?" Ginika leaned forward like Mama Chisom's answer was very important to her. Was it because of her parents? I had never seen her dad and she hardly ever spoke about him.

"Everybody stays. That's just how things are. At least he's not beating me. My neighbor's eye is always swollen. Poor woman. She was not even fine before the useless man started beating her. So even if she gets lucky and he dies she would not be able to find another husband. See *ehn*, all men do is give you high blood pressure. So the only thing you can do is manage yourself and manage your children."

"It's true. These men? Hmm? If you're not careful they'll use stress and wahala to kill you and the only thing that I am going to allow to kill me is enjoyment. Plantain and enjoyment," Mama E said.

Mama Chisom cackled and leaned forward to high-five

Mama E. The armpit of her shirt grazed the side of my head and I inhaled the stale stench of her body odor.

* * *

It took six hours to finish my medium-sized box braids. It would have taken less time but Mama Chisom kept stopping to tell stories. She talked with her hands, gesticulating wildly. I paid her double the amount she charged me even though I knew she had already inflated the cost. As Ginika and I walked towards the car, I could still hear her yelling prayers at me.

"It's not very hygienic to cook food in the same place that someone is braiding their hair," Ginika said when we got into the car. We were both holding small cellophane bags filled with plantain that Mama Chisom insisted we take with us.

"Are you going to eat it?" I asked.

Instead of answering she opened the bag and popped one oily piece into her mouth.

"Something must kill man," she said as she chewed.

Ginika was unusually quiet during the car ride and as much as I wanted to know why she was so interested in Mama Chisom's reason for staying with her husband, I didn't ask because I could feel a headache coming on. My head felt too heavy for my neck. Mama Chisom had a heavy hand and when I had complained that the braids were too tight, she just laughed and told me tight braids lasted longer. I got a tablet of

Panadol from Mr. Romieto to help with the headache when we got back home.

I was in my room trying to sleep off the headache when my door opened and Ginika entered. She said nothing as she got on my bed and lay on her back, her hands resting on her belly.

I watched her, waiting for her to speak.

"I'm never going to be like them," she finally said.

"Like who?"

"Like all of them. They wear their suffering like a badge of honor. 'Look at me, look at me, I'm so self-sacrificing. My husband mistreats me but I stay because I love my children. I'm such a good mother, such a good woman. Look at me.'" She was breathing hard.

"They're just making the best out of a bad situation."

"They're cowards." She stood up and began to pace. I watched as she walked back and forth for several minutes before turning around and kicking the door. Ginika had such an air of wisdom about her, I sometimes forgot she was a sixteen-year-old.

"Zam, there is no dignity in suffering. Those women are miserable," she said, her voice softer. She faced the door as she spoke and I wondered if it was because she didn't want me to see her cry.

"What do you want them to do? You heard what they said. If they leave their husbands, they can't go back to their father's house. They would have no money to feed their children or send them to school."

"It's not fair." Her voice broke.

"I know."

"That's never going to be me. If a man makes me miserable, I will leave him."

"I know." That I was sure of. Abuja was very different from the world I grew up in. Money flowed freely here. Though there were a lot of things money couldn't do, there was also a lot it could do. Ginika not only came from money, she also had a natural confidence. With confidence and money, she had the luxury of better choices.

We lay on my bed in silence for a long time. The sun went down and darkness engulfed the room. The steady hum of the air conditioner filled the space.

"I watched him punch her. So many times. Over and over. For no good reason. And the next day they both pretend like nothing happened," Ginika whispered.

Something cracked in my chest at her words. I knew she was talking about her parents. I held my breath and waited for her to say more, but she remained silent. I reached out and squeezed her hand. Nothing I said would have helped, so I let her know I was there the only way I could. I drifted off to sleep holding her hand.

SIXTEEN

Cheta

MAMA DID END up hiring a house girl when she got tired of shouting at me to do the chores. Only to fire her less than a week later. I knew she wouldn't last the first day I saw her. She didn't have the disposition necessary to deal with Mama's special brand of wahala. I could tell the second one would last longer than the first but not nearly long enough. She had lasted two weeks so far and I gave it one more week before she quit. But that wasn't my business. I spent most days out of the house, hiding in Papa's office, Ms. Okoye's house, or in the abandoned building with my friends.

Ms. Okoye didn't mind me coming over on days when I wasn't helping her with the shopping or cooking. I watched TV, used her internet, and I was sure she wouldn't mind if

I slept in her spare bedroom, but I thought that was taking things too far.

Papa's office was a small room in an ugly brown and white plaza. There was a desk, a cabinet with a lot of folders, and an old computer that took fifteen minutes to boot up. Uncle had built a block of flats at the edge of town, near the market, and gifted it to Papa. The rent money and the monthly maintenance fee were our main source of income and someone needed to manage it.

When Papa had stopped talking, and then working, two years ago, I stepped up because if Mama was in charge we would lose all our tenants in a matter of months. Before Papa shut down, I used to visit him in the office after school. I did my homework, drank Fanta, and listened as he dealt with the tenants. I knew which tenants paid their bills on time and which ones were always late. I knew which flats always had some kind of issue and I figured out when to anticipate their calls. I knew the tenants who liked to argue for argument's sake, complaining about rent, about the price of NEPA bill (as if I had anything to do with that), and a list of other stupid things.

The worst part of doing Papa's job was when the tenants couldn't pay their rent. I hated having to hound them to pay up and they hated it too. It must be hard having a teenager call you night and day and then show up at your door because you couldn't afford your rent, but there was no polite way to hound someone so I did what I had to do.

It always started the same way. They begged at first, voices soft and pleading. When I stood my ground that was when they got hostile. It was an elaborate, unnecessary struggle. One I would always win because I had the ultimate weapon—Mama. As much as they hated me demanding the rent, they hated it more when it was Mama. Mama was loud and unforgiving. No one wanted that.

"Cheta!"

I looked up to see Nne Michael, the woman who rented the space opposite mine. She sold office supplies and mostly wore shapeless Ankara dresses, but today her makeup was done in a garish shade of blue and she looked like she was going to a party.

"Ah ah! Nne Michael. You're looking fine o! Where are you going to?"

Nne Michael smiled at me as she twirled around the office, showing off her blue lace and silver gele and ipele.

"I know! I'm going to a wedding. Am I not looking like a hot cake?"

"The hottest cake in town."

She laughed, pleased at the compliment. "How are things?" she asked. I liked that she always asked how I was and seemed genuinely interested in the answer.

"Things are fine."

"And the family?"

"They're fine too."

"And your sister, I've not been seeing her in church."

"She's in Abuja with Uncle and Aunty." I didn't have to expand. She knew which uncle and aunty I was talking about.

"And they left you here?"

I had been getting that reaction since Zam left. It made me feel like I was defective. I was something that was easily left behind and discarded. "Na so I see am," I said.

"Eyah. I'm sure you're missing your sister."

"Yes," I said. I did miss Zam. I didn't think I would but she was a buffer. The sandpaper that dulled Mama's rough surface. The house was on edge without her.

"Ehen, go and visit your sister now. You, too, should go and enjoy Abuja."

I had thought about it. But I hadn't been looking forward to the argument it would cause with Mama. But Nne Michael was right, I should enjoy Abuja too.

Mama was not at home when I got there. I sat at the dining table and ate the fried rice the house girl had cooked while I waited for Mama to come home.

"Mama, I want to go to Abuja and visit Zam," I said, as soon as she walked through the door. I didn't really want to see Zam as much as I wanted to be away from Mama.

"You can't even greet?"

I breathed out slowly. "Good evening, Mama. I want to go to Abuja and visit Zam."

"No."

"Why?"

I didn't get an answer, instead she shouted to the house girl to warm her food. Why did she have to be so malicious? She didn't like me here but she didn't want me to leave.

"Mama, if you don't call Aunty, I'll call her myself and tell her I want to come. I'm sure she'll have no problem with me there."

* * *

The next evening when I came home from Papa's office, Mama said to me, "I've spoken to your Aunty. She said you can come. But only for a few days o! You have to find your way there and your way back, if you want to go. I'm not giving you any money to gallivant around the country."

"Okay, Mama. Thank you," I said and headed to my room. There was no need for her to know that she had logged into her email in Papa's office months ago and forgotten to sign out. I had seen the email Aunty Sophie had sent with details of the flight she had booked for me.

SEVENTEEN

Zam

AUNTY, KAIRA, GINIKA, and I were seated at the dining table having dinner. Aunty had come back the day before from her trip, and Uncle had travelled to Asaba for a meeting. Ginika and Aunty were carrying the conversation. Like me, Kaira silently ate her food. A few times I caught her raising her head to give her mother and Ginika a look filled with so much anger, it was a miracle their skin didn't burn from the intensity of it.

"I spoke to your mother today," Aunty said.

I didn't look up, assuming Aunty was talking to Ginika.

"Your sister asked if she could come and visit for a few days," Aunty continued and my head snapped up. Ginika was an only child.

"Cheta wants to come here?"

"Yes. She'll be staying for a week."

I smiled weakly. "Okay." One week wasn't that bad. Cheta and I shared a room for sixteen years. We could live in this house for one week.

After dinner, I was lying on my bed scrolling through social media when my door opened and Ginika came in. She plopped down on the other side of my bed, propped a pillow behind her head, and got comfortable.

"You don't like your sister," she said. It wasn't a question.

"She doesn't like me."

I didn't have to look at her to know Ginika was studying my face intently.

"Why?" she asked.

"Because she thinks Mama loves me more."

"Does she?"

I paused before answering, as though I were thinking about the answer, even though it wasn't something I needed to think about. "Yes. Mama prefers me."

"Why?"

Because I'm light-skinned, because I don't talk back, because I do as I'm told, because I listen to her complaints. There were a lot of reasons why I was Mama's favorite but I didn't voice them. Instead I said, "Cheta is stubborn."

"I'm stubborn."

"Yes. I'm very sure Mama won't like you too."

Ginika laughed. "Now I really want to meet your mum. Is she coming too?"

I hoped not. "I don't think so."

"Tell me about your sister, does she look like you? I always wanted a sister."

"Cheta is . . ." I searched for the right word but came up empty. "I can't think of a word to use."

For some reason that seemed to excite Ginika, she clapped her hands together and smiled, then stuck two fingers in her ear. "Actually no! Don't tell me. I want to meet her and come to my own conclusions. She might be an interesting character to add to my play. I need a good antihero."

"Is that what you're always scribbling in your notebook?" I asked.

She didn't answer. Instead she asked, "What do you think of Aunty Sophie?"

"Uh . . . she's nice," I said, but it came out sounding like a question.

"Do you find anything weird with how she acts?" Ginika cracked her knuckles, her eyes on the ceiling.

"What do you mean?"

"I don't know. The way she is with Kaira. There's something off about it. And sometimes it seems like she's carrying two different conversations. One in her head and one with everybody else."

"Isn't that called thinking?" I said.

Ginika rolled to her side, facing me. "Never mind. Someone like you wouldn't notice."

"Someone like me?"

"Yeah. Someone that looks at Aunty the way you do."

"How do I look at her?"

"Like you're obsessed or in love. It's creepy. Honestly. You people's obsession with mixed-race people is disgusting."

"Who is *you people*?"

"I don't know. All of you. Everybody." She pulled out her phone and opened a website. "See there's a whole website dedicated to mixed-race children. It's creepy how people fetishize them. Look at this comment." She read it out loud in an exaggerated American accent, "'Gotta get me a white chick, my daughter's gonna be the hottest chica on the block.' This person wants to marry someone from a different race just to have half-caste children. And his comment is also very creepy. He definitely has child molester tendencies. I'm reporting this comment as spam." Her thumb swept across the screen.

"It's better than some of the other reasons people get married," I said, thinking about Mama and Papa's marriage and how Mama only married Papa because his older brother was taken.

"Yeah but it still doesn't make it right. See, look at this picture." She thrust the phone so close to my face, I had to hold her wrist and move it away to actually see what she wanted to show me.

"That's a beautiful baby."

"Yes, but that not the point. It's just sad and a little bit pathetic how so many people worship light-skinned complexions. Damn colonialists. They succeeded in brainwashing an entire continent."

I didn't tell Ginika that I thought Aunty Sophie was one of the most beautiful women I had ever seen. I didn't mention my mother's love for skin-lightening products, or how she sometimes wore green contact lenses. I didn't talk about how she pored through the magazines that regularly printed pictures of Aunty Sophie at events, cut the pictures out, and gave them to her tailor, asking him to recreate the outfits. I didn't mention how my mother's breasts had turned pink and started to peel because of the chemical burn.

I didn't mention any of that because I couldn't stand Ginika thinking of my mother as pathetic.

* * *

Mama called me the next day. When she paused to take a deep breath after telling me she suspected Nne Chuk's new granddaughter was adopted because the baby was too fine to have been related to anyone in that family, I asked her why she didn't tell me Cheta was coming.

"Zam. So when I'm telling you about all the devilish behavior your sister has been exhibiting, do you not listen? Have I not been telling you that your sister has been giving me hypertension? Let her go and be somebody else's problem for some time."

After the call with Mama, I lay in bed and stared at the ceiling, thinking about Cheta's arrival. My door opened and

Ginika's head popped through. "What are you doing?" she asked me, her eyes roaming my room before settling on my face, as though she were looking for something.

"Nothing."

"I want to show you something in my room. Come," Ginika said.

I had never been in Ginika's room and I couldn't help the excitement that ran through me about being invited. Her room was cream and white like mine, but while mine had no personal touches, hers was a physical representation of her personality. Paintings—swirls and lashes of dark colors on canvas—hung from her walls. Picture frames rested on her desk, side table, and dressing table but half of them had no pictures. There was a poster board on the wall with no space left to pin anything. I took a step towards it, curious about what she had pinned, but she turned off the light, grabbed my hand, and pulled me to a corner of the room.

"See," she said, her hand outstretched, gesturing at the corner of her room.

There were candles on the floor in front of two straw mats.

"I think we're supposed to do it in the morning when the sun rises or maybe it's when the sun sets, but I don't think it should matter if our intentions are good. Right?" She looked at me, waiting for me to agree with her, but I had no idea what was going on.

"What is this?"

"We're going to commune with our chi and our ancestors."

168

"Isn't that idol worship? That's a sin," I said.

She rolled her eyes and took a deep breath before speaking. "It's not idol worship. Our chi is like our soul. It's like communing with your soul," she explained.

I knew I should walk out. This was traditional worship no matter what she called it. Good Christians weren't supposed to dabble in this sort of thing but I couldn't help the curiosity. Listening to Ginika talk over and over about the white man coming to rob of us our history, our religion, and our culture had made doubts grow in my mind. Doubts that I quickly stomped on and buried. But here in Ginika's dark room with the flickering candle lights casting shadows on the wall, and the smell of the burning incense, the buried doubts pushed through, demanding I pay attention, demanding I water them.

"What are we supposed to say?" I asked. Were we going to chant nonsensical words and paint our faces with white paint like the native doctors in Nollywood movies?

"I don't know exactly. I'm not really sure how any of this works, but I wanted to try."

She sat down cross-legged on one of the mats and looked up at me until I sat down on the mat next to her. "Just thank your chi, be grateful and ask for what you want. It's just like prayer."

I wanted to ask her why she just didn't go to church to pray if it was just like prayer, but her eyes were already closed and her lips were moving and I could tell that she was taking this very seriously. I wished she would speak out loud, I wanted to know what she was saying so I would know what I was supposed to say.

I closed my eyes, wondering how long this was going to take. I thought of Mama and Cheta. I wondered what dinner was like now that I wasn't there. Mama liked to talk and I was usually the one that listened. Cheta only talked back when she wanted to goad Mama. I was actually surprised that Uncle Emeke hadn't received a call informing him that Mama and Cheta had killed each other. Papa might as well be an ornament, with how little he spoke. I wondered how many words Papa had said since I left.

My eyes slowly fluttered open at the sound of my name.

"Were you sleeping?" Ginika asked. She was leaning over me, her face so close if I had the time I could count her pores and the little white dots on her nose.

"Not really," I said. I was in that in-between state, not quite awake, not quite asleep.

"Did you feel that?" she asked.

"What did you feel?"

"Peace," she said, smiling.

"Yes, I felt that too," I said honestly.

She smiled wider but I didn't tell her that it probably wasn't the same kind of peace she felt; the spiritual kind. No, it was the kind of peace that came when you were well rested.

"I'm not sure if we did it right and I'm not even sure if I understand what a chi is but it felt good. We should do it again," she said.

"Okay," I said without hesitation. It had been relaxing and it's not like I had been praying to another God, so I wasn't really doing anything wrong.

* * *

Cheta arrived on a Monday. I woke up early to sit on the balcony and await her arrival. Cheta came out of the car with a frown on her face. She looked different—older. I shrank back, even though I knew there was no way she could see me from where she stood. I heard the front door open below me and Mr. Romieto's voice say, "Our new madam. We have been expecting you. Unfortunately, Oga and Madam have travelled but Madam will be back before you leave." Cheta said something in response but I couldn't make it out because their voices faded as they stepped into the house.

When I heard their footsteps on the staircase, I quickly went into my room. I stood behind my door and listened as Mr. Romieto showed her the room she would be staying in. He said something I couldn't make out and I heard Cheta laugh. Cheta's laughs were low and abruptly short, as though her throat seized up halfway and refused to let the rest of it come out.

I heard one set of footsteps heading back towards the staircase. With my head resting against the door, I closed my eyes and slowly counted to sixty in Ika. Then I counted to one hundred in English, and stepped out of my room. My eyes immediately clashed with Cheta's. She was sitting in the living room, the TV remote in her hand.

"Cheta, welcome," I said. My fingers fidgeted at my sides. I didn't know what to do with my hands.

"Zam," she said with a chin lift.

We stood there staring at each other. I forced my legs to move and walked towards the couch farthest away from her.

"So, this is the big house you have been enjoying," she said. Her tone was neutral and her face was casually blank. I didn't know how to reply so I said nothing.

I watched as her eyes darted around the room, taking everything in.

Kaira came out of her room, saw Cheta and me sitting in the living room, and rolled her eyes. "My God. Are we running a hotel now? Is the entire village coming to live with us?" she said before retreating into her room and slamming the door with a force that shook the entire floor.

Ginika poked her head out of her room at the sound of Kaira's slammed door. A wide smile spread across her face when she saw Cheta and me. I had never seen Ginika smile so wide and it was not something I was sure I wanted to see again. She looked wild.

"Hello. I'm Ginika," she said, stepping out of her room. As always, her book was in her hand and there was a pen in her hair.

"I'm Cheta."

Ginika sat on the edge of the couch, her book balanced on her knees, pen in her hand, glasses buried in her afro. She looked like an amateur journalist who was conducting her first interview.

"So, what is there to do in this Abuja?" Cheta asked.

"I don't know. I don't really go out. You'll have to ask Kaira," Ginika said.

"That one?" She snorted, jerking her thumb in the direction of Kaira's room.

Ginika smiled then asked out of nowhere, "So Cheta, why do you think Zam is your mother's favorite child?"

Cheta's eyes widened at the unexpected question. Her head swung to me, then back to Ginika. Cheta looked at Ginika for a long time before getting up. As she walked past me, our eyes met. I watched as her lips twisted and for a second I swore she was about to spit at me, but she just shook her head and walked into her room.

"What is wrong with you? Why would you ask her that?" I whispered even though Cheta could not hear me.

Ginika shrugged. "I wanted to see how she would react."

Cheta spent the rest of the day in her room.

* * *

The next morning when I went to the kitchen to help with breakfast I pretended like I wasn't surprised when I saw Cheta standing by Ebuka, helping him chop vegetables. I smiled and picked up a knife and a chopping board and joined them.

As the day went on, I tried not to get angry when Ebuka laughed at her jokes, or when Mr. Gideon made her his taste tester for the day. When my palm itched with the urge to pull her hair, I reminded myself she was here for only a week.

The third day was the same as the second. I woke up to see Cheta had beaten me to the kitchen again. I gritted my teeth when Ebuka smiled at her, his dimple so deep, if he lay down and put water in it, the water would hold, like a little pond on his face.

Although we were both helping out in the kitchen, Cheta and I didn't speak. We talked to other people, we talked around each other, but we never actually talked to each other. After years of practice it was something we were both very skilled at.

I didn't say another word to Cheta, not until the evening of the fourth day. I was in my room looking for the deck of Whot cards when I noticed the manila envelope in my drawer wasn't in the same position I usually kept it. I picked it up and it felt lighter. Aunty was too generous with money and because I didn't go out anywhere and hardly spent money on anything, the envelope had gotten thick. I was used to the heavy weight of the money I had saved.

I opened the envelope and counted my money. Then I counted it a second time in case I had made a mistake. Then I counted it a third time just to be sure. After the fourth count I was sure my money was thousands of naira short and I knew exactly who took it.

"Cheta, please, where's my money," I said calmly when she opened the door after I knocked, my voice at odds with what I was feeling inside.

"What money?" she hissed.

"The money that was in my bedside table, where is it?"

"How am I supposed to know?

"It was there this morning. It's not there."

"Okay, so how is that my business? Go and ask your friend to help you look for it."

"Cheta. I know you took it."

"See this small girl. Are you calling me a thief?" She stepped out of her room and took a step closer to me, "Eh? Are you calling me a thief?'

"I'm not calling you anything, I just want my money. Please." I could feel the tears at the back of my eyes as frustration prickled my skin.

"I don't have your money. Leave me alone," she said, slamming the door.

"Cheta, please," I begged, knocking on her door but she didn't respond.

I spent the rest of the day in my room. When Ginika knocked on my door for Igbo lessons, I told her I had a headache.

I watched the clock and waited for 9 p.m. when I knew Chef Gideon and Mr. Romieto would head back to their rooms in the boys quarter, leaving Ebuka alone in the kitchen. Ebuka was the only person I wanted to be around. He was the kind of person who only spoke when he had something he really wanted to say. It was comforting. It was exactly what I needed. Ginika's silence was unnerving. Even when she didn't speak you could tell her mind was running on high speed. You could tell she was observing, analyzing, and filing everything around her.

Heading into the kitchen I expected to see Ebuka doing the prep for tomorrow's meals. What I was not expecting to see was Cheta sitting on Ebuka's lap, her hands wrapped around his neck and his hand on her thigh as they kissed. I watched them through the crack in the door. Watched his hand ride up and down her thigh. There was no hesitation in his movements and I knew it was because Aunty and Uncle were not at home, so there was no chance of them being caught on the security camera. I stood there and watched them until the image was imprinted in my mind. I walked away only when I was sure I would always be able to recall them intertwined with each other whenever I needed to remind myself why I shouldn't care if Cheta and I got along.

I went back upstairs and waited, pacing my room. The two hours between when I saw Cheta kissing Ebuka in the kitchen and when she finally came upstairs was more than enough time to nurture the anger I had kept tucked away in the darkest part of me.

The house was quiet. The television and ceiling lights were off. A lamp on one of the side tables cast a soft yellow glow in the living room. I heard Cheta's heavy footsteps climbing up the stairs. She was barely through the door when I got in her face. "Cheta, give me my money."

Her head jerked back in surprise but she recovered quickly. Cheta had never been the kind of person to let anything faze her. She clapped her hands and laughed. It was a scary laugh. "Are you deaf? Did you not hear me when I told you I don't have your money?" She began walking away from me, towards her room.

"Cheta, give me my money," I said again, following her.

"So because you have been living in this big house you have forgotten how to behave? You're calling me a liar and a thief?" she said.

"Cheta, give me my money," I said for a third time. I moved to block her from entering the bedroom door.

"Move. Let me enter my room." She tried to squeeze past me.

I grabbed at the hem of her T-shirt and held it tight in my fist, "Cheta, give me my money or we are going to fight this night."

She stared at me openmouthed, the disbelief on her face would have made me laugh any other time. "Zam. What is this? Have you gone mad? Leave my shirt."

I thought of Ebuka's hand on her thigh and my grip tightened. "Cheta, give me my money."

"Zam, leave my shirt." Her fingers tried to pry her shirt out of my grip but my hold was too tight.

I heard a door open and Ginika came out of her room. "What is going on?" Ginika asked.

Cheta looked at Ginika but my face didn't leave hers. "The devil has entered my sister. Either that or she has gone mad."

"Cheta, give me my money," I said a fifth time. I wanted to smack her but I was afraid if I did, I wouldn't stop.

"I don't have your money. What sort of disrespect is this? Am I your age mate? Who do you think you're talking to like this?"

"You are just a year older than me," I reminded her. She liked to bring up her seniority any chance she could. When we were younger, she used to complain to Mama that it was disrespectful for me to call her by name. She wanted me to call her Sister Cheta, like the way Mama called her older sister Sister Chinaza. Mama would laugh and tell Cheta that one year was not enough time to deserve that respect.

"Can you buy one year in the market? Eh? Can you go to the market and buy one year of life?" Cheta asked.

"Cheta, give me my money," I said a sixth time. I did not want to get off topic.

"Cheta, do you know that there are cameras in this house? When Aunty or Uncle come back we can just ask them to rewind the tapes and what do you think we will see when we watch it?" Ginika asked quietly.

Cheta said nothing.

"Just give Zam back her money," Ginika said.

Still, Cheta said nothing. Ginika stepped towards us and put a hand over my fist clenching Cheta's shirt. "Zam, leave her. She'll get your money."

I reluctantly let go of Cheta's shirt. I watched as she went into her room only to come back out a few seconds later. She threw a brown envelope at me and I caught it before it hit my face. I stood in front of her door and took the time to count the money—twice, to make sure every note was there, before going to my room to put it back where it belonged. Tomorrow I would find a new hiding place. Ginika followed me into my room and sat on my bed.

The bottle of oil that Mama Chisom had given me was on my bedside table. Ginika picked it up. "Have you oiled your scalp?" she asked.

When I shook my head, she offered to help. She sat on the edge of my bed and I sat on the floor between her legs. Ginika slowly massaged the oil into my scalp. The motion was soothing and I closed my eyes, then leaned my head against her warm thigh.

"I don't like your sister. I really don't like thieves," Ginika said.

That was exactly what I needed to hear. The tension slowly left my body and I let the anger roll off my skin.

"She kissed Ebuka," I said softly.

"What?"

"Cheta. I saw her kissing Ebuka."

Ginika huffed. "You can do far better than Ebuka. Even his mother warned you. Ebuka is trash and your sister is trash too. They can be trash together."

I liked that she did not point out that I had no right to be angry because he was not my boyfriend.

Cheta didn't step into the kitchen the next day. "Is your sister hiding from us?" Chef Gideon asked after the second day they didn't see her.

"I don't know," I said, without looking at him. I was still nursing some resentment that they had befriended her but I was not angry enough to stay away from the kitchen.

Two days later, Cheta left. I lay on my bed and listened to the sound of her small suitcase rolling on the marble floor. I didn't come out of my room to say goodbye. I waited until I heard the front door close, then I went to the balcony and watched her enter the car and leave the compound.

EIGHTEEN

Cheta

THERE WERE SOME people who were satisfied with their life. Chef Gideon was one of them. So was Mr. Romieto. Ebuka was not. He did everything with attitude. He tried to hide it, tried to be the meek houseboy he was expected to be. But some things can't be hidden. He carried his attitude on his shoulders. It was clear that he thought the Universe owed him more. It was interesting to watch; it was also painful because I recognized myself in him. I think he recognized himself in me too. I liked him. Apart from the attitude, he was funny and had a nice smile. Those two things didn't cancel the bitterness in him, but I didn't care. I didn't mind the way his eyes looked over my body. I knew what he wanted and I decided to see if I wanted the same thing.

His lips were chapped and firm. It tickled my skin as he pressed kisses into the side of my neck. I tried to focus, tried to lose myself in it, but I was too wound up. My muscles felt tight. I could tell he could sense it. His hands moved up and down my thigh, trying to persuade me to open up but his touch just made me stiffen. I hated that I felt this way, hated that I was so averse to touch. I never felt completely comfortable around other people. I was always so aware. I had no choice but to be; Mama had made me that way.

His hands slid from my thigh and trailed up into my shirt. His hand going around my side to rest on my back.

"What happened here?" he murmured against my neck, caressing the raised scar. I shuddered as the memory over-whelmed me. It was a muddled memory, wisps of belt buckles and screaming and pain. So much pain. I smacked his hand away, got off his lap, and said with a flirty confidence I didn't feel, "Shouldn't we be cleaning up?"

I turned away from him to gather myself and grabbed a plate in the sink. I felt disconnected from my body.

"Having a dishwasher makes everything so much easier. I wish we had this at home," I said. While my mouth moved and my hands scrubbed, I fought the tears gathering in my eyes and the shivers racing through me. By the time I had my emotions under control, Ebuka had left the kitchen. I was thankful for that. I walked up to my room, tired and overwhelmed, wanting nothing more than to lie down.

There stood Zam, arms crossed. "Cheta, give me my money," she said.

I steadied myself and laughed. It was a dark sound. I couldn't deal with being touched, but this—fighting with Zam—was something I could do.

*　*　*

"Cheta, how are you liking Abuja? Has Kaira been showing you around?" Aunty asked. She had arrived that morning, and after we all had breakfast together at her request, we were in the living room, pretending like last night's confrontation hadn't happened.

At the sound of her name, Kaira turned to me and tried to communicate something with her eyes. It wasn't hard to interpret. I ignored her.

"Actually, no Aunty. I haven't gone anywhere. I guess she has been busy." I used my tame voice. The deferent one that adults liked.

Kaira glared at me. I glared back. If she wanted to play the intimidation game, I would show her I was better.

"Kaira, didn't I tell you to show your cousin around?"

"I was busy," Kaira said.

"Busy doing what? Do you have some labor-intensive job I don't know about?" Aunty questioned.

Zam's lips twitched. I held in my laugh—barely. Ginika didn't bother. Unfortunately for her, she had just taken a sip of her 5 Alive and she choked in the process.

"Good for you," Kaira whispered under her breath.

Aunty Sophie ignored them. "Sorry, Cheta. Next time you'll have a better time," she said, picking up the newspaper on the coffee table.

"Thank you, Aunty," I said. I squeezed my legs to stop from bouncing on the couch. Next time. She said next time. She liked having me here. Her words gave me confidence in my plans.

I waited for the other girls to leave before I approached Aunty. I had everything figured out in a way that meant I could avoid Mama for the next four years. When I wasn't at university, every school break and holiday could be spent in Abuja. I would only have to deal with Mama on the phone. And when I graduated, I could get a job in Abuja or Lagos. I got excited thinking about the possibility of being away from Mama for good.

"Aunty, I've been reading about your foundation," I said.

She lowered the newspaper and looked at me. "Really?"

"Yes. I think the work you do is really amazing."

She smiled at me. That was all the encouragement I needed to go on.

"I was reading about the work you have done with the orphanage and how it started. The work the first director, Mr. Balogun, did was really inspiring and I want to follow in his footsteps. I'm studying psychology just like him and after I graduate I want to use my degree to help children in need.

Maybe on my breaks, I can stay here and volunteer at the orphanage. I read an interview Mr. Balogun did about . . ." I trailed off when I noticed the look on Aunty's face. I had said something wrong. But I didn't know what. Her eyes had glossed over and she was holding herself still. She was looking at me but it didn't seem like she was there.

"Aunty?" I said.

She blinked and came back into herself. Sharp eyes narrowed on me. "I don't think that's a good idea. University is a lot of work. You should focus on your schoolwork." Her words were stiff. Almost as if she were reading a speech. She stood up and walked out of the living room.

I found myself following her, confused about what was happening. Why was she angry at me?

"It doesn't have to be the orphanage," I said in a rush, "Mr. Balogun did—"

She grabbed the handle of the door to the west wing and whirled around. "Stop talking," she hissed at me, lips twisted in a look that made me take a step back.

I stared openmouthed as she slammed the door in my face.

* * *

"I want to greet Aunty before I go," I said to Mr. Romieto.

He grimaced. "Madam is not feeling well. She said to give this to you and to wish you a safe journey."

I took the money and stuffed it in my bag. "I'll be really quick. I just want to quickly speak to her." I spent the night going over everything I said to her, trying to pinpoint the moment her demeanor had changed. I was almost sure it had to do with James Balogun. I spent the night googling him until I came across an old Facebook post, written by some relative, commemorating the fifteenth anniversary of his death. I was so angry with myself. I should have done more research, looked deeper. Maybe reminding her about his death had triggered something in her. I needed to make things right because I needed Aunty to agree to my plan.

Mr. Romieto gave me a pitying smile. "Small madam. I'm sorry but Madam made it clear that she is not available this morning."

I had no choice but to leave without seeing Aunty. I called her when my plane landed in Benin. The call went unanswered. I sent a text message a few days later thanking her for her hospitality. I got no response.

NINETEEN

Zam

THINGS WITH EBUKA changed after Cheta's visit. I made sure
I was never alone with him in the kitchen. I still woke up early
but instead of going to the kitchen to help him start the day, I
stayed in my room and played games on my phone. At night, I
left the kitchen at the same time Chef Gideon and Mr. Romieto
did, leaving Ebuka alone to clean up.

"Are you angry with me?" he asked after the fourth day
while I was sorting beans. The smile on his face was both hesitant and expectant, like he already knew the answer was no. I
looked up and saw we were the only ones in the kitchen. Chef
Gideon had left without me noticing.

Instead of answering him I took the chance to study his
face. I noticed the sparse hair on his chin, the beard that refused

to connect. I noticed the pimples on his hairline and the tiny scar by his nose. His top lip was fuller than the bottom. The bottom lip was peeling and cracking. These were the lips Cheta kissed. I wondered if it was her first. How many other lips had she touched with hers? How many lips had he touched with his? Had their tongues slipped into each other's mouths? Did he like it? Did she want to kiss him again? I couldn't help but then compare him to my maths teacher, Mr. Oyeyemi, whose full pink lips I had never seen dry. I focused on everything that was wrong with his face so that later, when I thought of him, I would think of all these imperfections.

I turned back to the tray of beans balanced on my lap, ignoring his question. I saw his feet step closer to me.

"Zam. What did I do? Or are we not friends?" he asked.

"You didn't do anything," I said.

Ebuka was not an idiot. I was sure he knew how I felt about him. It was not a secret. His mother and Mama Chisom knew how I felt and they were not the kind of women who were capable of keeping their mouth shut. They would have definitely mentioned my feelings to Ebuka. Even though I had no claim to him, looking at him made my heart clench in my chest. He knew how I felt and he still kissed my sister. I had no right to be jealous, but I felt what I felt and I didn't care if it was unfair.

"So we're still friends?" he asked.

I looked up at him ready to lie and say yes but thankfully the kitchen phone rang. As he spoke to whoever was on the other end of the line, I left the tray of beans on the counter and slipped out of the kitchen.

Mr. Romieto and Chef Gideon noticed the tension between Ebuka and me, but they didn't say anything about it. Mr. Romieto's ears twitched constantly, his eyes darting from me to Ginika to Ebuka. Chef Gideon's stories became more unbelievable, using humor to ease the tension. Sometimes it worked, sometimes it didn't.

I didn't let my anger at Ebuka stop me from going to the market with him, though, because I liked being around his mother's nonstop chatter. Mama E noticed the change in my attitude and unlike Chef Gideon and Mr. Romieto, she was not the kind of person who knew how to bite her tongue.

"You are angry with my son," she said during one of my visits to the market. Ginika was not with me and I had never needed her presence more than in that moment.

"No. I'm not," I said, unable to lift my head to look at her.

"Don't insult me. Do I look like I was born yesterday?"

"Sorry, ma."

"I told you men are stupid. Whatever he did, you need to forgive him. He's a man. You know how these men are."

"Okay, ma," I lied. I didn't want to forgive him because I didn't want to like somebody who liked Cheta enough to kiss her.

"Good. I like you. My little in-law." She had taken to calling me her little in-law. It was one of the reasons I had let my imagination run wild, wondering what it would be like to be

Ebuka's girlfriend. Not that Uncle Emeke would ever allow it, but in my imagination anything was possible.

*　*　*

There was only so much self-pity Ginika could take. I could see her getting tired of listening to me complain about the same thing, but I couldn't stop my mouth from moving.

"I like you so I'm going to be honest with you," Ginika said when she finally had enough. "You need to get over it. I could understand why you were upset when you found out but it's been almost a month. Stop wallowing and move on. It's getting annoying. You guys make the atmosphere in the kitchen so awkward and you know how I like Chef Gideon's stories."

When I didn't say anything she sighed and continued, "Look. I get it's hard because you have to see him everyday. You need to find something to occupy your time. Go with Aunty to her next conference or something. Just find a way to get out of the house for a few days."

That evening I went to the west wing to talk to Aunty Sophie. She was scheduled to go to Asaba to talk at a seminar in two weeks. I spent the next hour reading about the seminar and coming up with reasons why I was interested in it. Reasons that sounded good enough to make her let me tag along.

"Aunty can I go with you to your conference in Asaba?" I asked her.

She was sitting on an armchair, looking at a newspaper but not reading it, that strange faraway look on her face. The television was on and the volume was so loud, I wondered how she could even think, let alone read the paper with all the noise.

She looked at me over her glasses. For a moment it didn't seem like she knew who I was, then she smiled and said, "Okay. Let Romieto know you will be accompanying me. He'll alter the arrangements accordingly."

TWENTY

Cheta

I RAN MY fingers down the mottled skin inside my arm. The scar had faded, and with it the pain, but the memory still followed me. Mama had pressed a hot knife into my skin because someone had told her I had been kissing a boy in the boy's toilet at school. The memories of all the scars that patterned my body followed me. No more. No more flayed skin and burnt flesh and broken bones. I grabbed the handle of the suitcase I had not bothered to unpack.

When I had stepped into the house after visiting Abuja and saw Mama's frowning face, something in me cracked. After spending a week away from her, living with Mama was now a hundred times more unbearable. Two days. I lasted only two days. I couldn't do it anymore. If I spent one more day in the same house as Mama, I would end up slitting her throat or slitting mine.

I didn't know where I was going. I didn't have enough money to go anywhere. The money I had taken from Zam's bedside table would have been enough to rent a small room in Benin City but she had to go and grow a backbone at the most inconvenient time.

But it didn't matter that I had no money, no job, and no place to go. I would find a way to make do. Zam was not the only one who got to be free. It was my turn now.

I lifted the suitcase a few inches off the ground and carried it downstairs. Mama was in the living room, a magazine balanced on her lap. She flipped the pages with one hand and held a pair of scissors in the other.

"What are you doing?" Mama asked, eyeing the luggage.

"I'm leaving, Mama."

"Leaving where? Where do you think you're going to?" She stood up, the magazine on her lap tumbling to the floor. Her hand clenched around the scissors and my body tensed, preparing to duck.

"Why are you asking? It's not like you care."

I was ready when the scissors flew. I dodged to the right in time and the scissors hit the wall behind me. I straightened and she took a step towards me, her hands outstretched. I took a quick step back. I knew how tightly her claws could dig into skin and draw blood. I grabbed the closest thing to me, an empty beer bottle on the coffee table.

"Mama, if you touch me, I will break this bottle on your head," I said it calmly, letting the weight and the seriousness of my words settle on her ears. I grabbed my suitcase and walked past her. She didn't follow me.

I walked out the front door and saw Papa sitting on the veranda. "Papa, I'm leaving."

His eyes went from mine to the luggage in my hand. He looked at it with such intense longing, almost as if he wished he could fold himself into it. I felt no sympathy for him. It was him and Mama now. Hopefully they ended up killing each other.

*　*　*

I was out of breath when I knocked on Anita's door. Rolling a heavy suitcase on uneven soil was harder than I thought. Thankfully Anita answered the door and not her mother.

Her eyes went wide when she took in me and the full suitcase by my side.

"Cheta, wetin?"

"Anita, dodo, I need a favor," I said.

"Are you going somewhere? Didn't you just get back from Abuja."

"Something came up," I said, waving my hand like it wasn't important. "I'm leaving right now and I need you to do something for me."

Anita turned to me with wide eyes and cut me off. "Leaving ke? To where? But why? Where are you rushing to? You can't leave me alone in this place o. Anwulika is leaving too. Who will I talk to?"

"I'm just tired of this place," I said vaguely. I didn't want to explain. My friends didn't know how bad it was at home and I preferred it that way. In the two days I'd been back, I spent most of my time in Ms. Okoye's place, going home only to sleep, and even then Mama found a reason to come into my room to complain about something. I had reached my limit. That was all there was to it. I simply could not handle any more.

"I want to be sure that Ms. Okoye will have help, can you do that for me. Look after her? Buy her foodstuff, cook, clean, and just do little things around the house. She'll pay you," I said.

"Yeah. As long as she pays. No wahala."

"She has some . . . she's not that comfortable with people. I'll make you a list of the things you can do and the things you can't."

"Hian! Her crase dey plenty like that?"

"She's not crazy," I defended. I was protective of Ms. Okoye. I didn't like the dismissive way people talked about her. It seemed they had forgotten the woman she used to be. She had been everyone's favorite teacher. The teacher who could take a joke and laugh with students. Everyone had forgotten her best traits and chose to focus on what her pain had turned her into.

"She's not bad. You'll get used to her. If you have any trouble just call me," I said.

Anita reached out and grabbed my hand. Her voice got serious. "Cheta, honestly, is everything okay? Where are you going to?"

"I've called Chizi. She said I can stay with her."

That was the wrong thing to say. Anita squeezed my hand. "Chizi! That anyhow babe? Wetin happen? Things can't be bad enough for you to go and stay with Chizi."

"Everything is fine. I have to get to the bus park and catch a bus to Benin. I'll call you later, okay?"

She studied me for a moment, her mouth turned down in a pronounced frown. "I can't believe you and Anwulika are leaving me in this place. And you're leaving me to live with Chizi. Of all people!"

"You'll be fine. I'll be fine. We'll all be fine," I said, more to myself than to her, because it was the only thing I could believe in.

TWENTY-ONE

Zam

THE ASABA AIRPORT was closed. According to Mr. Romieto, the plan was to fly to Benin and go by road to Asaba. Two cars had driven to Benin the day before, so they would be there to pick us up when we arrived. It was a short flight in a private plane. Aunty slept most of the way and I stared at the fluffy clouds. There was a Hilux truck with a driver and one MOPOL and a Mercedes with a driver and Mr. Boniface, waiting for us on the tarmac.

The car ride was as quiet as the plane ride. Aunty spent most of it with her eyes closed, her hands tapping in time to the beat of the song coming through the car speakers. Her wrists jangled as she moved. She wasn't wearing that much jewelry. Only a watch, a bracelet, a necklace, and a pair of small gold earrings. So simple. So classy. I wanted to be like her when I grew up.

"Do you like it?" Aunty asked.

I looked up, my face and neck immediately getting warm when I realized she had seen me staring at her jewelry.

"Yes. You wear that one all the time," I said, pointing at the bracelet she wore on the same wrist as her watch. It was a gold bracelet with hollow indents where stones should be. She had worn it the day she picked me up from Alihame.

"It was my mother's," she said. "She wore it all the time, so it's a little scratched up and some of the stones are missing. She lost three of them. I've only lost one so far." She touched the bracelet, a sad smile on her face. I was thinking about what kind of look I would have on my face if people brought up Mama after she passed away when the world suddenly went mad.

It started with the sound of fireworks. We had just passed Agbor and were driving through Umunede. It was a long stretch of road with nothing but thick bushes and trees. I looked out the window wondering why there would be fireworks in the middle of the day. From the corner of my eye, I saw the Hilux that was escorting us to Asaba swerve off the road, holes on the side that weren't there before.

Gunshots not fireworks, I thought, thick fear freezing my blood.

Something black flashed but before I could turn my head, the car started spinning. My face hit the seat in front of me and the force made my ears ring. Through the ringing I heard

Aunty screaming and the driver shouting. I looked up and saw Mr. Boniface frantically trying to get his rifle, which was awkwardly wedged between his door and his seat. The driver opened his door and ran out, shouting as he did. I tried to do the same but my hand wasn't cooperating.

A car door slammed and people wearing black masks exited the car that hit us, pointing guns and yelling instructions. Mr. Boniface dove over the console and escaped through the driver's door, leaving me and Aunty Sophie behind.

Aunty Sophie screamed at him and tried to reach over me to open my door, when suddenly her door was wrenched open and she was yanked out by her hair. I watched as they dragged her to the car and shoved her in.

Then the world went dark.

* * *

The sharp smell of antiseptic was the first thing I noticed when I woke up. The second thing was the moaning. The room was dark. There were fluorescent lights lined up on the ceiling, but only two were working, and one of those was flickering and looked like it would die out by the end of the day. There was a steady beating sound coming from the ceiling fan. I was in a large hospital room and I wasn't sure how I got there.

On the hospital bed beside me, a pregnant woman lay on her back. She was the one making the moaning noise. There was a small child, about two or three years, sitting on the edge of the bed, sucking on a SuperYogo and watching the woman.

I looked around the room and saw there were about thirty beds; more than half were filled. I stood up. Pain radiated through my arm as I moved and I slowly brought it to my chest and cradled it.

There was only one nurse in the room. She was seated behind a desk by the door, going through some hospital files. I walked up to her.

"Good afternoon, ma."

She looked up at me and nodded, then looked back down at the files.

"My arm is paining me," I said.

"It's broken. We can give you medication for the pain and put a cast but you have to pay up front. If you can't pay, there's nothing we can do for you." Her words were quick and toneless, like she had said that sentence so many times before.

"Can I just have something for the pain. My uncle can pay," I said through gritted teeth.

She put down the file in her hands and looked up at me. She looked angry but from the deep lines in her face I could tell this was her usual expression. "Did you not hear what I said? We only give medication after you pay. Now that you're awake you can go down to the reception and wait there for your uncle."

"Ma, do you know who brought me here?"

"A good Samaritan" was the only answer she gave.

I wondered why she was so angry. There needed to be some sort of rule against hospitals hiring such unfriendly nurses.

"Please. Do you have a phone I can use to call my uncle?"

She said nothing as she picked up the file and continued reading.

"Please, ma," I begged.

She closed her eyes and sighed before reaching into her pocket and bringing out a cell phone. "Stand here and call. Don't talk too long. I don't have credit," she said before handing me the phone.

I didn't have Uncle's number memorized so I called Ginika. I took a few steps away from the nurse as I dialed.

"Hello?"

"Hello Ginika. It's me," I whispered into the phone.

"Zam?"

"Yes. Is Uncle there?"

"I think he came home a few hours ago. Why?"

"Aunty has been kidnapped. Someone brought me to the hospital. I'm using a nurse's phone."

"Be fast o! I don't have credit!" the nurse called out. I turned around and saw her staring at me with narrowed eyes.

"Are you joking?" Ginika asked.

"I'm not joking. Give the phone to Uncle."

"Zam—" The phone call dropped. Just as I was about to call again, the phone beeped in my hand and a message stating that the phone was out of airtime flashed on the screen.

I stared at the phone in my hand, willing Ginika to call me back.

"Did you finish my credit?" The nurse asked. She stood up from behind the desk and snatched the phone from me. She put it in her pocket and walked towards the pregnant woman lying on the bed. As she was attending to the woman, the phone rang. I watched her pluck the phone out of her pocket and answer it. She spoke to whoever was on the line before turning around, her eyes searching the room. Her eyes stopped when they found me. She motioned me over and handed me the phone.

"Ginika?" I asked, putting the phone to my ear.

"Zam?" I heard Uncle's rough voice say. "What is this nonsense Ginika just told me? What is happening?"

I explained everything that happened and told him where I was.

"Give the phone to whoever is in charge," Uncle commanded quietly when I was done.

I gave the phone back to the nurse because she was the only hospital employee there. I couldn't hear what Uncle was telling her but she nodded and kept on saying, "Yes, sir."

When the call ended, she ordered me to wait where I was. I stood by the bed, watching her touch the pregnant lady's belly and ask some questions. When she was done, she took off her gloves and said, "Follow me."

I followed her out of the room, through a corridor, and up two flights of stairs. She stopped in front of a door. "You'll stay here. A doctor will be in to look at your hand." Then she whirled around and walked back in the direction we came from. I cautiously opened the door and saw it was a hospital room. It had a narrow hospital bed, a chair, and some sort of medical machine next to the bed. I wondered what Uncle said to her on the phone to make her break her no-treatment-before-payment rule. I got on the bed and quickly fell asleep.

I was awake when Uncle Emeke walked into the room. The nurse had come in hours ago to give me pain medication and to set my arm in a cast. Uncle's nostrils flared and his entire body seemed tense when his eyes landed on the cast. Behind him was a tall man wearing a suit. The man had a notepad in one hand and a pen in the other. The pen was poised above the unlined paper. He looked ready to take notes.

"Tell me what happened," the tall man said.

I looked at Uncle, silently seeking permission to answer. Uncle nodded and I started talking fast, repeating everything I had told Uncle earlier.

"Okay." The man looked at me as he wrote and I wondered if his sentences were straight. "Why didn't you get out of the car when you saw the driver and MOPOL running?" he asked.

I looked at my arm in the cast. "I couldn't move my arm and I hit my head on the window. I was confused. A lot of things were happening."

"Did they try to take you?" the man asked.

"No."

Uncle Emeke walked to the only chair in the room. It was tucked in a corner facing the bed. He was breathing noisily through his mouth, like someone who had just run a race. He sat down and watched as the tall man asked me questions.

"Did you see any of their faces? Did you recognize anyone?" the man writing notes asked without looking up from his notepad.

"They were wearing black masks. I didn't see their faces."

"What else do you remember?"

"I just told you everything."

The man opened his mouth to ask another question but Uncle spoke first. "Why wouldn't they take her too?" Uncle asked.

"Does she usually travel with your wife?" the tall man asked Uncle.

Uncle shook his head.

"They probably weren't expecting her to be there and planned to take only one person," the man said.

The man kept asking me the same questions. Questions like what car were they driving and how many kidnappers were there. I knew it was a black car but I hadn't paid attention to the car brand or license plate. I had only seen two kidnappers; the one that shot at the window and the one that opened Aunty's door and dragged her out. But from the shouts and the gunshots, there had to be more than two. I was too busy covering my head with my only functioning arm to notice anything helpful. He asked more questions I couldn't answer, and I could feel Uncle's frustration filling the room. I kept my eyes on the tall man, afraid of what I would see if I looked at Uncle.

When the man was finished with his questions, he nodded at Uncle and left the room.

Uncle stood up from his seat and came to stand beside my bed. "The doctors said that you'll be fine. They're going to give you some painkillers to take."

I nodded.

He leaned over me and I tried to shrink back but I had nowhere to go. "You cannot tell anybody. Do not say a word to anybody. Especially your parents. Do you understand me?" He was leaning over me and I knew when he said parents he really only meant my mother. Mama was the unofficial town crier. Everything that went into her ears came out of her mouth, usually at the moment where it could cause the most damage.

"Yes, Uncle," I said

"I've given Romieto instructions. Listen to him when you get home. I've made arrangements for you to fly back to Abuja," he said, before walking out of the room.

* * *

When I got off the private plane, there were three officers I had never seen waiting for me. They escorted me to the car. One of them climbed in the passenger seat and the other two sat in the back, with me in the middle. Being in a car with four men, three of whom had guns, was terrifying. The sounds of gunshots kept replaying in my head. I had never thought of what they would sound like in real life. I hadn't expected it to be so loud. My hand kept reaching up to roll the beads of my rosary. I kept my legs pressed together and my arms tucked into my sides, afraid of any body part accidentally touching the men beside me. No one spoke during the entire drive home.

When we got to the house, Mr. Romieto was standing by the front door. There were sweat drops beading his forehead and the underarms of his shirt were soaked. It was not a particularly hot day, there was no reason for him to be sweating that much. "Little madam, welcome back," he said. The laughter that usually danced in his eyes was gone, replaced by a sullen look that looked foreign on his round face.

"Mr. Romieto." I tried to smile but it was like my lips had forgotten how to.

He collected my small suitcase from the officer. "I'll carry it up for you," he said.

"I want to greet Chef Gideon and Ebuka," I said.

"Oga has forbidden it. No more spending time in the kitchen. You three girls are to stay upstairs from now on. When it's time to eat, one of us will bring food upstairs." I followed him through the hall and up the stairs. He looked back at me as he ascended. "Also, no more spending time on the balcony. The door has been locked and Oga has the key."

He carried my bag upstairs and set it in front of my room door, nodding at Kaira and Ginika, who were sitting on the couch watching us.

Once he headed back downstairs and the sound of his footsteps faded, Kaira pounced. "What happened? Tell us."

I told them everything I had told Uncle.

"What is Daddy doing about it?" Kaira asked when I was done. Before I could answer she asked another question. "Why didn't they take you?"

"Kaira! You make it seem like you wanted them to take her," Ginika said.

"What? They could have asked for more money if they took the two of them. It's just common sense."

"I don't think they were expecting me to be in the car."

"They probably didn't even know who she was. What's the point of kidnapping someone if you're not sure their family can pay?" Ginika said.

"What do you think is going to happen to my mum? Do you think they'll . . ." Kaira's sentence trailed off. I knew each of us were imagining all kinds of horrors, but none of us wanted to voice them. Kaira shook her head, as if she was trying to shake out the images her mind had conjured. "How much do you think they'll ask for?" she asked instead.

"Millions. Dollars or naira," Ginika said solemnly.

"Uncle said not to tell anyone. Not even my parents. They don't want the media to find out." It hadn't made any sense to me when Uncle had told me but I had nodded and promised not to tell anyone. "But why? If people know, can't they help? Someone might have some sort of information."

"Do you think this is abroad where you can issue an Amber Alert or use CCTV to track where the kidnapper's car went to? How will letting the media know help anyone? All it would do is let other kidnapping groups know that it is possible to snatch her," Kaira said.

"True," Ginika concurred. "That's how kidnapping works. People they return never talk to the news about it. Most people don't even go to the police. I heard my mum talking to her friend about an importer guy that got kidnapped. His family paid fifty million naira. They released him, he went to the police, the next day they kidnapped him again and asked for another twenty million. It was his punishment for going to the police."

"That's so messed up. Poor man. Getting kidnapped twice." Kaira started laughing. It wasn't really funny, but her laughter made me smile and suddenly the three of us were laughing uncontrollably.

"Aunty is going to be fine. Uncle will pay and they'll return her," Ginika said with false confidence, when our laughter gradually died. I could tell she was trying to convince herself as much as she was trying to convince us.

"Why didn't they call Uncle when they took her. He didn't know anything had happened until I spoke to him."

Ginika shrugged. "They probably just do that so that the family panics. Maybe people are more likely to pay when they've been worrying for hours."

We spent the rest of the day in the living room. The TV was on but no one was watching it. We were all lost in our own thoughts. The lights were off and the sunlight streaming through the windows was the only source of light. When the sun set, the room was slowly plunged into darkness, and still none of us moved.

"I'm sleeping here," Ginika announced abruptly into the darkness. She went into her bedroom and came out holding her duvet. Kaira and I followed her lead and went to fetch our own duvets. We didn't talk about the reason why none of us wanted to be alone that night.

I woke up in the middle of the night when I heard sniffling. It was coming from the couch beside me and I knew it was Kaira crying.

The three of us spent most of the next day in the living room, only leaving to take a shower and use the bathroom. For breakfast, lunch, and dinner, Ebuka brought trays of food upstairs. An hour later he was back to collect the trays. Each time he came up he tried to subtly get my attention, but I refused.

Ginika commandeered the remote and absentmindedly flipped through channels. Occasionally she stumbled on something and we all watched. Sometimes one of us made a random comment but for the most part, we were quiet. I knew they were both thinking the same thing I was, but it was as if we had made a silent pact not to talk about Aunty and whatever horrors she may or may not be suffering.

In the middle of a documentary about crocodiles, Ginika abruptly stood up and tossed the remote on the couch. "Let's commune with our chi," she said.

"What?" Kaira looked confused.

"Me and Zam do it sometimes. We commune with our chi. You guys stay here. I'll get it ready." She headed to her room.

"What is she talking about?" Kaira whispered to me, as if she was scared Ginika would hear her behind the closed door.

"She builds a shrine so we can commune with our chi," I whispered back.

"Shrine? Like idol worship?" Kaira asked. She seemed excited.

"She says it's not idol worship."

Ginika opened her door and stuck her head out a few minutes later. "It's ready."

Walking into her room, my nostrils were assaulted by the strong scent of burning candles. It was far more candles than she usually used. There were three straw mats on the floor. Kaira sat on one mat at the end and Ginika took the mat on the other end, leaving the middle mat for me.

"Just think about what you want and try to be at one with your spirit. Your chi is your spirit on a different plane. You are your chi. Or something like that," Ginika explained to Kaira.

I was expecting Kaira to have more questions but she seemed eager to begin.

"Do we sit or do we lie down?" she asked.

"I think we're supposed to sit but we always lie down."

Kaira nodded and settled on her back. Her eyes closed and arms straight at her side. I looked at Ginika, who had also lain down, eyes closed, hands clasped together on her tummy. I ignored the burning pain in my broken arm and stared at the ceiling as I replayed the scene in my head, wondering if there was anything I could have done differently to help Aunty.

*　*　*

My phone rang. The ringtone sounded so much louder in the dark. I checked the display, saw it was my mother, and quickly decided to ignore it. Uncle's warning rang in my mind. I put my phone on silent and stuck it under the pillow. I didn't want to accidentally tell Mama something I shouldn't.

"Do you talk to your mum every day?" Kaira asked. She was lying next to me and must have seen the display. We were on Ginika's bed. Somehow we all ended up there after communing with our chi. The candles had been blown out but the fragrant scent still lingered.

"Yes. No. Not every day. Almost every day."

"What do you talk about?"

"Nothing really. She talks and I listen. She just mostly complains about my sister."

"And your dad?"

"He doesn't talk."

"What? Since when? Is he mute or something?"

"No. He just . . . he doesn't really speak."

"Why?" Ginika rolled onto her side to face me. It made me uncomfortable knowing they were both watching me, waiting for an answer.

"I don't know. He just slowly stopped talking."

"To you or to anybody," Kaira asked.

"To anybody." I hesitated before deciding to tell the truth. "I used to count the days he went without speaking. The longest was eight days."

"I count the days too," Kaira whispered. "At least you're lucky. My mum doesn't speak to me. Just me. The longest has been twelve days. And we live in the same house."

"She doesn't look at you. Sometimes it's almost like she's scared to look at you," Ginika whispered.

"I know," Kaira said. She sounded like she was holding back tears but I couldn't see her face in the dark.

"Is she like that with Akubundu?" I asked.

"No. He has always been the favorite." The tears in her voice were gone. It seemed to have hardened very quickly and turned into bitterness—a bitterness I was familiar with. It was the same kind of bitterness that flavored Cheta's voice.

"I'm my mother's favorite," I said. "Most of the time I wish I wasn't. It's why my sister doesn't like me. It makes living in the house so difficult. That was why I was so happy to come here. There was so much hatred in the house and it always felt like it was my fault." There was something freeing about letting the words out of my mouth.

There was silence for a few minutes and I was already beginning to regret saying anything when Ginika said, "I win. I haven't spoken to my dad in three years."

"So, basically, we're all fucked up," Kaira whispered.

TWENTY-TWO

Cheta

I DUG THE earphones deeper into my ear and increased the volume, but there was no point. No matter how loud the music was, it was never loud enough to drown out the sounds of Chizi's moaning. It was the third night in a row I was forced to listen to her and her boyfriend having sex. But I couldn't complain—at least not out loud. Chizi was nice enough to let me stay with her rent-free in her one-bedroom face-me-I-face-you apartment. I had shared her bed with her the first night, but if I had known what she got up to in that bed, I would have slept on the couch. My second night there, her boyfriend, Obinna, had shown up smelling of gin and sweat. He was a short and bulky man with a shaved head and a scraggly goatee. When Chizi introduced us, I pretended not to notice his wedding ring or the fact that he was old enough to be her father. The caliber of man Chizi wanted to allow between her legs was not my business. After spending a few minutes making polite small talk, Chizi and Obinna disappeared into the bedroom. The noises came soon after. I slept on the couch that night, though Obinna did not spend the night. He had come out of the room looking disheveled, the smell of sex following him. The same thing happened the next night and the night after.

I closed my eyes and burrowed into the couch, focusing all my energy on the music pounding in my ears and not on the noise coming from the bedroom. Listening to Chizi haw like a donkey was better than being beaten, I reminded myself when I began to wonder if I should just go back to Alihame.

* * *

Early in the morning, like I had done every day since I got to Benin, I took a cold shower and got ready in the dark because there was no power and Chizi didn't have enough money to buy petrol for her small generator. I put on my most professional-looking clothes and trekked to town. An okada would have been faster but I needed to save all my money for food. I went into every salon, every buka, every store and asked them if they were looking for help. I left my contact details at every place. I needed to make money quick. I was completely dependent on Chizi and I hated it. I was waiting for an opening at the restaurant Chizi worked in. It was in one of the latest hotels, the one all the people with money stayed in. People with too much money didn't have the patience to wait for waiters to bring back change, and according to Chizi she could earn up to five thousand naira in free change on a good night. But until a spot opened, I had to find a place to work.

Hours later I was back at Chizi's apartment, hot, tired, and still jobless.

"Where have you been?" Chizi asked me when I walked in. She was sitting on a small plastic chair that rested against her peeling cream walls. It was where she sat when she smoked, so she could blow the smoke out of the window. There were two men in the living room with her. One of them had a baby face and was sitting on the ground, a bowl of garri topped with groundnut between his spread legs. The other one was on his back on the couch, a hand flung on his forehead. He looked like he could be sleeping but I could see his right foot rocking slightly.

"I was looking for a job," I said, handing her one of the SuperYogos I had bought. I couldn't pay rent but at least I could buy her yogurt.

"Thanks. These are my cousins, Nnamdi and Johnson." She pointed at the baby-faced one and then the one lying on the couch.

I gave them a small wave. The baby-faced one smiled at me, the other one opened one eye, nodded at me, and then closed it again.

I sat on a small wooden stool in the corner of the room.

"Guys, this is Cheta, the friend I was talking about, the one wey no sharp."

I narrowed my eyes at her. "What?"

She laughed and puffed on her cigarette. "Yes now. You no be sharp babe, o." She turned to Johnson and explained, "Her uncle is rich enough to buy this country and she's here soaking garri and hopping okada with me. If I had a rich uncle, do you know the type of life I would be living?"

Nnamdi laughed as he brought a spoonful of garri to his mouth. "Who be her uncle?" he asked, his mouth full. His words were directed at Chizi, but his curious gaze was focused on me.

"Iweka," said Chizi.

Johnson finally opened both eyes, running them up and down my body, taking in my outfit. "Iweka as in Iweka Oil?"

"Yes o," Chizi said, stubbing out her cigarette and lighting a new one.

"Why you dey squat with Chizi? Your uncle no fit get you apartment?" he asked.

I bristled at his tone. "I like to find my own way," I said.

"How did the job search go?" Chizi asked.

"Not well," I said.

"Which kind job you dey find?" he asked.

I opened my mouth to say it was none of his business but Chizi answered first. "She's looking for anything really. She just wants to have small money in hand when uni starts."

"Hmm," he said. "I might have something for you."

I looked at him, taking the time to study him like he had studied me, and I didn't like what I saw. I learned how to read people a long time ago; it was a skill I had no choice but to hone when living with Mama. There was something dodgy about his demeanor. I also hadn't missed the way he perked up when Chizi mentioned my uncle's name.

"No, thanks. I'll find something on my own," I said.

"You don't even know what the job is," he said.

I tore open a corner of the SuperYogo with my teeth and sucked, not bothering to respond.

Chizi laughed. "Johnson, leave her alone. Cheta is very stubborn. Her head is like cement."

* * *

After almost two weeks of searching, I was ready to give up. The job I thought I was going to get as a cashier at Chicken Republic had fallen through, and to make things worse it started raining on my way home.

I entered a supermarket and pretended to browse the aisles just to get away from the rain. My phone rang in the dairy aisle.

"Anita, what's up," I said, holding my phone to my ear with one hand and absentmindedly picking up a carton of milk with the other.

"Your mum just left my house," she said.

I set the milk down. "What did she want?" I hadn't been in contact with Mama or Papa since I left. I definitely wasn't going to call them and they hadn't called me. I wasn't surprised but a part of me still hurt and I hated that part of me because it meant I cared and I didn't want to care.

"She was asking me if I had heard from you," Anita said.

"Wetin you tell am?"

"I told her last time we spoke you said you were in Lagos trying to make it as a musician."

A surprise laugh escaped. An old woman walking by me jerked in surprise. I mouthed an apology.

"I wish I saw her face when you said that."

Anita laughed. "She was not happy at all."

"I can imagine," I said, laughed along with her.

When the laughing died down, Anita got serious. "Cheta, honestly, what is going on? Why don't you want your mother to know where you are? She seemed very worried."

I snorted. I had made Anita promise not to tell anyone where I was going because it would inevitably get to Mama and I knew Mama. Her needing to know my whereabouts was about control not concern. I didn't want her showing up in Chizi's apartment with her nonsense. I told Anita a half-truth, "Nothing is going on. I'm just trying to hustle here and you know how my mum is. If she knows I'm in Benin, she'll come here and try to drag me back to Alihame."

I could tell Anita wanted to know more but thankfully she let it go. We spoke for a few more minutes and she caught me

218

up with all the new gist after assuring me she was taking care of Ms. Okoye.

The rain was still coming down hard when I got off the phone and it didn't look like it was going to stop anytime soon.

I returned to Chizi's house with chattering teeth, soaked clothes, and muddy shoes.

"What happened to you?" Johnson said when he saw me. He was lounging on the couch with a bottle of Gulder in his hand.

"Nothing," I said. I wasn't interested in discussing my failures with him.

"Are you still looking for a job?" he asked, watching as I took off my shoes. He was always watching me. It made me uncomfortable but I had learned to ignore it.

I closed my eyes and inhaled, making a conscious decision to let go of my pride as I exhaled. "Maybe. Do you have something for me?"

Johnson's head jerked in surprise before a slow smile spread across his face. He was always over at Chizi's place, so he had a front row seat to my dejection. Every day I walked through the door still jobless, he asked me if I was interested in working for him. I always said no—on principle. But now I was desperate and out of options.

"*Maybe* isn't an answer," he said.

I rolled my eyes. "Yes, I'm still looking for a job."

He started to explain what I'd be doing for him. You didn't have to be a genius to figure out Johnson was into yahoo-yahoo.

He wore expensive clothes but spent most of his time lazing around Chizi's apartment acting like he had no care in the world. He didn't seem to have a job and yet somehow he always had money to spend. There were only two explanations: his parents either had money or he was into some sort of 419. I knew his parents were just as broke as Chizi's, so I wasn't surprised when he started explaining what he did and what he wanted me to do. He was surprisingly eloquent. I could almost pretend he wasn't trying to convince me to sell drugs.

TWENTY-THREE

Zam

WE DEVELOPED A routine. During the days we pretended everything was fine. We huddled in the living room, alternating between playing Whot and binge watching *Gossip Girl* and old-school Nollywood movies featuring Osuofia. We forced ourselves to laugh, we communed with our chi, we listened to music and danced around the room. But the subject of Aunty's kidnapping lingered in the air like a bad smell that refused to dissipate. Sometimes we were forced to face reality, like when Akubundu called Kaira to ask for updates and she told him the same thing Uncle Emeke had told us, "They had people working to get her back, ASAP."

We stopped pretending when the sun set and the lights went off. It was in those quiet moments that we spilled our secrets and discovered that we hurt the same way and wanted the same things—parents that cared.

On the morning of the fourth day, Kaira's phone rang.

"Dad?" Kaira answered out of breath, laughter resonating in that one word. She had been laughing as Ginika chased me around the living room holding a wall gecko she had found in her room. I watched Kaira, trying to ignore how itchy my arm was underneath the cast.

Whatever Uncle said made Kaira's spine snap straight. A look of disgust flashed across her face and I knew what she was feeling. The same thing was rumbling through my belly. Guilt. Like me, she had forgotten—for a brief moment—that her mother had been kidnapped. For a few minutes, as Ginika threatened to put the gecko on my head, our joy had been genuine.

"They've returned her. A car is coming to pick us up to take us to the hospital," Kaira said when the phone call ended. Her voice was flat. No emotion.

Ginika set the gecko on the floor and it climbed up the wall, disappearing into a small crack near the ceiling. "I'll wash my hands," Ginika said.

The ride to the hospital was quiet. I sat in the middle, with Ginika and Kaira on either side of me. Once there, we were directed to the private wing on the seventh floor. Kaira paused outside Aunty's room. We watched her take a deep breath before reaching for the handle. My stomach clenched as the door creaked open. I braced myself, terrified at what I might see.

The room was big, well lit, and far cleaner than the hospital I had found myself in when I woke up after the abduction. Aunty lay on her side, eyes closed, facing the door. She wore a light blue hospital gown that was several sizes too big. I couldn't see bruises on any visible body part. She looked normal. I would have expected someone who had been kidnapped to look rough, but she looked as serene as she usually did.

"Mum?" Kaira said.

Aunty didn't stir.

Kaira glanced at us. "Should I wake her?" she mouthed to us.

I shook my head and Ginika shrugged.

Kaira took a step forward and placed her hand on Aunty's arm. "Mum?"

Aunty's body jerked and her eyes opened. She blinked at us, as if trying to place us, before sitting up. She moved slowly; an IV drip was connected to her right hand.

"Hi, Mum," Kaira said. The words came out stilted. It was obvious she didn't know what to say. What could she say? There was no guide on how to talk to a person after they had been kidnapped.

"Girls, how are you?" Aunty asked. Her tone was off. It was the kind of tone you used when talking to an acquaintance you didn't particularly like but you had to be polite to.

"We're fine," Kaira said.

Aunty nodded. She craned her head to the left, trying to see past us. "Where's my son?"

After a long pause, when it became obvious Kaira wasn't going to answer, Ginika said, "He's still in London. Uncle thought it would be better if he stayed there for now."

"Hmm. Good, good. Please call the doctor back. I want to ask him some questions." She carefully lay back on the bed and closed her eyes, clasping her hands above her stomach, the way dead bodies were positioned in caskets.

Kaira took a stuttered breath next to me. Aunty's dismissal clearly hurt her. We quietly left the room.

"That was . . ." I trailed off. I wasn't sure what word to describe it.

"Weird," Ginika said.

Kaira said nothing. I wasn't sure what she was feeling and her face gave nothing away.

When we got back home, Kaira headed to her room and slammed the door shut. I knew she was crying behind that closed door. Ginika and I sat in the living room, watching the TV on mute.

* * *

Aunty spent six days in the hospital. She had been cleared to leave on the third day but she insisted on being tested over and over again despite all the tests coming back negative. I could see Uncle's frustration mounting as he tried to reason with Aunty. But it was clear she wasn't going to budge. She was so sure something had to be wrong with her and nothing any doctor said or test results showed could convince her otherwise.

Uncle made us visit her every day. The visits were short and strange. Some days she spoke to us, asking the same questions over and over, making it obvious she hadn't bothered to listen to our answers. Other days she said nothing. Uncle's concern for his wife was quickly turning into irritation and it was hard for him to hide it. There was no button he could press to turn his wife back to the way she was and Uncle was not a patient man. He took his frustration out on the doctors, yelling at them and demanding answers. We listened as the doctors spoke to Uncle Emeke using words like psychological trauma and PTSD and therapy.

And every day we went to the hospital, something in Kaira cracked. For three nights, while Aunty was taken, Kaira had whispered her wishes to us. She wished that her relationship with her mum was different. She wished that when Aunty came back they could work towards something healthier—something normal. It was obvious that was not going to happen. Not with this version of Aunty, a version who was broken in a way no one was sure how to fix. The kidnappers had damaged something in her. In the past, when Aunty got that faraway look, a word or a nudge had her snapping back to the present with a smile on her face. Now nothing seemed to snap her out of it.

"I always knew something was off with Aunty Sophie. She hid it well but I could tell. Now it's almost as if she can't be bothered to pretend anymore," Ginika whispered to me one evening after a very unproductive visit. Aunty had said only a handful of words during the entire two hours. She seemed to speak fewer words every day. And the worse Aunty got, the more Kaira distanced herself from us, returning to the snobby girl who didn't speak to anyone and locked herself in her room.

"What should we do?" I asked. I didn't want things to go back to the way they had been.

"Let's give her one more day," Ginika said to me.

The next morning Ginika pounded on Kaira's door.

"What do you want?" Kaira demanded when she finally opened the door.

"I want you to stop being a little bitch. Your mum doesn't like you. Big bloody deal. We all have problems. Woman up and stop crying. You're annoying me."

"Fuck off, joh." Kaira tried to slam the door on our faces but Ginika pushed past her, entering the room.

"No. Dress up and follow me."

Kaira ignored Ginika and flopped on her bed, burrowing under the duvet. Ginika, not being the kind of person who gave up, simply snatched the duvet off her and threw it on the floor.

"Ginika! Leave me alone!"

"You know I can do this all day. Get up and come with us," Ginika said, hands on her hips, looking like a disapproving mother.

Kaira reluctantly got off her bed, grumbling behind us as we made our way to the kitchen. Mr. Romieto and Chef Gideon were there. I wanted to ask where Ebuka was. I hadn't spoken a word to him in weeks and a part of me missed talking to him.

"Have you boiled the yam?" Ginika asked Chef Gideon. Chef Gideon nodded. Mr. Romieto went into the pantry to drag out the pestle and mortar.

"What are we doing?" Kaira asked, sounding more curious than annoyed.

"I was reading about ways to let out anger. And all the websites suggest things like throwing plates and boxing. I asked Mr. Romieto and he's not going to allow us to break plates and there's no punching bag in the house so I came up with the next best thing. Pounded yam!"

"I can see that you're mad."

Kaira shook her head and whirled around. I blocked her path. "Zam, move joh," she said.

"No. You're going to pound that yam and stop acting like a child," I said.

"See small Zam of yesterday. You've grown wings o!" Kaira smiled as she spoke. I didn't miss the pride in her voice. She liked that I wasn't letting her bully me.

Ginika handed Kaira the pestle. It was bigger and longer than the one I used at home.

"God, this thing is heavy," Kaira grunted.

"Oya, start pounding. And pound well o! I'm hungry and I like smooth pounded yam."

* * *

Aunty came home in a bulletproof car surrounded by a six-car convoy. She walked into the house and went straight to the west wing. Uncle came out of the west wing half an hour later, with his shoes in one hand and a briefcase in another, grumbling to no one in particular, "Keep an eye on her." He didn't wait for a response before he slammed the door and made his escape.

Kaira went in to check on Aunty a few hours later.

"She's in the shower," Kaira reported back to us.

We were on the floor of the living room having Igbo lessons. Ginika's notebooks and textbooks were spread across the coffee table.

"Igbo class is the only class I've ever failed," Kaira said, flipping through the Igbo dictionary Ginika had found on one of Uncle's bookshelves.

Ginika snatched it from her. "Well, pay attention and maybe you can pass Igbo next term."

"Isn't school supposed to start in like a week?" I asked. No one had said anything about it. I didn't have any uniforms or textbooks and I didn't know how to bring it up to Uncle with everything going on.

Ginika shrugged. "I can bet my parents don't even know when school starts. I have to call my dad's secretary and ask if he remembered to pay my school fees."

"Ugh. Don't talk about school. I don't know how all this shit is going to work because I can't go to school every day with four policemen and a convoy. That is just like a different level of obnoxious. And if my dad says something crazy like we should be homeschooled, I will literally die," Kaira said.

My phone rang and cut off Kaira's whining. I didn't have to look at it to know it was Mama. She was the only one who ever called me.

"Is that your mum again?" Ginika asked.

"Yeah," I said with a sigh. Anytime my phone rang and I saw Mama's name on the screen, my heart jumped in my chest. There was already so much going on with Aunty, I couldn't deal with Mama's wahala on top of it. Regulating the frequency of the calls with Mama had been Ginika's suggestion. Now, I only picked up Mama's calls every other day.

"Ma nne," I answered.

"Zam, did you not see that I called you yesterday?" she asked. Mama hardly ever bothered with greetings. She got right to whatever she wanted to say.

"Sorry, ma. My phone was on silent," I lied.

"Why is your phone always on silent now? Did I not tell you to stop that bad habit? Don't be behaving like your sister, o. I did not send you to Abuja so you can spoil there. You know that wicked child has still not come back! Only God knows what she is doing. Did I tell you I heard from one of her friends that Cheta is gallivanting around Lagos disgracing our family. I'm not even surprised. I was talking to Nne Chuks yesterday about . . ." Mama jumped from topic to topic without pausing to take a breath and never really gave me a chance to speak. I was like a living diary and I was tired of it. All she did was talk about herself and complain about Cheta. I couldn't blame Cheta for leaving. Honestly, I was more surprised she hadn't done it sooner. I let Mama go on for a few minutes before I couldn't take it anymore.

"Mama, Uncle is calling me. I have to go," I said, cutting her off. It was my go-to lie to get off the phone.

Kaira and Ginika were smiling and shaking their heads at me when I ended the call.

"What?"

"Nothing. Your face when you talk to your mum is just funny," Kaira said.

Ginika nodded. "Yeah, you always look like you're smelling something stinky."

I stuck my tongue out at them. "Let's continue," I said to Ginika, picking up one of the language books.

Kaira went to check on Aunty about an hour later. "She's still in the shower," she reported, unable to hide the worry in her voice.

Fifteen minutes later Kaira went to the west wing and came back with the same answer. "She's still in there." The worry had spread from her voice to her face.

"What is she doing in there?" I asked.

"Trying to drown herself?" Ginika said.

Kaira gasped and ran back to the west wing.

"What is wrong with you?" I jabbed her with an elbow before getting up and running after Kaira.

I had never gone beyond the living room in the west wing, so I followed Kaira's screams through an open door that led to a large bedroom. Kaira was at the other end of the room, pounding on a closed door with her fists. "Mummy! Mummy! Open up! Mummy, please!"

She turned around when she heard me come in. "The door is locked. What should I do?"

The door suddenly swung open and Aunty stood there, dripping wet with a fluffy towel around her. Her hair was plastered to her face and her eyes were red and puffy. "What?" she asked.

"I-I-I . . . you . . ." Kaira stammered, unable to get her words out. She leaned forward and braced her hands on her knees, panting as she tried to get her breathing under control. I could see her pulse throbbing in her neck.

"You were in there for a long time and we were scared that you might be hurt," I said.

"I'm fine. The water pressure in the hospital was abysmal," Aunty said before shutting the door and locking it.

When Aunty wasn't taking three-hour-long showers she spent her time watching the security feed. There were cameras placed strategically around the house before the kidnapping; after it, the number of cameras doubled. Every entrance of the house was monitored and Aunty sat in front of the screen and made sure everything was as it was supposed to be. She never left the west wing so Mr. Romieto delivered a tray of food to her three times a day.

231

Sound carried in the mansion, you just needed to know the right places to listen, and Kaira knew all the right places. When the men in suits came by the house to talk to Aunty about what happened, Ginika, Kaira, and I had huddled close together, listening to Aunty describe the kidnappers and the room they kept her in. We listened as she described everything she overheard the kidnappers say. She spoke in a flat and removed voice, as if she was discussing a movie she didn't particularly enjoy.

More days passed with no improvement from Aunty. We heard Uncle try to coax her to return to the land of the living with different methods. His voice went from soothing and understanding to demanding and vaguely threatening. *Today is your cousin's birthday, what time do you want us to leave? You can't stay in this room forever you know, get up let's do something. There's a new Indian restaurant, let's go out for lunch. Sophie, are you planning on spending the rest of your life on that bed? Are you going into your office today? You're better than this, get up! Get up now or you wouldn't like what I will do.* Nothing worked.

* * *

It was early in the morning and the rainy season was in full effect. Abuja rain was almost apocalyptic in its intensity. It started with no warning, accompanied by lightning that brightened the sky and thunder that shook the earth, before stopping just as quickly as it started. It was strangely soothing.

I liked to lie in bed and listen to the sounds of the storms. The ebb and flow of it. The sky had settled and the storm had turned into a drizzle when my door was flung open and Kaira rushed in, Ginika behind her. "They have Mr. Boniface. I saw two policemen dragging him out of the car through my window," she said as she rushed to my window and drew back the curtains.

My window overlooked the back garden. Kaira opened it slowly. I got off my bed and walked over, curiosity urging my feet to hurry. We watched as two policemen dragged Mr. Boniface to the center of the garden. The back patio door opened and Uncle Emeke stepped out, walking with a vicious purpose. To our surprise, Aunty Sophie trailed behind him.

"This is the first time she's stepped out of the house," Kaira whispered, voicing something we all knew.

"Why is Uncle wearing construction boots?" Ginika asked.

"Shh!" Kaira hushed her.

Ginika rolled her eyes.

"Madam! Thank God you're okay," Mr. Boniface said when he saw Aunty. His hands were tied in front of him and his face was swollen. His T-shirt was caked with mud and blood.

Uncle Emeke walked forward and kicked him in the face. Ah, so that's why he was wearing those boots. "Shut up. Don't talk to my wife. Don't look at my wife."

Mr. Boniface brought his hands over his head, attempting to block the kicks. "Oga, sorry. Please, no vex. Na panic, I panic."

233

"Panic? Panic?" Emeke laughed. "Were you not trained? Did you not have a gun? You ran away and left my wife and niece there? After everything we've done for you and your family?"

"Oga, sorry, Oga, please!" he begged.

"Gbankiti!" Emeke punctuated the command with another kick to the head. "Did you plan it with the kidnappers? Eh? Are you working with them?" Another kick, this time to his kidney.

Mr. Boniface whimpered. It was fascinating and terrifying to watch a big man reduced to whimpers. "No, sah. Oga, I'm not working with them sah. Oga, please. Na panic, I panic. I dey think of my wife and pikin."

"Have we not been good to you? Has my wife not been good to you? Better confess now o. If you were working with the kidnappers and we find out later, you will not like what I do to you."

"Oga, I swear to God. I'm not working with them. If I'm lying let thunder fire me. Oga, I'm sorry." Mr. Boniface burst into tears, sobs racking his big body. His tears seemed to ignite Uncle Emeke's anger. Uncle went wild. Kicking and punching Mr. Boniface with a cold, ruthless efficiency. Over and over, until Mr. Boniface's T-shirt was soaked in blood. I looked away, unable to stomach any more. But I could still hear the sound of shoes against flesh, the desperate pleas of a broken man, the vicious words of an angry man.

"Take him away," Uncle said to the officers, finally. I turned back to the scene. Uncle took off his bloody shoes, and walked into the house barefoot.

Aunty stayed outside, standing opposite Mr. Boniface. I couldn't see her face so I couldn't guess what she was thinking. Mr. Boniface begged, "Madam, I'm sorry. I dey use God beg you. Forgive me. I get pikin." One of his eyes had swollen shut and a gash on his forehead was bleeding into his other eye. I had never seen anyone that badly beaten before. If this was what Uncle Emeke did to Mr. Boniface, I wondered what he would do if they ever found the kidnappers. Aunty said nothing before she turned to walk back into the house.

Kaira snickered. "He's going to be pissing blood for a while."

"Kaira!" Ginika exclaimed, smacking her on the arm.

Kaira shrugged, unfazed by the brutality we had just witnessed. "What? It's not like he doesn't deserve it." She rolled her eyes and walked out of the room.

I looked out the window and saw the drizzle had turned into steady rain. Mr. Boniface was still on the ground, his head facing the clouds. I wondered if he found the rain as soothing as I did.

TWENTY-FOUR

Cheta

WHEN THE HEAT was oppressive, the flies out in full force and the customers scarce, I liked to close my eyes and pretend I was Tony Montana. Selling cough syrup, untested penis enhancement pills, and other drugs (some illegal, some not) in a ramshackle stall next to a meat market was not the same as smuggling millions of dollars of cocaine across borders but it was nice to daydream. I spent most of my time sitting on an uncomfortable wooden bench at the back of a small stall at the edge of the market. The meat sellers were in a large canopy on the left and the air was scented with fresh blood and meat. The small portable battery-operated fan pointed straight at my face was a small reprieve from the stuffy heat.

I could be charming when I was motivated. I knew how to talk to people, knew how to convince them to do things they might not have wanted to do. When people came in wanting a bottle of cough syrup, they sometimes ended up leaving with two or three and maybe a ten-tablet strip of tramadol. The thing about sales is, you need to know your buyer. You need to know who can afford more and who can't. That way you don't end up wasting your time up-selling. I could tell Peter was impressed by me, even though he hardly said anything. Peter, a burly forty-something-year-old man with a large forehead and yellow eyes, sat at the front of the stall in a plastic chair. He had a small radio that was always tuned to Wazobia FM. He hardly spoke, so I wasn't sure what exactly his role was. He wasn't a particularly tall or muscular man but he had a no-nonsense air about him that made people wary. I didn't know if he was there to monitor me and report back to Johnson or to monitor the customers.

I still wasn't sure what Johnson's motives were. There was a reason he was so insistent on giving me a job and a high cut of profits. Whatever Johnson wanted from me, it wasn't good, but I just didn't have it in me to care. I simply wanted to save up money and leave.

* * *

At work, I always I wore a red wig with a fringe and covered my nose and mouth with a blue bandana. Peter snorted the first time he saw me tie the bandana at the back of my head but he didn't comment. I was being as careful as I could be. This wasn't going to be my life forever. When I left this place, I didn't want anyone associating me with it.

Nothing I sold was that bad. Except for the cough syrup and a few of the other pills. It was illegal to sell codeine without a doctor's prescription. The NDLEA had calmed down with the arrests but all it would take was one newspaper article or a viral tweet or an overeager politician wanting to show his constituents that he was concerned about the youth, and the arrests would start up again. I knew at the end of the day, if the police decided to crack down and I somehow got caught up in it, no one would help me. Johnson and Peter would not hesitate to throw me under the bus.

I had no moral dilemmas about what I was doing. As far as I was concerned, cough syrup and tramadol once in a while was fine. Everyone needed something to make them feel good from time to time. Most of my customers were young adult males who popped tramadol pills and washed them down with a mixture of cough syrup and soft drinks. If they became addicted in the process, that was their own personal problem. People did it for fun, for the mild high, to help them last longer in bed, to get them through their strenuous jobs, to make them forget their problems. Whatever their reason, I didn't particularly care to know. I had my own problems.

But once in a while the reality of what I was doing hit me in the face. The first time I actually thought about the consequences of my actions was the morning a young boy who looked malnourished came by. I spotted him from afar. It was obvious he was on something, or maybe several somethings. He twitched and itched as he approached, his eyes darting around nervously. The boy could not have been much older than thirteen and he was obviously going through withdrawals. He wore a dirty, tattered oversized T-shirt but I knew that if he lifted it, I would be able to count his ribs.

"One bottle," the boy said, pulling out a heap of crumpled notes from his pocket.

I counted it carefully even though I could tell it was not enough. "The money is not complete," I said.

"Count am again," he insisted, picking at a scab on his arm.

"Price don increase," I said

"Abeg, I no get money," he pleaded.

"You no get money, you no buy. This no be charity. Commot," Peter said.

"Oga, abeg—"

"I said commot for here! Are you deaf?" Peter stood up and towered over the skinny boy.

The boy snatched his money from my hand and stuffed it back in his pocket before running away. I watched his skinny frame disappear into the crowd and I hoped he used the money to buy food.

Peter watched him run away with disgust. "Dirty addict," Peter muttered, also watching the boy, as if we were not part of the reason the boy had ended up like that.

The second time I thought about the consequences was the woman who had a baby tied to her back. The woman was unkempt and the baby looked even worse. The baby had angry-looking red rashes all over his face and dried catarrh around his nose and mouth. His eyes were red and swollen like he had been crying all day. The baby could not have been more than nine months but I swear he stared at me with accusing eyes, breathing loudly. He sounded like an old man with lung cancer and I wanted to ask the woman if her money was better spent in a hospital but again, I had to remind myself it wasn't my business. Guilt gathered in my belly as I watched the mother walk away with four bottles of cough syrup and two 100-mg strips of tramadol. I prayed to God that the mother's breast milk had dried up. I wasn't sure what effects the drugs would have on breast milk but whatever it was, it couldn't be good. People who wanted drugs always found a way to get them, I reasoned with myself, trying to make myself feel better about what I had just done.

* * *

The restaurant Chizi worked at was close to the market. Once in a while she showed up to hang out with me. I knew Peter liked it when Chizi came around. His round face broke out in an uneven smile when she entertained us with stories of the rich people she waited on. She always had juicy gist and delicious leftovers.

"I'm so annoyed," she announced one afternoon, as she dropped down beside me on the bench.

"What happened," Peter asked eagerly. The man was such a gossip.

Before Chizi could speak, her phone started ringing.

"This man is disturbing my life," she said.

"Who?" I asked as I separated the money I had made that day by denominations.

"Obinna! I asked him to buy me one bag I've been eyeing for my birthday and he told me he cannot afford it. Ordinary bag, o! It's not like it was even that expensive. Stingy man. He has been calling me since morning and I refused to pick up," she said with a frown as she watched her phone ring.

I didn't point out that Obinna was a mid-level local government employee and probably spent most of his money on his wife and three children.

"After all the things I do for him, he can't buy me a bag? Can you imagine that?"

"All you girls. Always wanting something. All of you have longthroat. Buy me this, buy me that. No be prostitution, be that? You no know say prostitution na sin?" Peter said.

"How is it prostitution if he's my boyfriend? You sef, you fit talk? You tink say I no see you and Cynthia for beer parlor? Cynthia na your wife?"

"I'm a man," he said with finality. Like that absolved him of all his sins.

Chizi rolled her eyes. "Ehen? And? Sin na sin. No dey judge me if you too dey sin." Chizi said.

She turned to me. "Anyways, I'm thinking of breaking up with him."

"Why?" I asked.

"Because I'm a fine girl and I can do better than him."

I laughed. God, I loved Chizi's confidence.

She snapped her fingers, "Ehen! I almost forgot to tell you. I saw Paulina today."

"Paulina Oko?" I asked. I only knew one Paulina. The social prefect who graduated when I was in JSS3.

"Yes. You know when I woke up today, I told you I had a good feeling. I was right. Paulina is a big girl o! If you see the car she was driving! Brand-new Mercedes. She came to the restaurant with a few friends. I thought she would pretend like she didn't know me because I was working there but she was so friendly!"

"Paulina was always nice."

"She gave me her number and said that she may have an opportunity for me. She said I should come see her this weekend. I asked her if I could bring you and she said yes. Paulina is going to change our lives. I can feel it." Chizi was vibrating with excitement and it was so contagious I let myself get excited, too.

TWENTY-FIVE

Zam

I COULDN'T SEE anything. I gave my eyes a moment to adjust to the dark. Tilted my head and listened, trying to figure out what had woken me.

Thump.

There it was again. The sound of something heavy falling. I looked at my phone. 3:19 a.m. Who was awake?

I opened my door and poked my head out. The storage room next to mine was open and the light was on. Aunty Sophie was on the floor looking through a suitcase. What was she searching for in the middle of the night?

"Good evening, Aunty," I said softly.

She looked up, her face blank for a moment as if trying to

place me, before she gave me a small smile and turned back to what she was doing.

The suitcase was filled with clothes, books, and old toys.

"Yes!" she said when she lifted a coat and saw a photo album underneath.

She made a strange sound, hugged the album to her chest, closed her eyes, and rocked her body back and forth.

"Aunty, are you okay?"

She stopped rocking and looked up at me. "God. I hate that question. Are you okay? Are you fine? What does that even mean?"

I took a step back, stunned at the anger in her voice. She narrowed her eyes at me and got off the floor. "My husband thinks I've gone mad. Do you think I'm crazy, too?"

I froze. Did she want me to answer that honestly?

"I like you," she said. "You remind me of someone I used to know. James. He was quiet—observant. Like you."

She walked into the living room and sat on the couch. I followed her, sitting on the other end and twisting my body to look at her. She opened the photo album, flipping through it carefully. The spine was cracked and the edges worn.

"James Balogun. He was one of the directors of the foundation."

Her finger stroked the picture. It was uncomfortable to watch. It felt like I was intruding on an intimate moment.

"Do you think you're a good person?"

"I . . . umm," I stammered, thrown off by the question. Why was she saying all this to me? Was she drunk?

"James was a good person. The best. I'm not. People think I am, but I'm not," she continued, without waiting for my response. "He's dead. Car accident. Third Mainland bridge. They say he died instantly. I wonder if that actually happens. Instant death. How instant is instant? Was there a moment, a second when he realized he was going to die? What were his last thoughts? I always think about that."

She turned to me, her eyes locking on mine, and I knew then she was completely sober. It wasn't alcohol that had loosened her tongue, it was grief. Whoever James was, he must have been important to her.

"Have you ever had a boyfriend?" she asked.

I shook my head, the rapid change in topic making my brain spin.

"When you marry someone make sure you choose a good man. Not someone who is good to you. Someone who is good to everyone. The kind of goodness that seeps out of his pores. The unadulterated, unfiltered kind." Her eyes had a distant look but it was different from the zombie gaze she had worn since she returned, this look was softer, like she was daydreaming.

I scooted closer, to get a better look at the picture. It was old and browning at the edges despite the protection of the clear film. They looked young. James was dark-skinned with a thin moustache and a little afro. They were standing together, their bodies tilted towards each other as he bent to whisper something in her ear. I couldn't see the expression on his face but I could see the wide smile on Aunty's face. She was younger, her hair a curly halo framing her face. She looked so happy. I had never seen Aunty smile like that.

"Was James your boyfriend?" I asked.

It was the wrong thing to say. My question shook her out of her daydream.

"He was my employee," she said, snapping the album shut. She looked disgusted.

"It's late. You should go to bed." She hugged the photo album to her chest and walked out of the room.

✳　✳　✳

"Did you know anybody named James that worked in your mother's foundation?" I asked Kaira later that day, meeting her eyes in the mirror. I was seated on a chair in front of my bedroom vanity, while she borrowed my head to use as a wig stand. She was behind me, curling the ends of the hair.

"James who?"

"James Balogun."

"No, why?"

"Nothing, just asking. Read something about the foundation in the newspaper," I lied. I couldn't bring myself to tell her about my conversation with Aunty. It felt like I was betraying Aunty in some way, and I liked sharing a secret with her. I liked knowing that to a certain degree Aunty felt she could confide in me.

"Are you ever going to show us what you're doing?" I asked, watching Ginika in the mirror. She was on my bed, writing in her notebook.

"No," Ginika said.

"She writes short stories about us, or fictionalized versions of us. She also has poems and drawings and some other things in there."

Ginika's head snapped up. "You read it?"

Kaira shrugged unapologetically. "You left it on the table when you went to shower a few days ago."

"And you read it?" Ginika's voice was low but it rang with anger.

"I was curious."

I watched Ginika's heaving chest and braced myself for her next move, really hoping things wouldn't turn physical. I didn't think either of them knew how to fight. Ginika had anger on her side but Kaira seemed like someone who fought dirty and I did not want to get between that. Thankfully, Ginika stood up and left the room, slamming the door after her.

"You shouldn't have read it," I said.

"Honestly, it's not that big a deal. It really wasn't that interesting. With the way she guards that thing I was expecting to read some juicy secrets."

"Still. You should apologize."

"Ugh. Fine. Everyone is so bloody sensitive." She dropped the curler and went after Ginika.

* * *

I looked around. Was anyone else as uncomfortable as I was? We were gathered at the dinner table at the request of Uncle Emeke. The gentle humming of the air conditioner and the scraping of cutlery against ceramic were the only sounds breaking through the heavy silence.

Halfway through the meal, Uncle Emeke cleared his throat. "We have something to tell you girls," he said.

All eyes except Aunty Sophie's went to him. He put down his fork. "We've decided that it will be best if the family relocates to England. I've started looking into boarding schools for you two," he said, pointing at Kaira and me.

There was a delay between Uncle's words and my brain processing them but when I finally did, I couldn't breathe. He said you two. He pointed at me.

"It's going to take some time to get Zam's visa and other documents so you'll start school a few weeks late. I've spoken to the schools about it and they say that's okay."

"Can I come too?" Ginika asked.

Uncle Emeke shrugged. "You have an EU passport so

there'll be no visa issues with you. If you want to and your parents agree you can."

"I'm going to school in England?" I clarified, pointing at myself.

"Yes. I've spoken to your parents. They've agreed. The schools we're looking at are top tier. You'll get a superior education at whichever one we choose. I think a change of scenery would be good for everyone," he said, looking pointedly at Aunty Sophie.

Was that what Mama had been calling about? She had called me five times that morning. Five calls in one morning was typical when I first moved to Abuja but over the past two weeks, I had slowly weaned Mama off calling me. I just didn't pick up. I spoke to her every two days now and I planned to stretch it to every three days by the end of next week. Mama was a serpent. A giant serpent that wrapped around your soul, injecting its venom with sharp fangs and crushing your will with its heft. I had spent my whole life feeling constricted. Now, I finally understood existing shouldn't be painful. Speaking to her just made me feel the squeeze of the serpent again.

"Why?" Kaira asked suddenly, slamming her fork on her plate. Spaghetti sauce splattered across the table.

Uncle jerked back, surprised at the anger in her voice. "Excuse me?"

"I'm not stupid. Do you think I'm stupid?" Kaira asked her

mother, ignoring her father. I glanced at Ginika, wondering if she knew what was going on.

Kaira pointed at me. "The day after Akubundu got into MIT, you started talking about Zam living with us. Do you think I'm too stupid to put two and two together? You need her here as a buffer. You need Ginika too. So you don't have to talk to me. Or look at me. *Why won't you look at me?*" Kaira screamed the last sentence, her voice cracking on the last word.

"Kaira! That's enough. Your mother has been through enough. She does not need this nonsense from you. What kind of disrespectful behavior is this?" Uncle said.

"What about me? What about what I've been through?" Kaira jabbed at her chest.

"Jesus Christ!" Uncle Emeke threw his hands up and pushed away from the table. "I said it. I said we should have slapped these children more when they were younger," he said to no one in particular. He walked away muttering under his breath about women, wahala, and spoiled children.

Through everything, Aunty Sophie's face remained on her spaghetti.

Kaira pushed away from the table and Ginika followed her. I wanted to go with them but for some reason I couldn't pull myself away from the table.

"She's always been a difficult child. From the moment she was conceived. She came out screaming and never stopped. I thought things with her would get easier when she grew up. They didn't," Aunty said, twirling her spaghetti on the fork.

* * *

"We don't have to go if you don't want us to," I said when we gathered in Kaira's room hours later.

"Shut up," Kaira sniffled. "It's not like I don't want you to go. I just wanted her to admit the reason she needs to have both of you around."

I exhaled. "Okay. Thank God. I really want to go to England. I was just trying to be nice."

Ginika and Kaira burst out laughing.

* * *

I opened the kitchen door to see Mr. Romieto and Ebuka playing Ludo while Chef Gideon stirred something in the big pot.

"Little madam! We thought you had forgotten us!" Mr. Romieto said when he noticed me by the door.

"That's impossible," I said. They were my first friends in the house. If not for them I would have spent my first few weeks in my room feeling sorry for myself.

"You're just in time to taste Chef Gideon's latest concoction. He swears he got this recipe from a sheik's favorite wife. Not sure where Giddyboy here would meet a sheik's wife and he has refused to tell us."

"I was sworn to secrecy," Chef Gideon huffed.

"Of course you were," Mr. Romieto said, with a disbelieving shake of his head.

I smiled, realizing in the moment just how much I had missed them.

I stayed in the kitchen for hours, listening to Chef Gideon's familiar stories, eating his delicious food, and laughing at Mr. Romieto's funny commentary. Ebuka mostly stayed quiet, only speaking when Chef Gideon or Mr. Romieto asked him a direct question.

"Settle things with him," Mr. Romieto whispered to me, when it got late and it was time for them to retire to their quarters.

Ebuka was by the sink, washing up. I joined him, effortlessly falling into the cleaning groove we had perfected my first week in the house.

The air between us vibrated with the things unsaid. I could feel the restless energy coming off him. I hated it. Why did Cheta have to ruin everything?

"I'm going to the market tomorrow. Do you want to come?" He was trying to keep his tone casual but there was a sense of something strained—barely contained—underneath.

"I can't," I said. We were still on lockdown. Now that Aunty was back, Uncle refused to let any of us out of the house.

"Did your sister say something to you?"

"What? No," I said, confused.

"You stopped talking to me after she left. Did she say something about me to make you hate me?"

"I don't hate you."

He slammed the glass against the sink. The musical tone of the crystal vibrated through the kitchen. A single crack appeared, snaking from the rim to the middle of the glass.

"Don't talk to me like I'm a fool. Do you think I don't notice how you've changed?"

"Ebuka—"

"Or is it because of that girl? She started talking to you and you abandoned us. Mama has been asking about you. Have you forgotten her too?" He took a step towards me and I stepped back, wanting some distance from his anger.

"Kaira is my cousin," I reminded him, starting to get upset. I hadn't abandoned anybody. I wasn't allowed to go anywhere. None of us were and he knew that.

"You think you're better than us. Better than me."

I took another step back and I hit the wall. He had backed me into the corner. I could feel his hot breath fan across my face, I could smell the stew on his breath, feel the heat of his skin. I shrank back, trying to become one with the wall.

"I don't think that," I said, my heart racing.

"Yes, you do!" he roared. Drops of spittle landing on me.

The kitchen phone rang, making me jump. "The phone," I whispered.

Ebuka took a step back, breathing heavily, nostrils flaring, visibly trying to calm himself.

He turned away from me and answered the phone. He listened for a moment then said, "Yes, ma."

"Madam is looking for you," he said to me, without turning around.

I slowly edged around him, careful not to touch him. Once I was out of the kitchen, I ran through the hall and up the stairs. I leaned against the wall and took a moment to breathe and get my hands to stop shaking before I entered the west wing.

Aunty sat on the couch, a glass of wine in her hand.

"Aunty, you were looking for me?"

"Come, sit with me," she said. "Do you want to taste?"

I nodded and grabbed a glass from one of the cabinets over the bar. She poured a little of the deep red wine into the glass. The heavy smell hit me first. I took a small sip and the strong taste and silky texture soaked my tongue. It was somehow fruity and bitter, an odd combination.

I looked at her, trying not to squeeze my face. "Hmm," I said.

Aunty laughed. "I had my first taste of wine when I was fourteen. My mother gave me a sip when my father wasn't looking. I'm sure I had the same expression you have now."

She took another sip. "Don't worry, you'll get used to the taste."

I watched her in shock. She laughed. She was present. This

was the Aunty Sophie I knew, not the woman who seemed to always be in a daze.

"Do you know the worst thing about being kidnapped?" she asked suddenly.

She raised her head and looked me in the eye. "It's the violation, the sense of helplessness that comes with having your personal space tampered with."

She picked up the remote and switched on the TV. Ebuka was on the screen, standing by the sink with his hands on his hips. It hadn't been luck that the phone had rung at the right time. Aunty Sophie had seen everything.

"Did anything happen between you two?" she asked.

My hands started shaking again. I slowly set the wine glass on the coffee table. "No, Aunty."

"Whatever the case may be, it was inappropriate for him to get that close to you and yell in your face. He'll be gone by tomorrow."

"Aunty please, he needs the job," I said. I knew how hard Mama E worked and I knew it wasn't enough. Ebuka's income helped take care of his siblings. His family needed that money.

"There will be people lining up to replace him and they all need the job," she said.

"Aunty please, his family relies on him," I tried to explain.

"I've made my decision," she said.

* * *

Ebuka was gone by the time I woke up and headed down to the kitchen the next morning.

"I told you not to get that boy in trouble," Mr. Romieto said before turning back to sorting the pantry and pretending I wasn't there. Chef Gideon said nothing to me and refused to make eye contact.

"They blame me," I wailed, bursting into Kaira's room. She was sitting on her bed next to Ginika, playing a video game on the Xbox they had taken from Akubundu's room.

"Of course they blame you. What did you expect?" Kaira said, tapping furiously on the controller.

"But they're my friends."

Kaira paused the game and looked at me. "Zam, you're still acting like you're some poor village girl and you're not. You're one of us now. It's like in *Downton Abbey* when Branson married Sybil and became part of the family. His relationship with the staff changed because he went from pleb life to dining with gentry and all that fancy stuff."

"I don't know what you're talking about," I said.

"Ginika, educate her."

Ginika sighed and put down her controller. "What this snob is trying to say is that whether you acknowledge it or not, there is a class divide. They know it and they're aware of it and a part of them may resent it. You know, I don't even think Uncle knows Ebuka's name. He always called him the boy or that boy."

"They're my friends," I said again. "If they just give me a chance to explain what happened—"

"No. They're employees," said Kaira. "For all you know they might find you very annoying and just humor you so you don't go crying to my parents. Or they might really enjoy your company. But either way, we're us and they're them and when the wealth war starts and it's time to eat the rich, they might hesitate but at the end, they'll turn you into a pot of stew. But if it makes you feel better you should know they won't hesitate to fry me."

"True. They'll definitely chow Kaira first," Ginika agreed.

I stared at them, unable to think of what to say in response to that.

"So what should I do?" I asked. "I've tried calling Ebuka but he's not picking up."

Kaira wrinkled her nose. "Eww. Why do you even have his number?"

I ignored her. "Do you think I should call his mum?" I asked Ginika.

"Why do you have her number?" Kaira said, sounding confused.

"Call her in a day or two," Ginika said.

Kaira sat up and clapped her hands. "Call her now. I want to hear what she'll say."

I brought up Mama E's contact information. I needed to explain. I knew how much their family relied on Ebuka's income and I needed her and Ebuka to know that I hadn't wanted any of this to happen.

"Call her," Kaira said.

I took a breath and called.

"I bet a thousand naira she'll call you a witch," Kaira whispered as the phone rang.

"Hello?"

"Mama E, it's Zam."

There was silence for a moment. Then the shouting started. "Gini? So you have the liver to call me after what you did. Amusu, who sent you to destroy my family? Look at what you did to my son! Onye iberibe—"

I hung up before she could continue with her insults.

"What does *amusu* mean?" Kaira asked Ginika.

"Witch."

Kaira cackled. "Ha! I said it! Oya, pay me my money."

TWENTY-SIX

Cheta

PAULINA LIVED IN a duplex in GRA. There were two cars parked in the compound, the Mercedes Chizi talked about and a Toyota. Bright red and orange flowers lined the front of the house, complementing the front door painted a deep wine color. A house girl opened the door and led us into the living room. Paulina's house was elegantly furnished in shades of blue and grey. It wasn't as spectacular as Uncle Emeke's house in Abuja but for a woman who had only graduated from university a few months ago, it was perfect. Paulina rose from the couch, her movements sure and graceful.

"Wow! Look at you girls all grown up," she said. She leaned into Chizi first and air-kissed both cheeks before doing the same to me. She smelled citrusy and expensive.

She rested her hands on my shoulders and smiled at me. "Last time I saw you, you were still wearing pinafore and blouse. God, I hated that school uniform. Take a seat, help yourself," Paulina said, gesturing at the food spread on the table. I did just that, having learned in the past few weeks not to say no to free food.

This Paulina was different from the soft-spoken one who timidly patrolled the assembly making sure our top buttons were fastened and our ties properly knotted. She was confident in a worldly sort of way. It was surprisingly easy to talk to her. We reminisced about school days, smiling as we remembered hustling for tuckshop, laughing as we recalled how couples would secure their spot on the wall during social night so they could grind comfortably, giggling as we mimicked Sister Benedicta's funny way of speaking.

Her phone rang, interrupting us. She silenced it without looking at it. "Sorry, it's my work phone. I don't know why they're calling me on a Saturday and I don't want to know."

"Where do you work? You must have a really great job to afford a place like this," I said.

Paulina smiled and shook her head. It was the kind of look you gave a naïve child. "What kind of job could I possibly get right out of university that would allow me to afford this place? This is all thanks to the Senator. I thank God for him every day. He has really changed my life."

Why did girls who dated men in power always refer to them by their titles? The Senator. The Commissioner. The Chief. The Director.

Chizi looked impressed. "You're enjoying, o. My own useless boyfriend is refusing to buy me ordinary bag for my birthday."

"She has been complaining about this man and this bag for a week," I said, shaking my head.

Paulina laughed. "If you know what I went through before I caught this senator. Finding men like him is not easy. You have to make him fall in love with you and make sure he stays in love with you. You have to anticipate their needs in and out of the bedroom. All men are different. Some want someone to listen, some just want to fuck. Some want a woman to stroke their ego, others want a woman to take control. You have to watch and listen, figure out what they want and mold yourself in that image."

"So where did you meet the Senator?" I asked.

"Hook a girl up," Chizi said.

"A friend introduced us. Men like the Senator are very hard to find. Most of his friends are looking for a different girl every night. I'm lucky. I found a good one. The Senator is a simple man. He just wants someone to have sex with and tell him how smart he is, before going back home to his ugly wife and ungrateful children. But some of these other men? Bastards. Evil bastards. They lure you in and then next thing you know they're making you sleep with their dogs."

I choked on my orange juice. Chizi reached over to smack my back while Paulina just laughed.

"What?" I wheezed, when my coughing fit died down.

"That's not even the worst part. You wouldn't believe the stories I've heard." She shuddered, shaking her head as if trying to dislodge the memory. "I can't even say it out loud."

I was glad for that. I didn't want to know what was worse than being forced to sleep with a dog.

"Why are you working when the Senator can take care of you?" Chizi asked.

"Ah! What kind of question is that? My dear, you should know by now that you cannot rely on a man. You have to be making your own money on the side because if he wakes up one morning and decides he is done with you, you need a backup plan. So you have to save every single kobo. Don't let him buy you things, collect the money and buy it yourself. Make sure you price it well and then pocket the change. You have to be smart about these things. Senator bought me this house and those cars but they're both in my name. I own everything you see, but at the end of the day, I'm a woman sleeping with a married man in a lawless country. The fact that everything is in my name doesn't matter. If he should ever decide that he wants everything back, there is nothing I can do. So you have to look out for yourself first and foremost. Always."

"So do you have anyone you can introduce us to?" Chizi asked.

Paulina was quiet as she studied us. A long moment passed before she said, "There's a party next weekend. Very private party. Not just anybody can come. All the big men in Benin will be there. If I vouch for you, you will be representing me. So you have to dress accordingly, be discrete and not do anything to embarrass me."

Chizi lit up, barely holding herself back from jumping on her seat. "Paulina, trust, we will represent you very well. We're not small girls. We know how these things work."

Paulina didn't look totally convinced. "This life is not easy, o. You think you can just wake up one morning and snag a senator? Look anyone can sleep with a married man, but to hook a man of that caliber you must put in the work. Makeup must be flawless, your outfit has to be on point, your skin has to be blemish-free. You have to always look perfect."

In that moment, I noticed the difference between us and Paulina. Chizi and I were both wearing jeans and a simple blouse, though Chizi looked like she had made more of an effort than I did—and she had. While I lounged on the couch after breakfast, she had spent the time putting on makeup. When she asked me how she looked, I told her she looked good, but now sitting next to Paulina, she looked garish—over the top. I looked down at my chipped month-old nail polish and I couldn't help the embarrassment that heated my skin. We looked like kids next to Paulina in her fitted dress and tasteful makeup. I was generally a confident person and feeling inadequate made me uncomfortable.

"We won't let you down," Chizi promised.

Chizi was unusually silent on the way back to her flat. Later that night when Obinna showed up, she refused to open the door. After thirty minutes of knocking, one of her neighbors came out and threatened to beat him up if he didn't stop making noise.

He left her fifty-six text messages and called her eighteen times. The nineteenth time she picked up and threatened to show his wife the messages he was sending her if he didn't leave her alone. The calls stopped after that.

"Finally," she said when no call came after twenty minutes. "I don't even know why I wasted my time with him. He could not buy me anything and he wasn't even good in bed. Don't you just hate it when men don't know what they're doing?"

Chizi, like most of my friends, assumed I had sex. I didn't bother to tell her she was wrong. I couldn't stand most people's touch. I enjoyed kissing, I liked the intimacy of it, but I never let it go further. I lay in bed, thinking about everything Paulina said, and I wondered if it was possible to be a sugar baby without giving up any sugar.

TWENTY-SEVEN

Zam

I DISCOVERED I had never truly been cold when we finally moved to England. London was endless grey skies, sudden flashes of rain, and chilly winds. I didn't own a warm jacket so I borrowed one of Kaira's. Ginika and Kaira laughed at me when I wrapped myself in multiple layers of socks, sweaters, and scarves. "It's not even that cold," Kaira said, shaking her head. "Just wait till it starts snowing."

Two days after we arrived, Uncle Emeke hired a car and driver to take us to Somerset to visit the school he wanted us to attend. It was a three-hour car ride from London. We piled into the back seat of the SUV and Uncle took the front seat. I could see the worry in his eyes when we left. Aunty Sophie had managed to get herself out of bed and see us off, and he kept on glancing back as the car pulled away from the house, even after the car took a bend and Aunty Sophie was out of sight.

The school was in the countryside. The scenery soon changed from clustered brick buildings to green pastures. The farther we got, the farther apart the houses were. There were kilometers of land separating neighbors. I watched herds of black and brown cows graze on the open fields and wondered if cows got cold.

"That's it," the driver said hours after the journey began, pointing to a large building looming in the distance. I was eager to get out of the car and stretch my legs. I shifted forward, the seat belt straining against my chest as I tried to look out the windshield in the direction he was pointing.

It wasn't a school. It was a castle. It stood high on a hill, its grey stone riddled with dark green moss and cracked from the hundreds of years it had withstood British weather. The overcast skies gave the building a shadowy, forbidden appearance. Towers with pointed caps jutted from the top at the four corners of the building. Trees with bare branches and thick trunks lined the long road that led to the front of the building like soldiers standing at attention.

A petite blond girl met us at the entrance in front of a tall thick door that looked like it had been carved for giants. She was wearing the school uniform. Dark-blue-and-green-plaid pleated skirt and a white shirt. "I'm Emilia. I'm the Head Girl and I'll be showing you around today. Follow me, please," she said. Her smile was so wide and her green eyes were so sparkly I couldn't help but wonder if she was on drugs.

The halls were filled with students carrying books and chattering with friends. We followed Emilia, trying to keep up with her hectic energy. Her high-pitched voice, rapid-fire speech, and thick accent made it hard to understand her. She talked nonstop as she took us on a tour through the school, showing us all the amenities and facilities. There were three tennis courts, an indoor and outdoor pool, two libraries, five common rooms, a basketball court, a football field, and so much more. There were so many rooms, it would have been easy to get lost. The school was magnificent. They had stables. Stables with horses! I couldn't believe this was going to be my life. Earlier in the year, I had been in class with forty other students, enclosed in a room with peeling walls and sagging ceilings, and now I was touring a castle. I said a quick, silent prayer of thanks for Aunty Sophie. She had no idea how much she had changed my life.

"How did you like the school?" Uncle asked, when the tour was over.

"It's great," I said.

"It's good," Ginika said.

"Why do we have to be in boarding school. Can't we just find a school closer to home and be day students?" Kaira whined.

Uncle closed his eyes, as if trying to summon patience. "Why are you so ungrateful? Do you have to complain about everything?"

Kaira didn't respond.

The ride home was quiet. Uncle fell asleep, Ginika wrote in her notebook, Kaira listened to music on her phone, and I stared out the window.

* * *

Uncle left for Nigeria the next day. Once again, commanding us to keep an eye on his wife, like it wasn't supposed to be the other way round. She was the adult. I knew Kaira wanted to say something rude at Uncle's decree but thankfully she held her tongue.

We had a few days before we had to be at school and Kaira intended to make the most of it. We left the house early every morning and didn't return home until it was dark out. We spent most days exploring the city, the girls eager to show me their favorite places. We went shopping in Oxford Circus. For the experience, Ginika said, as we navigated the rowdy streets. Kaira trailed behind us complaining about the crowd and the tourists. I loved it. I loved the controlled chaos. I loved navigating the Underground and getting on buses that actually had breathing room. It was a luxury I didn't think the British fully appreciated.

We visited London Bridge and took pictures outside Buckingham Palace. We went to a theatre in Soho and watched a ballet performance in Convent Garden. Kaira and I both fell asleep halfway through and Ginika spent the rest of the night teasing us about being uncultured. We paddled pedalos down the Serpentine and posed with the lion statues at Trafalgar Square. Afternoon tea quickly became my favorite pastime. We visited a different restaurant every day. I gorged on scones, macarons, cakes, and sandwiches and sipped tea till I felt bloated.

When we were exploring London, all the issues with Aunty Sophie faded away. It felt like we were wrapped in one of those transparent covers Mama used to protect her favorite chairs from dust and visitor's bums. But when the day was over and it was time to go home, it was as though the cover was being slowly and painfully ripped away the closer the bus got to our stop.

Some days the change in environment seemed to help Aunty. There were brief moments where her old personality shone through, where she seemed like she was back to normal—laughing at something funny on TV or talking to her cousin, Aunty Carol, on the phone. Then Kaira would walk in the room and any progress Aunty made seemed like something I had imagined. Of course Kaira noticed that her presence seemed to put her mother in a bad mood. That didn't stop Kaira from trying. She asked Aunty to watch her favorite show, asked her to come shopping with us, offered to cook her favorite meal. Kaira couldn't cook and she gave up after the fire alarm went off and ordered takeaway instead, but the thought was there. Aunty either didn't notice or didn't care. It was painful to watch the way a part of Kaira shriveled every time Aunty dismissed her. And now that we were all friends I could see Ginika getting annoyed on Kaira's behalf. Ginika was the kind of person who carried other people's matters on her head and she didn't know how to keep her thoughts to herself. I saw the way she frowned at Aunty, her mouth itching to say something.

"Why are you trying so hard with her?" Ginika asked one day after Aunty had dismissed Kaira with an annoyed sigh and locked herself in her room.

Kaira closed her eyes and took a moment to think about it. "I don't know. She's my mum. I also kinda feel kinda bad about yelling at her that time in Abuja. I mean she had just been kidnapped. And it's not as if yelling changed anything. I thought maybe if I tried something else, tried to be less . . . difficult, at least I can say I tried my best, you know? But it's not working so why do I even bother?"

Kaira turned away from us, acting like she was looking at something interesting on her phone. Ginika and I pretended not to notice the way her shoulders shook because we knew Kaira wouldn't want us to see her cry.

* * *

The day before we left for boarding school Aunty Carol came over to make sure we had everything we needed. Aunty Carol was Aunty Sophie's cousin on her dad's side. She was a plump woman with full cheeks and one droopy eye. She was staying over at the house and heading out with us early the next morning.

We ordered takeaway from an Italian restaurant and congregated at the dining table for dinner.

"Aunty, did you hear her?" Ginika asked when Aunty Sophie had no reaction to a funny story Kaira was telling.

Aunty Sophie blinked out of her daze and looked at Ginika. "Sorry, what?"

"I asked if you heard what Kaira said."

"Sorry. I wasn't paying attention," Aunty Sophie said.

"You never pay attention when I speak. Why?" Kaira asked. Her tone was carefully calm and curious. Too calm. I knew then that Kaira was done with trying. I noticed a change the day before when she had wiped her face and pretended like she hadn't been crying. Her face had been blank and angry, almost as if her tears had washed away her patience with her mum. Lord, just once I would like to have a dinner that didn't end with people angry at each other.

"Aunty, do you know that since I've known you, you have never once looked Kaira in the eye," Ginika said.

"Yes, Mum. Why is that?" Kaira asked.

"Kaira, eat your food," Aunty said. Her voice was weak and lacked authority.

"No! Answer my question," Kaira demanded, slamming her fist on the table. The air in the room froze. I think everyone forgot how to breathe for a second. I stared open-mouthed at

Kaira. Her ombre wig framed her face, her nostrils flared like she was preparing to breathe fire.

"Kaira. Shut up your mouth and eat your food. Osanubua! You modern children are so rude. As old as I am I cannot speak to my mother like that," Aunty Carol said, her voice laced with a strict disapproval that dared Kaira to disobey.

Kaira ignored her. "I was looking at photo albums yesterday. You have so many pictures of Akubundu as a baby. And so few of me. Why?" Kaira asked, voice shaky with anger that had turned to pain.

I looked around the table and saw everyone, including Aunty Carol, looking at Aunty Sophie, waiting for an answer.

"Can you at least look at me?" Kaira asked.

Aunty unraveled. She pushed her chair back and stood up, the chair tumbled to the ground. "I'm looking at you. Are you happy?" she shouted at Kaira.

Kaira got to her feet and faced her mother. "No!"

My hand reached up to the rosary around my neck. It felt like I was back in our house in Alihame, with its sad walls pressing down on me. Across from me Ginika caught my eye and mouthed *breathe*.

Kaira closed her eyes and when she spoke her voice was soft in a way I had never heard. "No matter what I do, you always make me feel like I don't matter."

Aunty said nothing, she just stared at Kaira, her chest heaving, face was twisted in a way I hadn't seen before. She looked scared. I realized then that she had never seen Kaira like this—completely open—everything she was feeling spilling out of her. Kaira dressed her hurt as anger and used it to protect herself. Aunty had never truly looked at Kaira and now that she was, she could see the pain she had caused and she couldn't handle it. She fled the room. The table was quiet. No one knew what to say. Aunty Sophie had taken our collective appetites with her. Aunty Carol broke the silence. "Your mother has been through a lot in her life. You should be gentle with her."

"What about me? Don't I deserve gentle too?" Kaira asked, staring at the door Aunty Sophie had slammed shut.

Aunty Carol sighed and reached up to rub her temple. "Have you ever asked about your grandmother?"

"She died when I was a baby."

"Did you know Sophie was the one who found her mother's body?"

Kaira slammed back in her seat. "She did?"

The door creaked open and we all turned to see Aunty Sophie storming in holding something in her arms. She dumped it on the table, making the plates rattle, and stomped away again. Aunty Carol grabbed the unopened bottle of wine and followed her. "I'll talk to her," she said to Kaira.

"Open it or I will," Ginika said, when Kaira didn't move.

We gathered around Kaira. The first page was a polaroid of Aunty Sophie lying on a hospital bed looking exhausted, holding a pink bundle in her arms. The album was filled with pictures of Kaira's childhood. She carefully flipped the pages, taking her time to study each picture and trace the faces with her fingers.

Kaira as a baby, being held by her grandmother. Kaira in a swing, her dad pushing her in the park. Kaira and Akubundu playing in the snow, a young Aunty Carol kneeling next to them, her head thrown back in laughter. Aunty Sophie was in very few of the photos and the ones she was in, she wasn't smiling.

*　*　*

Kaira spent hours looking at the pictures. I didn't want to leave her alone, so I lay on the couch, saying nothing, keeping her company. Aunty Carol was still in Aunty Sophie's room and Ginika had gone to meditate before bed.

A door creaked open and Aunty Sophie appeared in the hallway. She walked by without looking at us and headed to the kitchen. Aunty Sophie was standing behind the kitchen island pouring juice into a glass when she spoke. "I haven't thought about my mum in a while. I try not to. It's easier that way." She swayed slightly and it was obvious she and Aunty Carol had opened that bottle of wine. She placed her hands on the island to steady herself.

"Carol said she thinks my mother would be ashamed of me," Aunty whispered into her glass. In an even quieter voice she added, "I think she's right."

Kaira glanced at me. *What do I say,* her eyes asked. This was the openness Kaira wanted from her mother and now that she had it, she didn't know what to do with it. Neither did I.

"Kaira, I don't hate you," Aunty Sophie said after a long moment of silence. I felt like an intruder. I didn't belong in this moment but it seemed wrong to get up and draw more attention to myself. I sat still and tried to blend in with the couch.

"You were born a few days after I learned a good friend of mine died." Aunty closed her eyes and rolled her neck, taking a moment to compose herself. She was talking about James from the picture, who was definitely more than a friend.

She cleared her throat. "It was such a difficult birth and then you came out and it seemed like you never stopped crying. I blamed myself in a way. I don't know the science around it but I'm guessing it can't be healthy for a baby to be . . . I don't know . . . marinating in all that grief. I felt like I was going mad, I had all these negative feelings inside me I didn't know how to handle and when my mother came for omugwo I gratefully handed you over to her.

"She was amazing with you. She gave you all the love I couldn't. I didn't need to be a mother to you because she was doing such a great job at being the mother you needed. And then one morning I . . . I . . ." Aunty's voice hitched. Kaira grabbed my hand and I knew I made the right decision to stay. We knew what was coming next. Aunty's grief had risen and spread across the room. I loved my mother, because it was what I was taught to do. Blood was blood and that kind of bond came with unconditional strings. I didn't particularly like Mama but I couldn't imagine walking in her room and finding her dead. Just the thought of it made me feel sick.

It took a moment for Aunty to gather herself and continue. "My mother had the magic touch. She could always calm you down when you were crying. One morning I woke up and heard you crying and it just didn't stop. I went to the nursery to check on you and my mum was holding you in her arms. You were crying but her eyes were closed and she wasn't moving. I didn't realize I was screaming until your father came running in still covered with soap from the shower." Aunty laughed at the memory. It was a scratchy, cheerless sound.

"I think I just got used to blaming you. When I look at you sometimes I see my mother's dead body holding you in that rocking chair. It's not fair to you but I don't know how to be around you."

*　*　*

The next morning, Kaira was running around the house doing last-minute packing. Ginika was in her room blasting weird chanting music that she said she needed to resettle her core. I didn't even bother asking her what that meant. We were leaving the house in thirty minutes. Kaira kept looking at the locked door and pretending she wasn't hoping her mum would come out to see us off.

I was seated at the kitchen island, swiveling on a stool and flipping through the album, looking for one picture in particular. I had seen it last night and it had taken a lot to not snatch the album away to study it. But yesterday had been about Kaira.

I froze and stopped flipping when I saw it, that feeling punching me in the chest again. I carefully pulled it out of the page, needing to study it without any plastic sheet in the way.

"I took that picture, you know?" Aunty Carol said, climbing on the stool next to me. She smelled of the cigarette she had just been smoking outside.

"You did?" I turned to her, eager to hear more, needing her to tell me something that would shake a memory loose. Cheta and I were wearing matching Minnie Mouse dresses. I had a shy smile on my face, my hand around the neck of a blue teddy bear. Cheta's little hand was on my shoulder and she was frowning at someone out of the frame.

"You were holding that teddy all day. You just refused to let it go. Akubundu decided he wanted to play with it and grabbed it from you. You started crying and your sister marched right to him, snatched the teddy back, and shouted something at him. I'm not sure what it was, she was speaking Ika and I don't speak the language. Then she walked back to you, gave you the teddy, and wiped your tears. It was the cutest thing. I just had to take a photo." She looked at the photo album on the table and ran her finger down the cover. "I took most of these photos."

Aunty Carol shook her head and looked at me. "How is your sister by the way?"

"She's fine," I lied. I had no idea how Cheta was and for the first time I felt guilty about it.

We filed out of the house about twenty minutes later when the hired SUV arrived. Beside me, Kaira kept tapping her leg and glancing at the door, as we watched the driver load our suitcases into the boot. I could almost feel her willing Aunty to come out and say goodbye.

The driver slammed the boot. "Is that all?"

"Yes. That's everything. Girls get in," Aunty Carol said.

Ginika grabbed Kaira's arm. "Look," she said pointing at the house. Aunty Sophie was standing by a window watching us.

Ginika cupped her hand around her mouth. "Bye, Aunty," she shouted.

Aunty took a step back and the curtain fell. Then she reappeared again, and even from the distance we could see the smile on her face she couldn't squash.

"Ginika!" Aunty Carol reprimanded. "The neighbours."

Kaira laughed. "Bye, Mum!" she shouted, following Ginika's lead.

Aunty Sophie gave a small, almost shy wave and stepped away from the window.

"That's progress," Ginika said, getting into the car.

TWENTY-EIGHT

Cheta

LIVING WITH CHIZI was nowhere near as bad as living with Mama but it was still hard. Mostly because I couldn't say anything when she annoyed me. I was a guest in her home and as welcome as she made me feel, I knew hospitality only stretched so far. I couldn't complain when she left toothpaste in the bathroom sink or dishes in the kitchen sink. I stayed silent when she smoked her cigarettes in the house, the smoky smell clinging to walls, to clothes, to wigs, never really fading. Chizi was a social butterfly; her flat was one big revolving door of different kinds of people, which was what I disliked the most. I didn't like people and I didn't want them in my personal space.

I discovered very early in life that my loud mouth was the only thing that kept me sane. When something annoyed me,

I let it be known. I complained and I ranted. I expelled the negativity in my body using my words. Going from expressing everything I felt to biting my tongue made my soul feel constipated. I wanted freedom. More than anything, I wanted a home to call my own.

I looked at myself in the full-length mirror behind Chizi's door. What was I doing? Was I just trading one shackle for another? I was uncertain about the whole sugar baby thing and I had let Chizi sweep me up with her excitement. The peach dress Paulina lent to me was fitted in all the right places and stopped right above my knees. Paulina had arranged for a professional makeup artist to stop by Chizi's apartment to give us a makeover. I was contoured, highlighted, and powdered until I couldn't recognize myself. I looked sophisticated. I looked like a cosmopolitan woman who travelled the world and brunched at upscale restaurants.

"The driver is here. Are you ready?" Chizi asked.

"Yes," I said, though everything in me was screaming no.

The skeptic in me would not allow me to be excited, like Chizi. Paulina had spent a lot of money on us and I had learned a long time ago that kindness often came at a cost.

The car pulled up in front of a gated mansion. Security guards checked the boot and scanned our tickets before letting the car drive in.

Paulina was there when we arrived, her senator by her side. I had imagined him as an old man with a beer belly. He was anything but. He looked like he was in his mid-forties and was fitter than most men his age. When he was drawn into conversation by a man who looked like he had barely managed to stuff himself into his navy suit, Paulina used the opportunity to drag us aside.

"You both look good. Well done," she said.

Chizi preened, basking in the praise.

In a soft voice, Paulina gave us a brief rundown of the men in the room. She pointed out the ones to stay away from because their fetishes were on the darker side, the ones that already had a harem and wouldn't be worth our time, the ones that beat their girls, and the ones whose wives dedicated their time to making their husbands' mistresses miserable.

"Who is that?" Chizi asked, pointing at an older man with greying hair, surrounded by a throng of women. He looked like a grandfather.

"That's Chief Omozusi. Very wealthy and very generous. He paid for his last girlfriend's master's program in the States, now he's on the look out for a new one and everyone wants him."

Chizi adjusted her dress and straightened her shoulders. "I'm going to talk to him," she said, before walking in his direction.

A woman wearing a gold sequin dress that clashed with her bleached skin and ash-blond hair entered the room. There was something about her that drew all eyes in her direction. Paulina turned away and stepped closer to me as the woman walked past us.

"Who is that?"

"That's Natasha. Don't accept anything she offers you. Don't even shake her hand. She's a witch. She'll steal your destiny and put it inside calabash," Paulina whispered.

I blinked. "What?"

But Paulina was already sashaying away, her eyes locked on her senator, who had beckoned her. She was so in tune with him. While she spoke to us, she never really let him out of her sight. I watched them interact. Paulina called him honey and darling in a saccharine sweet voice that was somehow both sensual and comical. He ate it all up like a starving man. If I didn't already know he had a wife and two grown children at home, I would have mistaken them for newlyweds. As over-the-top as their affection was, there was something surprisingly genuine about it.

I stood in the corner, feeling unsure. The women in the room outnumbered the men at least four to one. Men like having variety, Paulina had said. I didn't know what to do, who to talk to. I wasn't even sure I wanted to be here. I was about to walk around and look for Chizi when a man appeared at my side, holding two flutes of champagne.

"Would you care for one?" the man asked.

I nodded and accepted it, just because it gave me something to do.

"My name is Samson," he said, handing me one of the flutes.

"Elizabeth," I said, giving the name I had chosen for my first Holy Communion. Chizi and I both agreed to use fake names. I picked a name I knew would be easy for me to remember.

I brought the glass to my lips. The bubbles tickled my nose as I pretended to take a sip. I wasn't stupid enough to accept a drink from a stranger.

"So what are you looking for here?" he said.

"I could ask you the same thing."

"Do you know why I came over to talk to you?"

I said nothing, waiting for him to continue.

"You look as uncomfortable as I feel."

I looked up at him then. Taking the time to study his face. He had a prominent jaw and an even more prominent Adam's apple. He could have been in his late thirties or early forties. I couldn't tell.

"Are you old enough to be here?" he asked me.

"Are you?" I shot back.

"I'll take that as a no."

"I'm in two-hundred level," I lied.

"That doesn't mean anything. My cousin started university when she was fifteen. She was sixteen in two-hundred level."

"Good for your cousin," I said, looking around. Chizi was in a corner, talking to the chief. She was so close to him, her chest was brushing his arm, and he didn't seem to mind. He was surrounded by other women, but Chizi had shouldered her way to his front, keeping all his attention on her.

"I'm sure some men here are into that sort of nonsense, but I'm not interested in fucking a child," the man said.

"And I'm not interested in fucking you, so that's not a problem you have."

"You have to be careful how you speak. Some men will take offense to your tone." Coming from someone else, that would have sounded like a threat, but he just sounded concerned.

"I know. I also know you're not one of those men."

"How do you know that?"

I looked at him. "Because you asked my age." Men had approached me since my breasts sprouted. None of them had ever been concerned about my age, even back when I was clearly a child. "Why are you here? If you care about my age, this doesn't seem like your kind of scene."

"Why are you here? This doesn't seem like yours," he countered.

"I need money," I said simply. The words came out breezily like I didn't have a knot the size of a fist in my stomach, making me want to throw up. What was I doing here? This wasn't me. I watched him take me in slowly, his eyes making their way up my body, from my shoes until they reached my narrowed eyes.

"I can help you with that," he said with a smirk.

I opened my mouth to say something sarcastic but Chizi materialized at my side, cutting me off. "Chief, let me introduce you to my friend. Chief, this is Liz. We're coursemates in UNIBEN. Liz, this Chief Omozusi."

"I see UNIBEN is full of beautiful girls," Chief said with a wide smile.

"Chief!" Chizi gasped, laughing, like he had made some hilarious joke. His arm snaked around her hips, drawing her closer.

"Hello," I said. I gestured at the man next to me, "This is . . ."

"Samson Emmanuel," he said, not in the least offended that I had forgotten his name.

Chief nodded at him, before asking me, "Liz, so are you studying finance like your friend here?" His hand squeezed Chizi's hip.

"No. Psychology," I blurted out, shocking myself.

Chief Omozusi's drunken laughter echoed through the room. I could smell the alcohol on his breath from where I stood.

"A doctor for mad people? Fine girl like you? And your father let you study that? Does he not want you to marry so you can go to your husband's house and stop spending his money? No man wants to marry a woman who spends her days surrounded by mad people." He smacked the hand that wasn't wrapped around Chizi against his thigh and howled at his own joke.

His ignorance was giving me a headache. I gave him a tight smile. It was the first time I had ever spoken my dream out loud and I didn't like that this fat buffoon thought it was funny.

"Psychology is not about madness. Mental health is important. So many people are suffering in silence with issues like depression and—"

"Depression?" he exclaimed, cutting me off. "That's a white man disease! See, the thing is they don't have problems, so they create problems for themselves. The problem is that they're too comfortable. When you don't have to worry about NEPA or petrol scarcity or corruption you get bored, so you create new diseases to cry about."

"I think it's a noble profession," Samson said, drawing my attention away from Chief Omozusi. "My company works with a nonprofit that helps people in need. Maybe we can meet up sometime to discuss how we can help each other. If you're looking for a job I'm sure I can help you find a position."

I snorted. "I know how these things work. I'll show up and the next thing I know you're carving out my heart for a juju ritual to increase your wealth. No, thank you."

Samson threw his head back and laughed. Everyone turned around to look at us.

"I like you," he said.

From the corner of my eye I saw Paulina give me an approving nod.

Samson left the party soon after, giving me his business card before slipping away. I pretended to drink champagne and pretended not to be repulsed when men older than my father flirted with me. I laughed at jokes that weren't funny while I counted the minutes until it was time to leave.

Chizi chattered all the way home, tipsy on attention and champagne. While she spoke about the chief and the connection she felt with him, I put my hand in my purse and ran my fingers along the embossed letters on Samson's business card.

Chizi kept on yammering as we got to the flat, shed our layers, and got ready for bed. I wiped off my makeup and washed my face at the bathroom sink, watching myself in the mirror. I shook my head at what I saw. We might have worn sexy dresses, flirted with rich men, and drank expensive champagne, but when the wigs and the fake lashes came off and the hair bonnet came on, we looked like what we were, confused seventeen-year-olds, living in a rubbish flat and making the best of a bad situation.

TWENTY-NINE

Zam

I ROLLED IN bed, away from my phone's ringing—not that I could get very far in a twin bed. A lumpy bed. With the thousands of pounds Uncle and every other parent was paying, you would think the boarding school would at least invest in better mattresses. I drifted off when the ringing stopped, only to be yanked awake when the ringing began again.

I took a moment to fortify my inner strength before answering the call. "Hello?"

"She has done it! She has finally disgraced this family's name! After everything I've done. Eh? What did I do to deserve this?" Mama screamed into the phone. I could hear thwacking noises in the background and I knew it was Mama's hand smacking against her thigh.

I sat up, rubbing my hand against my forehead. Did she have to be so loud? "Mama, what are you talking about?"

"Your sister is an igbaraja now o!" Mama shouted, sounding more out of control than usual.

"Cheta?"

"Which other sister do you have?"

"You have seen Cheta?" It had been months since she disappeared. Every time I spoke with Mama, she told me a new rumor she had heard about Cheta's whereabouts.

"Two different people called me and told me they saw her on campus. They said she's a big girl now, hanging out with some wayward boys that have dirty money. What would she be doing with them except selling her body? She has become a sugar baby. That girl does not have shame."

"Are you sure?" I asked. From what I knew about sugar relationships from Nollywood movies, sugar babies tended to be subservient, or they pretended to be subservient. It was the only way to cater to the whims of rich men. Cheta was the least submissive person I knew and she was incapable of pretending to be anything other than who she was.

"Do I not know what my child looks like? Adaibe took a picture of her and sent it to her mother who sent it to me. And you know how big Nne Adaibe's mouth is. Now everybody in the village knows my shame. I can't show my face outside anymore!"

I spent the next hour trying to convince Mama to calm down. It didn't work. When the call finally ended she was just as irate as when it began.

* * *

"You've been quiet all day," Ginika said. She was seated at the edge of my bed eating a pack of biscuits she bought from the tuckshop. We had a little bit of free time before the bell rang for high tea.

"I'm just thinking."

"About?" Kaira prodded. She was standing in front of the small mirror over my desk, detangling her hair.

"I spoke to my mum last night."

Ginika sighed. "Are you going to tell us what's wrong or do we have to keep prompting you?"

"There's something wrong with my mother," I said.

Ginika sat up straight. "Is she sick?"

"No. I mean . . . You know how Aunty Sophie kind of explained why she acts the way she does around Kaira?"

Ginika nodded. Kaira stopped brushing her hair and looked at me through the mirror.

"There has to be a reason Mama is the way she is. When I was younger, I heard her sisters making a joke about how people used to think my mum was adopted because she was darker than all her sisters. Now with all the bleaching she's lighter than them. They used to call her 'Blackie.' I've just been thinking about what it must have been like for her as a child, feeling like she didn't belong with her family," I said.

"Yeah, I can see how things like that could lower her self-esteem. It still doesn't excuse the way she treated you and your sister. Whether or not she intended, she pit you against each other," Ginika said, licking crumbs from her fingers.

"Yeah. That's like me and Akubundu. He's never actually done anything to me but I kinda hate him for being Mum's favorite. I think we're going to talk about that in our next session," Kaira said. She now had once-a-week family therapy with her mum. Uncle Emeke, being a strongheaded Nigerian man, refused to go, but at least it was a start. I had even seen Aunty Sophie make eye contact with Kaira the week before when she had come to school to sign an exeat that gave Kaira a day pass to attend a session. It was quick, but it happened and I was so happy for Kaira.

"I spoke to my mum and she told me my sister is now an ashawo," I said, spilling the other thing that was on my mind.

"What?" Kaira and Ginika gasped in unison.

I told them what Mama had told me. "I keep thinking about the money Cheta stole from me. I was so angry, I never asked why she needed it. What if she owed some bad people money? What if I had just given her the money?"

"Your sister's decisions are hers alone," Kaira said.

I nodded, though I didn't believe her words. "You don't understand because you never experienced it. But living in that house was horrible. It was so toxic. Do you know what it feels like to live your entire life feeling like you can't breathe? And I left her there . . . I left her alone to deal with Mama. I left her—"

Ginika shook me. "Zam, breathe!"

I shook my head. What was she talking about? There was no air! And why was my heart beating this fast? Were hearts supposed to beat this fast?

"Deep breaths. Close your eyes and breathe with me. Focus on me," Ginika commanded. I struggled against the buzzing in my ears and tried to focus on her voice.

"That's it. Just breathe with me."

When I finally got my panic under control, Ginika said, "Zam. You need to learn that you cannot blame yourself for other people's actions. You were offered an opportunity and you took it. You did what was best for you. Cheta would have done the same thing without thinking twice."

I nodded, trying to let her words sink in, trying to make myself believe them. But while I remembered all the ways Cheta made me feel small with her unkind words, I couldn't help but remember the little ways she had also looked out for me.

After the bedtime bell rang and Kaira and Ginika left to go to their rooms, I opened my bedside drawer and picked up the photo I had taken from the photo album, the one of me and Cheta with the teddy bear. I didn't think anyone would care the photo was missing and for some reason, it was important I had that picture with me. I needed to get a frame for it. Did Cheta remember this day? I placed it on the bedside drawer, lined it up perfectly, and took a picture of it with my phone. Without giving myself even a second to second-guess what I was about to do, I texted it to Cheta.

THIRTY

Cheta

IT TOOK THREE days for me to gather the courage to call Samson.

"Hello."

"Samson, it's Liz."

Silence.

"We met at the party, a few days ago," I said, already regretting my decision to call. Did he not remember me?

"Yes. I've been expecting your call. Are you free today?" he asked.

I didn't want to appear too eager but it was a Friday, I had sold most of the product I had on hand and there was nothing else to do, so I made arrangements with him, and two hours later, a taxi dropped me off in front of a small bungalow off Sapele Road.

The door was slightly open and I could see the reception area was empty.

"Hello?" I called out into the empty room. Was I in the wrong place?

"Cheta!" I heard Samson's voice call out. He appeared round the corner. He was wearing a blue button-up shirt and navy trousers.

"Where is everybody?"

"There wasn't much to do and it's Friday so most people went home early today," he explained. "Let's go to my office."

We walked past the reception area, through the empty room that had three desks with computers and papers on them, into a hallway with flickering fluorescent lights. No warning bells sounded in my head, not until he ushered me into the room at the end of the hallway and, instead of walking into the room with me, shut it and stood in front of the door like a guard. I knew that tactic. It was what Mama always did when she didn't want me to escape her abuse. That was when I began to realize just how stupid I had been. I didn't know this Samson from Adam. I didn't know if Samson was his real name. I knew absolutely nothing about him except for the fact that he attended a private party where men were looking for young girls to sleep with. That was when it dawned on me that he had called me Cheta when I arrived, not Liz.

"Why are you blocking the door?" I demanded.

"Is she here?" a voice called out. I swung my head around, surprised by the second voice.

"What is going on?"

Samson smiled at me. "Yes, she's here."

Fear seized my body, making it hard to breathe. *Chineke!*
What the hell had I gotten myself into?

Instilling fear was addictive, Mama taught me that. I could
see it in the way her eyes smiled every time she came near
me and I flinched. The satisfaction on her face when my eyes
begged for mercy before my tongue did. She enjoyed it. When
I realized that, I took that power from her. I refused to flinch,
even if I was trembling inside. I refused to feed her addiction.

When Samson had used his body to block the door, every
cell in my body itched to scream—but I didn't. I knew that
second voice. There was no mistaking the rumbling tone and
the Bini accent that highlighted every word. I turned my head
and saw Johnson reclining on a brown couch in the corner of
the large office. What was he doing here? He had been lazing
about on Chizi's couch when I left the flat that morning.

"What is going on?" I asked. I was proud of myself for
keeping my voice steady even though it felt like someone was
playing basketball in my chest.

"Johnson and I have a proposition for you," Samson said.

"What kind of proposition?" I asked, one eye on him, the
other on Johnson. I had a knife in my bag. I always carried
one with me. If I stabbed him in the throat, I could use all my
strength to kick the door open and flee before Johnson had a
chance to cross the room. It happened in movies all the time.
It could work. Couldn't it?

"You said your Uncle is Iweka? As in Iweka Oil right?" Johnson said.

"Yes," I said, still trying to figure out the logistics of my escape plan.

Johnson sat up on the couch. "Cheta, I've been good to you? Haven't I? I helped you when you needed it. Gave you a job. Looked after you."

I knew he was going to use that line one day. I knew he had an agenda when he gave me that job. I just didn't expect it to be this soon. It took every bit of self-control not to laugh. Selling illegal drugs in a hot market stall was not looking out for me. But I wasn't stupid enough to disagree with him before knowing exactly what he wanted from me.

"Yes," I said.

Johnson smiled, looking pleased with himself.

"We have a business proposal for you. Johnson mentioned you and his cousin were attending the party last week and I found a way in. I was there to see you," Samson said, in a way that implied I should feel special.

"What is this business proposal?" I asked, still on edge at being confined in a room with two men I didn't know very well.

Samson laid out his plan. I listened as he explained how he and Johnson were partners who had made some bad business deals and now had debt that needed to be paid. They wanted to use me as an in to Uncle Emeke. When he was done I finally understood why his business failed. I didn't know if he was naïve or just an idiot. Maybe a little bit of both.

Uncle wasn't some local chief who gave out small contracts to people he liked and had his hands in local businesses. Uncle was international. He dined with heads of state, had business meetings with sheiks, had met European royalty. Yes, he sometimes came to Alihame and dined with the common folk. Yes, he sometimes helped people with their small businesses but those people were usually older relatives—and only because that was how things were done.

I knew the kind of man Uncle truly was. I had overheard the conversations between him and my father. I listened to the way he talked down to Papa and made him feel less than. He never missed a chance to remind Papa that he would never reach his level of success. Uncle did not help his people out of the kindness of his heart. He did it because it was good for business. He wanted people to see him as a man of the people—a son of the soil. It was for his public image and nothing more. The only people Uncle probably cared about were Aunty Sophie and his children, and maybe Zam now that she lived with them.

"How much do you think my uncle is worth?" I asked.

"At least thirty billion naira," Johnson said.

I laughed. *Thirty* billion *naira*?

I walked over to the couch and sat down. "Google it," I said.

Samson pulled out his phone and typed. "Five hundred million," he said, looking at me.

"I thought he would have more than that with all that oil money," Johnson said, looking confused.

I looked at Samson and waited.

"Dollars. Five hundred million *dollars*," Samson clarified.

"That's about two hundred and five billion naira," I said. I googled my uncle often. I knew his worth had dropped when the stock price in his company did, but Uncle was smart. You didn't get that rich by not being smart. He was probably hiding billions more in offshore accounts.

"So we should ask for more money? Go for a bigger contract?" Samson asked.

Jesus Christ this man was an idiot. "No. I think I have a better idea," I said with a smile.

In that moment, standing in front of two men with dubious morals and questionable ethics, I realized I could turn my life around. Most people think greed is in the eyes, but they're wrong. It's in the curve of the lips. I knew they were on board with my plan from the way their lips curled as I spoke.

* * *

That night, I went to bed with so much excitement running through me, I felt my heart would burst. This was it. This was what was going to change my life. No more hopping okada to look for dead-end jobs, no more selling drugs under the boiling sun, no more sugar baby meetups. This was a once-in-a-lifetime thing. I wasn't interested in making a career of it. I was going to do it once, do it big, do it right, and disappear.

THIRTY-ONE

Zam

THE CAR TURNED onto the familiar street and the first thing I noticed was how unusually smooth the ride was. I wound down the window and looked out of the car, my seatbelt straining against my chest. The road was tarred; the potholes filled. I wondered which politician had done it and if he had won the election.

With the window down, the breeze wafted into the car and I inhaled the smells of my childhood. The air here was different, heavier but sweeter. It was my first time back in Alihame since I left in June and apart from the road, it looked like nothing had changed in the past six months.

I was back for two weeks to spend Christmas with my parents. Christmas meant presents and I had four suitcases of them in the boot of the car. Mama had given me a list of things to buy. The list included items for everyone from my primary school teacher to Father Charles to Sister Benedicta to Nne Lota, the woman whose shop was opposite Mama's. Ginika, Kaira, and I trekked up and down Oxford Street buying everything on Mama's list. Before I even handed her my passport, the airline employee who weighed my suitcases said, "Why do Africans always have overweight luggage?" She called out to her colleague who was checking in someone else at the other counter. "Martha, this box is ten kilograms over the limit." Martha didn't look up as she said, "Let me guess, Nigerian?"

With the window down I heard the generator before the house came into view. This was definitely a special occasion. There was a crowd of about thirty people gathered in front of the house. The car came to a stop and I saw familiar faces peering in the tinted windows. Mama's multicoloured face was leading the horde. When I stepped out of the car, Mama rushed forward and grabbed me by my shoulders. "My pikin. My daughter." Her arms wrapped around me and drew me into her.

"Ma nne," I murmured into her chest, trying not to choke on the smell coming off her skin. Mama always smelled like the bleaching creams she used, but the chemical stench had gotten stronger. I was crushed against her, her arms wrapped around me so tightly I couldn't move if I tried. After a long minute, she pulled me away to look down at me, but she kept a hold on me, her fingers digging into my shoulders. Mama looked different. She was far lighter than she had been the last time I had seen her. Her skin, the odd mix of yellow and brown, now had angry-looking red patches.

I looked over Mama's shoulder and saw the crowd gathering around us, everyone speaking over each other and yelling out words of welcome, but one face in particular stood out. Papa stood by the front door, a rare smile on his face. "Nwam oma," he said. *My beautiful child.*

Conversations with Papa happened far less often than those with Mama. They were short and filled with awkward pauses. So to see Papa standing in front of our home, smiling at me, made my entire body warm. The fact that with one sentence I knew Papa had missed me made me feel unbelievably good. I ran towards him and wrapped my arms around him, squeezing him as tight as I could. His belly was bigger than it was before I left, making it hard to wrap my arms around him. He smelt like kola nut and sun and sweat. I felt Papa pat me on my back. I didn't have enough time to enjoy the moment before a hand wrapped around my upper arm and yanked me away.

"Come. Let's see what my daughter bought for us from London," Mama said, stretching out the vowels in *London*, her voice rising higher on the word. She pulled me into the house, the crowd of people following close behind.

Mama was in her element, holding court in front of everyone she knew. Gifts were opened, praises to God were sung, questions about London were asked, food was served and eaten, and finally hours later guests began leaving.

When night fell and the last of the crowd had dispersed, I carried my now mostly empty suitcases upstairs to my room. The room smelled and looked different. It no longer felt like an extension of Cheta. Everything that had made the room Cheta's was gone. It seemed Mama and Papa did not think she was ever coming back. The walls no longer leaked with her personality. The pictures she had on the wall were no longer there. The two twin beds had been pushed together to make one big bed. The side table no longer held Cheta's cosmetics, instead it had a handful of kola nut and two empty bottles of Orijin. Lined up against the wall were Papa's shoes and hanging from the closet door was a familiar blue and orange wrapper.

This was Papa's room now. It should not have surprised me that Papa had used the first opportunity to put some distance between him and Mama, but it did. In the corner of the room was a mini mountain of books, clothes, and other random items, balancing precariously and covered with several layers of dust. It looked like after Cheta left, someone had shoved everything she left behind in the corner and forgot about it.

"I should have thrown that out a long time ago. I'll tell the house girl to do it tomorrow," Mama said. I whirled around and saw Mama standing by the door, her eyes on the pile of dusty items.

"You know your sister is back?" Mama said, shifting her eyes to me.

"What?"

"Yes o. Nne Adaibe just told me before she left. She saw Cheta entering Ms. Okoye's house. It's not enough for her that she went to Benin to disgrace our family. She had to come here and disgrace us too."

I didn't know how to feel knowing Cheta was back. "Do you think she'll come here?" I asked Mama.

"She better not try it if she knows what's good for her."

* * *

It was strange being in the house and having no responsibility. I woke up the morning after I arrived and I looked out the window to see the house girl had already begun sweeping the compound. By the time I showered and got dressed, she had already made breakfast.

As the days passed I got used to being back and I realized just how much I missed Alihame. The house girl Mama hired was an amazing cook and everyday I gorged on Nigerian food. I knew once I got back to England, it would be back to pasta and burgers and pizza and other boarding school food, which tended to be bland and underwhelming. I feasted on jollof rice and plantain, pounded yam and oha, eba and okra, akamu and akara, fanyogo, icheku, suya, agabalumo, malt and anything else I could get my hands on. I ate until I had to unbutton my jeans.

But the thing I missed most of all was the language. I loved the way Ika flowed off my tongue, the way I didn't have to think twice about pronunciation or accent. It felt good to be back in a place where everyone was like me. We all sounded the same and there was a freedom in being one of many, a certain kind of peace that came with not being the odd one out.

I followed Mama to her shop everyday. Before Abuja and England, when I went to the shop with Mama, I would sit in the back and do homework, only popping out occasionally to help Mama with a customer. This time I was front and center. Mama made sure to let everyone know that I was her daughter back from overseas. It took me about a week to get used to being on display. No matter what the conversation was about, Mama found a way to let the customer know that I went to school in London.

On a Tuesday afternoon, during a lull in customers, while Mama and I were taking an inventory of materials, a familiar voice said, "Ma nne."

Mama and I turned. Cheta stood at the entrance of the store. It was the first time I had seen her since Abuja. She looked skinnier and she had bags under her eyes.

Something in Mama came alive at the sound of Cheta's voice, like a current under her skin had sparked to life. The violence in Mama was a living thing and it was hungry. Cheta happened to be its favorite meal. Mama was the first to speak. "What are you doing here?"

"I came to greet you, Mama," Cheta said. Her voice was soft. Softer than I had ever heard it.

"You've been here for many days? It's just now you're remembering your mother?"

Cheta opened her mouth, then closed it, then opened it again.

Mama got impatient. "What do you want or are you just going to stand there?"

"I brought some things for you. They're in the car."

Mama leaned to the side and craned her neck to see past Cheta. Ms. Okoye's rundown car was in front of the store.

"I don't want anything you bought with your igbaraja money," Mama spat.

Cheta took a step back, almost as if Mama had hit her.

"Mama, I'm not an igbaraja."

Mama laughed. "Do you think I was born yesterday? Eh? Cheta, do I look like a child? I heard about the boys you are running around with in Benin?"

Cheta's chin lifted and her jaw clenched. She had that look on her face, the one that said she wasn't backing down and that never ended well.

I stepped in between them, trying to calm things down. "Mama, maybe we should—"

Mama shoved me aside and focused on Cheta. "Chetachi, do you know what people are saying about you? You think I have not heard your gist? Everyone in this village knows what you are. Have you not embarrassed me enough? Look, if it is the devil that sent you here, go back to where you came from and tell him you didn't find me. *Dodo*, take your igbaraja money and be going." Mama turned around and continued counting inventory.

"Why do you hate me, Mama? What have I ever done to you?" Cheta asked, her eyes fixed on Mama's back.

The question stunned me. Not the boldness of it, but the sincerity. The usual sarcasm that coated most of the words uttered by Cheta was absent. Just as Mama carried violence, Cheta carried pride. But she had none of it with her, like she had shed it somewhere on the way. Mama seemed as surprised as I was because a response wasn't quick off her tongue. Her mouth opened, momentarily silent. Cheta was doing something she had never done, letting herself be exposed the way Kaira had done the night before we left for school. That night had ended with hope for Kaira but I knew this would not end well. I didn't know how Mama could live with so much negativity stewing inside her. How she didn't collapse under the weight of it.

"Zam, is the igbaraja still there?" Mama finally said, knowing fully well that Cheta hadn't moved.

A customer walked up to the store, eyeing Cheta as she walked by her. "Nne Zam, how are you?" the woman said. She was one of the women from Mama's church group. One of the women who always seemed to know the latest news of Cheta and never hesitated to inform my mother. As she spoke her eyes were fixed on Cheta, knowing the impact her words would have.

That was the last straw for Cheta. *Nne Zam*, as if Mama's firstborn wasn't standing right there. The look on Cheta's face made something splinter in my chest. She got into the car and drove off. I walked out of the shop and watched the car navigate the potholes and the pedestrians who crossed roads with no regard to their life. There was no way I could catch up to it on foot.

While Mama spoke to the customer, I grabbed my bag and left the shop. I was about to turn the corner when Mama shouted my name. I pretended not to hear her and kept walking towards the fruit section of the market. From afar I spotted Ezinne's distinctive head. It was flat and angular at the crown with a steep drop from the top, giving her the illusion of an abnormally long neck.

"Ezinne? How are things?" I asked.

She looked up at me and her eyes widened. "Cuzzo! I heard you were back." She was one of the few people who hadn't shown up to welcome me home because Mama had banned her from the house. You would think having a daughter who was known around the village as an igbaraja would have softened Mama's attitude about Ezinne but it seemed to make it worse.

Ezinne had a scar on her face from where Uncle Festus had hit her with his belt buckle. It was an ugly scar that cut across her left eye and trailed down her cheekbone.

If anyone knew where Cheta was staying, it would be Ezinne. Everyone knew what Ezinne had done. Everyone knew how she got that scar. Wherever she went, she was trailed by whispers and taunts. Since then, it seemed Ezinne had taken it upon herself to become the town gossip. She found out whatever she could about people and spread it far and wide, whispering into the ears of whoever listened. If people were talking about someone else, then they weren't talking about her. But people had long memories and the scar on her face was a constant reminder. No matter how much time passed or how much new gossip surpassed old ones, they would never forget how she got that scar.

According to Ezinne, Cheta was staying at the Plazafield hotel, a small hotel that hadn't been completed the last time I was in Alihame. I hailed an okada and the ten-minute ride to the hotel did nothing but tighten the knot in my belly. The girl at the front desk was the older sister of one of my classmates and one of the people who had gathered at my house the day I arrived. She didn't hesitate to give me Cheta's room number. I stood in front of the door and stared at it. It took a few moments and several deep breaths before I gathered the courage to knock.

"What do you want?" Cheta asked when she answered the door.

"I wanted to talk to you."

"Oh? You want to talk now? When I saw you earlier you didn't have anything to say."

"You know how Mama is. She never lets anyone talk." I tried to smile, tried to make light of the situation but my words came out flat. "Cheta, please let me come in, let's talk."

She crossed her arms, refusing to budge. Her body solidly

blocked the door. "What do you want? Or are you here to insult me too?"

"I don't believe anything Mama said. I know you. I know you're not an igbaraja."

She eyed me with suspicion. "So why are you here?"

I took a deep breath and rolled the words around in my mind. The words Ginika and I had practiced. "Cheta. We're sisters. We need to stick together. I know Mama made things difficult but—"

"*Gbankiti*! Shut up your dirty mouth! Can you imagine this nonsense?" She turned her head around, seeking an answer from an audience that wasn't there. "Tell me Zam, was it you Mama beat with a wooden spoon, eh? Was it your leg she burnt with hot soup? Tell me, was it you?" She gesticulated wildly with her arms. The bracelets on her wrist clanking together, the sound echoing in the hallway.

I could feel the frustration welling up in my throat, threatening to burst out.

Cheta continued. "Today, was it you she called igbaraja? Was it you she refused to look at? And you . . . you just stood there. Just stood there and watched."

"I tried to—"

"You didn't try hard enough. You never did," she yelled.

"What did you want me to do?" I yelled back. "Mama didn't beat me because I know when to shut up. I know when to keep quiet and mind my business. That's all you had to do. Shut up and face your front, but you always have to talk. You always have to be right. Always have to win." Even through the anger flowing through me, heating my blood and making my chest tight, there was a lightness in my limbs, a looseness on my tongue. It was freeing to stand in front of Cheta and tell her what I really thought.

Cheta studied me with narrowed eyes then laughed. It was a low and bitter sound that cut off abruptly. "You feel good? You feel proud of yourself for telling me what you think, don't you? So you have the guts to confront me but you can't open your mouth and confront Mama, the person who actually deserves it."

She shook her head. "You're a coward. You know how Mama treated me growing up was not right, but you never spoke up for me. You just sat there and watched it happen and you didn't care because it wasn't happening to you." She took a step back. One hand on the door frame and the other curving around the edge of the door. Her bracelets slid down her arm, one in particular caught my eye. It was a familiar scratched gold with missing stones, glinting in the light of the hallway. My mouth went dry and my heart began to gallop in my chest. The last time I saw that bracelet, it had been on a different wrist.

"I'm leaving tomorrow. I just wanted to say goodbye. I'm going as far away as I can from this toxic place. Tell Mama she never has to see her igbaraja daughter again," Cheta said, drawing my attention back to her eyes that were glassy with unshed tears. There was a heaviness in her tone, a finality in her voice. She slammed the door and the hallway shook.

Goosebumps broke out on my skin. I rested my forehead against the wall. *Slow breath in through my nose. Pause. Three seconds. Out through the mouth.* Just like Ginika had taught me.

When I finally felt like I wasn't going to throw up, I sat down in the hallway and thought about what I was going to do. Aunty Sophie deserved to know that the people who had traumatized her were dealt with and would never harm her again but how would she react if she knew her niece was behind it? She was slowly getting better and I didn't want to be the messenger that unraveled her progress. And what about Cheta? What would happen to her? More than once, I had heard Uncle Emeke talk about *killing those bastards*. There was something cold and bloodthirsty about the way he said it that made me believe it wasn't an idle threat, especially after seeing what he did to Mr. Boniface. The image was still so clear in my mind—Mr. Boniface, bruised and bloody and curled up in a ball, pleading as Uncle kicked him mercilessly. If Uncle could do that to a man whose only crime was reacting like a human and protecting himself from gunfire, I didn't want to think about what he would do to Cheta. He wouldn't sit back and hand Cheta over to the police. No. He would do something much more vicious. The panic was bubbling up again. I gently rubbed my chest with my palm and focused on breathing.

Why did I have to notice that stupid bracelet? I didn't want the burden of this knowledge. At best this would ruin Cheta's life and at worst it would end it. Cheta had already been through so much. I couldn't stop picturing the pain on her face when Mama had called her an igbaraja. Or the sound of betrayal in her voice when she accused me of never standing up for her. She was right. I never did. No matter what Mama did, no matter how wicked she was to Cheta, I just kept quiet and looked away. I always chose protecting myself over protecting her. Now I had another choice to make. Aunty Sophie deserved justice, but Cheta deserved to have someone protect her for once.

* * *

Papa was on the veranda when I got home, eating kola nut and staring at the sunset. I got a chair from the living room and dragged it to sit beside him. Once the sky darkened and shadows shrouded his face, I gathered the courage to ask him the question I had always wanted to ask.

"Papa, why don't you talk?"

His big belly rose and fell as he breathed. His eyes were focused on something in the distance when he said, "My daughter. At my age you realize that you have said everything you wanted to say."

It wasn't a good enough answer, but I knew it was the best he could give. Turning my head to look at Papa—*really look at him*—I saw a man who had let life beat him. A man whose spirit had disintegrated and turned to dust in the shadow of his brother's success. Papa was a deeply unhappy man who seemed to be comfortable wallowing in his unhappiness and there was nothing anyone could do to pull him out.

"Zam!" Mama screamed from upstairs, "Come and help me rub cream on my back."

I gave Papa a small smile and squeezed his hand before going upstairs to help Mama.

Mama stood in front of the mirror, the bottle of bleaching cream in her hand. "What were you looking for in Cheta's hotel?" Mama asked, her voice unusually controlled. I wasn't surprised she already knew I went there. I looked up and our eyes met in the mirror. Her gaze was so intense, my eyes dropped down to her back, unable to hold her stare. Red, yellow, and brown patches were scattered across her back. It looked as though a child had gotten into paint cans and crawled all over her.

"Eh, Zam what were you looking for there?"

My tongue felt heavy in my mouth as I thought about all the things I could say to her, all the ways I wanted to scream at her.

I wanted to lie. I wanted to tell her that I hadn't seen Cheta because I knew that was what she wanted to hear but when my tongue unstuck from the roof of my mouth, I heard my voice say, "She's my sister. I just wanted to talk to her."

Mama narrowed her eyes, studying me. "Have you not been hearing all the things I've been telling you about her?"

"Mama, she's my sister. I haven't seen her in months. I just wanted to talk to her and there's nothing wrong with that," I said, barely able to hear my voice over the pounding in my ears. I was rarely ever on the receiving end of Mama's vicious looks. I could feel it burning my skin. How had Cheta lived with this for years? I wanted to look away but I forced myself not to.

Mama's hand squeezed the bottle of skin bleach. The cream spurted out and ran over her fingers. "I see you want to be like your wayward sister. Get out of my room before you annoy me this evening."

I didn't need to be told twice. I ran out of her room with a small smile on my face. For the first time I hadn't let Mama walk all over me. I knew it was the confrontation with Cheta that gingered me. I didn't want to be a coward. Not anymore. There was so much more I wanted to say. Maybe tomorrow, I would find the courage to talk to Mama about how the cream was destroying her skin or how she had been a horrible mother to Cheta. Tonight was a start.

THIRTY-TWO

Cheta

I LEFT MS. Okoye's house while it was still dark, shutting the door quietly behind me. She was still the same fidgety woman who looked like she was about to pafuka at any moment. Her house was clean and she had food in her fridge, so it was good to know that Anita was taking care of her. She had even gotten herself together enough to tell me she missed me.

The street was quiet except for the occasional rooster crow. I knew Papa would be awake and I wanted to see him before the neighborhood busybodies woke and started their days. He was in the same spot I last saw him in when I left Alihame months ago. It was a familiar sight—Papa seated at the veranda watching the sun rise. He gave me a small smile as I approached. I was so stunned, I almost tripped. That was

315

the most reaction I had gotten from him in a very long time. I walked up and sat on the bench next to him.

"The tenants are not happy without you," he said, biting into his kola nut.

When last had I heard him speak? His soft voice made my ears tingle. After the initial shock, a startled laugh fell from my mouth. I wasn't surprised the tenants were unhappy. I would be, too, if Mama was my landlady.

"This is for you, Papa," I said, retrieving the bundle from my handbag. Papa unwrapped the brown paper bag and peered inside. He nodded and put it aside.

"You were always a good girl. A hard worker," he said. His voice was scratchy and low. Rusty with underuse.

We lapsed into silence. I sat there and soaked up Papa's presence. For the first time his silence wasn't oppressive, it was easy. I let myself bask in that realization for a few minutes.

"Goodbye, Papa," I said, standing up to leave. I knew Mama would be up soon and I needed to be gone when she emerged. I didn't need to hear anymore of her nastiness. The things she had said to me the day before were more than enough.

"Chetachi."

I turned around to look at him. He patted the bundle next to him. "I don't know where you got this money from and I don't want to know, but you've always been a smart girl. Continue being smart."

I nodded. It was the most fatherly thing he had said to me in years. I hadn't told him I was leaving for good but I think some part of him knew it. We stared at each other. An understanding passed between us. I would always resent him for his neglect and he knew that. Just like I knew he would always hate himself for the man he had become. We were both resigned to our truths. I left with a smile on my face. It wasn't much, but the few words I had exchanged with Papa let me know that he cared and that knowledge meant a lot to me.

With Papa crossed off the list, I had done almost everything I had set out to do. I had caught up with Anita and the rest earlier as they were all back for Christmas. It was nice to sit at our old spot in the abandoned building sipping chilled Malta Guinness, chowing on Cabin biscuit, and catching up.

Now, there was only one more place left to visit. It was just past dawn. The street was still quiet but I looked over my shoulder to make sure no one was watching before I scaled the fence. I used my key to enter the house. I coughed as I stepped in. The house was musty. Dust particles danced in the stale air.

So much had happened in the five months since I left Alihame. So many things in my life had changed. But Uncle Emeke's house was still the same. I had to head to Benin to catch a flight to Lagos and from there get a flight to Canada, but I couldn't leave without seeing the house one more time. I walked slowly around. For so many years the empty house had been my refuge. I sat at the edge of the bed in the guest room and stared at the wall. This was the room where I would come to cry, to hide, to be alone.

This was my last time here. I placed the key on the bedside table. It had been a life raft but I didn't need it anymore. I had a new one tucked in my pocket. I pulled the folded paper out of my pocket and read the words again, though I had it memorized. I had printed a copy of the email and kept it on me at all times. When the guilt got too much, I read the words and I reminded myself I had my reasons. The email had come in the day after we released Aunty Sophie. No matter how many times I read it, the words sucked out the air from my lungs and left me feeling light-headed. There it was, written in bold, *Congratulations on your acceptance.*

No one knew about the acceptance. None of my coursemates at UNIBEN knew I wasn't coming back after the Christmas break. I lied to Chizi, Johnson, and Samson about heading to Lagos to start a business with a family friend. Apart from Mama, they were the ones I needed distance from the most. I was done. My criminal life was short-lived and eventful but it was time to retire and move on to better things. Johnson and Samson were not ready to do the same. They were already talking about the next target, already eager to get their hands on someone else's money. I had enough self-preservation to know you stopped when you were ahead. Always.

It was time to leave. Maybe once I got on the plane, the fear that was a recent but constant companion would lessen. It sat in my chest, right next to the resentment and the guilt. Aunty Sophie had chosen to take Zam and when I had proposed an arrangement that would keep me away from Mama, she had walked away. Still, I knew that wasn't a good enough reason to do what I did. It made it hard to sleep or eat. Though the resentment had mostly faded. Stacks of money had a way of doing that.

Aunty was kept in a room with a mattress and given food three times a day. She refused to eat but at least we offered and it wasn't like we were going to force-feed her. It took three days for Uncle Emeke to get the cash and pay the ransom, and in those three days we treated her well. As for the fear—nothing could ease that. I spent most of my time looking over my shoulder, waiting for the day armed men would knock down my door and arrest me. There was no CCTV to track us and no obscure clues that could lead to us, but Uncle was a rich man. He could hire professional investigators to track us down, people more competent than the local police, whose ranks included some officers that probably couldn't spell DNA. If they did find us, at least I could say that as hostage situations went, Aunty had it good. Maybe that would count for something. If she had any lingering trauma, I'm sure she had doctors to manage it. Didn't all rich people have that? At least, that was what I told myself.

Sometimes, I still couldn't believe we pulled it off. The thought had come to me one hot night in Chizi's apartment. NEPA had taken light and I was sitting in the dark, fanning myself with one of the resumes I had printed out, listening to the battery-powered radio. The presenter was talking about an ad he had seen on social media for a course on how to survive if you're kidnapped. Apparently, the man running the course had been kidnapped twice so he was somewhat of an expert on the matter. *The only person in my life worth anything is Uncle Emeke*, I thought, but you couldn't take Uncle because he had access to the money and someone had to pay the ransom. Akubundu was out of the country. So that left Aunty Sophie and Kaira. Planning a kidnapping was nothing more than an outrageous daydream, a way to pass the time. But in that room with Samson and Johnson it became more. It became possible.

Crooked people moved in flocks. Samson and Johnson knew people with guns and greed and once the firearms and crew were secure, everything else was just details. It all happened so fast, I didn't have time to pause and think about what I was doing, not even when I called Ebuka to get information on Aunty's movements. I kept in touch with the staff in Abuja and casually called to gist. It wasn't unusual for me to ask about how everyone was doing and what everyone was up to.

We were a crew of eight. Samson's apartment became our base. We spent most of our time there going over the plan, making sure every probability was thought of and planned for. I felt high, like I was floating on a never-ending buzz of adrenaline and hope. The days moved fast and before I knew it, I was crouched in a bush, gripping a gun I didn't know how to use and calling Johnson on a stolen phone to tell him Aunty's convoy had just sped past me and was heading his way.

Minutes later, I heard the gunshots and a chill descended on me. I moved on autopilot, following the plan we had carefully laid out. Nothing penetrated the chill. Not even Johnson telling me they had left a young girl unconscious in the back seat. I didn't ask him to describe her. I didn't want to know who the girl was. Even Aunty Sophie's screams didn't faze me. I felt nothing but annoyance at the sound. I was relieved when someone gagged her with a bandana.

It had been decided that I would mostly stay out of the way. Even with the black ski masks and code names, we couldn't risk Aunty Sophie noticing me. I sat outside, on the other side of the room we had put her in. It was a one-storey uncompleted building in the middle of undeveloped land. There was nothing but insects and frogs around us. Samson and I were on look-out duty. We sat on a long wooden bench, our guns resting beside us, against the wall.

I was nodding off to the sound of nature and Samson's snores when a sound that didn't belong jerked me awake. It was a faint, stuttered sound that I recognized because it felt like I had spent most of my life making that noise. It was the sound you made when you were trying desperately to hold tears in, when you were using everything inside you to keep yourself together. I thought I was ready for Aunty's pain, thought I had hardened myself against it. But that sound pierced through the chill that had settled inside me and that was when I forgot how to breathe. My chest got so tight I had to rub it with a fist. I mumbled something I didn't remember to a still sleeping Samson and walked around the building, away from Aunty's pitiful sounds.

It was Johnson's voice asking "you dey okay?" that pulled me out of the crippling fear I had slipped into. I straightened and turned around to face him. I couldn't show doubt or fear around them, so I smiled and said with confidence I didn't feel, "I go dey okay when money enter hand."

I was wrong.

* * *

The sound of footsteps caught my attention. I knew who it was. I recognized the hesitant shuffle. When we were kids, I knew sometimes she followed me here to Uncle's house. She wasn't as quiet as she thought she was. I had never called her out on it because even when I was angry at the world and at her, there was something slightly reassuring about her presence. It made me feel like I wasn't completely alone.

"What do you want?" I called out. If she was here for another confrontation, I would give her what she was looking for.

Zam appeared in the doorway, her face squeezed in a mix of determination and doubt. Her newfound confidence fighting with the ingrained habit of hiding in her shell.

"I went to the hotel and you weren't there," she said.

"What do you want?" I said with a sigh.

"I wanted to talk to you," she said.

"I've said all I wanted to say to you. Pu ebeni." *Go away.*

322

She stared at me and her eyes dropped down to my wrist.

"You shouldn't be wearing that."

"What?"

"Aunty Sophie's bracelet. The one she was wearing the day she was kidnapped. You shouldn't be wearing it."

I reflexively put my hand behind my back. She knew. *Shit. Shit. Shit.* She *knew.* I knew the look on my face was ugly. Everything I had been working towards for months was about to blow up in my face. The bracelet was supposed to be a reminder of the risk I took to be free of my family forever, a reminder to be a better person as I began my new life, and now this reminder was going to be my downfall. I felt the panic burning through me. It was unlike anything I had ever felt. It seized my limbs; I felt fragile, exposed, unspooled, like one of Papa's old cassette tapes.

"I'm not going to tell anybody," Zam said. Her voice was soft, the tone you used when you come across a rabid animal braced to attack.

I couldn't say anything. The panic had clogged my throat, sealing my voice.

Zam continued, "I swear, Cheta. I swear I won't tell anybody. I promise you."

I let her words penetrate. I used them to anchor me against the wave of panic that was sweeping through me. It took some time for it to clear and when it did, shock registered.

I studied Zam. Really studied her. She was telling the truth. Zam had never been a good liar. She just didn't have the face or the character for it.

"Why?" I asked suspiciously. Why would Miss Goody Goody who always followed the rules keep my secret?

"It's an apology."

"For what?"

"For everything," She looked at the floor. "I know you hate me because I never said anything about the way Mama treated you."

I opened my mouth but said nothing. I seemed to have forgotten how to speak.

She raised her head and looked me in the eye. "I texted you a picture I found of us when we were younger," she said.

"I changed my number. I didn't get any text," I said, wondering where she was going with this.

She took her phone out of her pocket and showed me the picture.

I studied it. The teddy bear was vaguely familiar but that was all. "I don't remember this."

"Me too. I've been staring at the picture trying to remember, but then I remembered something else. Do you remember when Belinda was bullying me in church and you helped me?"

I snorted. How could I forget. "Sister Benedicta made me sweep the side chapel for three weeks and made someone else head of the youth choir." I still wasn't over that.

Her hand reached up to stroke the rosary around her neck. "I'm sorry, Cheta," she said.

I felt the air whoosh out of my lungs. I didn't realize how much I needed to hear her say that. How much I needed her to be on my side for once. It didn't change the past. But it was something. It felt good to hear an apology, to know that I wasn't crazy to believe she had wronged me.

"That wasn't the only time. There were so many times you protected me. Now, it's my turn. I can do this for you." She paused and then said with more conviction. "I will do this for you. I swear on everything. I won't tell anybody."

I saw the resolve on her face and I believed her. "Thank you," I said.

"If you have anything else from that day you have to throw it away. Uncle cannot find out what you did. He's not a merciful man," Zam said, her eyes serious and unblinking. There was a warning in her voice that made me uneasy. I had never heard Zam sound so serious.

She hesitated before she asked, "Yesterday. You said you were leaving forever. Where are you going to?"

"Abroad," I said, keeping it vague.

She nodded in approval. "Good. Go where he can't reach you because if Uncle finds out what you did, he . . . he will make you pay. Do you understand?" Her voice trembled in a blend of emotions. Fear and sadness maybe. Like she was both scared for me and sad she would never see me again.

"I understand." My mouth felt dry. Zam's distress had leaked into me and my body itched with the need to get far away. "I have to head to the airport."

She opened her mouth, then closed it, biting her bottom lip.

"Zam, say what you want to say."

"Why did you come to Mama's shop yesterday?"

I wanted to say something offhand because just thinking about the way Mama had spoken to me yesterday made my chest hot, but it felt wrong in the moment. I answered honestly. "I don't know. The entire time I was driving there, I was asking myself what I was doing. I just . . . wanted to try. One more time. I don't know why. It's not like Mama deserves it."

"I'm sorry," Zam whispered.

I shrugged. Mama was who she was.

"Can I hug you?" Zam asked, still whispering.

I blinked in surprise.

"Umm . . . okay." I really didn't want to, but it seemed wrong to refuse after she had apologized and promised to keep my secret.

She stepped forward and wrapped her arms around me. It was awkward, neither of us really knew where to place our hands or adjust our bodies. But seconds passed and something started to happen. A long-forgotten familiarity slowly filtered in. An old memory of Zam and me when we were younger. Before we grew apart under the pressure of Mama's parenting, Zam would climb into my bed at night and we would play pretend with the one-legged Barbie doll we shared.

I settled into the hug and let it soothe me.

I'm scared, I wanted to whisper to her, but I swallowed the words.

Zam slowly pulled away from me to look at my face. She took my wrist and unclasped Auntie Sophie's bracelet. She put it into her pocket then reached up and pulled her rosary over her head. The same rosary she wore for years. The one she would clutch when she got overwhelmed and started to shake. I never asked why she did it. I just knew that rosary was her life raft just like this empty house was mine. She grabbed my wrist again and wound the rosary around it—once, twice, three times. The beads pressed into my skin.

"Ijen ewere," she whispered. *Safe journey.* She twined her fingers with mine and squeezed. I squeezed hers in return.

"Ye meye ke," I said. *Thank you.*

I left Zam standing in the middle of the room. I heard her sniffle as I walked away. If we had grown up in a different home, maybe Zam and I would have been the kind of sisters that laughed and had inside jokes and told each other everything and kept in touch even if we had continents between us. But that wasn't us and that would never be us and for the first time that realization filled me with regret. I didn't look back because I knew that if I watched her cry, I would cry, too, and I had done enough of that. I had to focus on the future and the new life I wanted to create for myself. Maybe one day the things I had done would catch up to me but until then, I was going to make the most out of my fresh start and do my best to be happy.

Acknowledgments

I am so thankful for the many people who brought *How You Grow Wings* to life.

Sarah LaPolla, for seeing the potential in this book and for being its first champion: You saw what *How You Grow Wings* could be and I am forever grateful. My incredible agent, Kari Sutherland, for believing in this story and for finding it a perfect home: Your enthusiasm and incredible understanding of the characters and the story means everything. I am very lucky to have you and the Bradford Literary team. My editor, Krestyna Lypen: From our first call, I knew my book would be in good hands. Thank you for your editorial feedback and the care you have shown towards the characters and spirit of the story.

Adriana Bellet and Karina Granda, for bringing Cheta and Zam to life in such an incredible way. The cover makes my heart happy. Amanda Dissinger and Kelly Doyle, for helping usher this story into the world and getting it into the hands of readers and booksellers. Ashley Mason, Christina Yates, and Chris Stamey, for being great at what you do and catching everything I missed, and the rest of the talented Algonquin Young Readers team: Shae McDaniel, Caitlin Rubinstein, Elise Howard, Adah Morales, Laura Essex, Laura Williams, and Julie Primavera.

Libraries have a very special place in my heart. A good chunk of this book was written at the Tempe Public Library, and I am thankful for librarians everywhere for the work they do and for providing a safe space for people to discover new worlds.

My fellow 2022 Debuts, I am happy to be on this journey with you all.

Mum and Dad, I love you and I am grateful for your endless support and guidance. You have always believed in me and my writing. You were my very first cheerleaders and I could not do this without you. Thank you for all the trips to libraries and bookstores. Thank you for encouraging and nurturing my love of books and storytelling.

Shout-out to my people: my siblings, Nkem, Omam, Orieka, and Erica, and my adorable nieces and nephew, Amara, Ijemma, and Cairo. Mama Agbor, thank you for your prayers. The Ovienmhada and Ojougboh family. My incredibly supportive aunties, Omoye, Oyenwen, Big Mummy, Flora, and Ozigbo, and my uncles, Enahoro, Brother Dan, Meekey, and Sonny. Aunty Jumi, my personal person, you're the best.

The friends who read early versions, who sent messages of support, who have cheered me on and encouraged me: Tobi, Heidi, Dayo, Rume, Louisa, Tobi, Emikele, Vanessa, Shasha, Roselle, Amelie, Tomi, and many others. Funmi Elegba, you're a real one. Lagos would not be the same without you. Ocheme Saleh, my favorite person, thank you for being you, for believing in me on days I don't believe in myself, for reading everything I write, and always asking about my word count.

To the readers, booksellers, librarians, bloggers, and anyone who picked up this book, thank you for giving it a chance.

And lastly, to young Nigerians for whom home is not a safe place. There are kind people in the world who will treat you with care and respect. Family is more than blood. I hope you find your tribe and the loving home you deserve.